THE LEAGUE OF EXTRAORDINARY GENTLEMEN

LXG

THE LEAGUE OF EXTRAORDINARY GENTLEMEN

NOVELIZATION BY
K. J. ANDERSON

BASED ON THE SCREENPLAY BY
JAMES DALE ROBINSON

ADAPTED FROM THE COMIC BOOK BY
ALAN MOORE

POCKET STAR BOOKS

New York   London   Toronto   Sydney   Singapore

The sale of this book without its cover is unauthorized. If you purchased this book without a cover, you should be aware that it was reported to the publisher as "unsold and destroyed." Neither the author nor the publisher has received payment for the sale of this "stripped book."

This book is a work of fiction. Names, characters, places and incidents are products of the author's imagination or are used fictitiously. Any resemblance to actual events or locales or persons living or dead is entirely coincidental.

An *Original* Publication of POCKET BOOKS

A Pocket Star Book published by
POCKET BOOKS, a division of Simon & Schuster, Inc.
1230 Avenue of the Americas, New York, NY 10020

™ and © 2003 Twentieth Century Fox Film Corporation.
All rights reserved.

Cover art ™ and © 2003 Twentieth Century Fox Film Corporation.
All rights reserved.

All rights reserved, including the right to reproduce
this book or portions thereof in any form whatsoever.
For information address Pocket Books, 1230 Avenue
of the Americas, New York, NY 10020

ISBN: 0-7434-7676-X

First Pocket Books printing July 2003

10 9 8 7 6 5 4 3

POCKET STAR BOOKS and colophon are registered
trademarks of Simon & Schuster, Inc.

Manufactured in the United States of America

For information regarding special discounts for bulk purchases,
please contact Simon & Schuster Special Sales at 1-800-456-6798
or business@simonandschuster.com.

THE LEAGUE OF EXTRAORDINARY GENTLEMEN

1

On the edge of a century's turning, London was a sprawling mosaic of crooked tile roofs, shuttered windows, cobblestone streets, and garbage-strewn alleyways. Fog crept through the city like pestilence, mixing with the foul breaths of smoke from coal grates and great belches from factory smokestacks. Cold buildings huddled together as if seeking warmth against the night's chill.

Nearly two millenia of history had seen London evolve from a Roman settlement to a Saxon stronghold, then a burgeoning commercial center and religious axis. Ultimately, London became a pinnacle of European political might as well as a powerful industrial hub. World-shaking events would begin—or end—here.

For decades now this place had endured the turns of the industrial revolution, which had transformed it from a grand city of one million inhabitants into a vast metropolis teeming with more than four times as many people, all of them trying their best to survive.

In the distance Big Ben chimed its lonely but predictable tones. Most people no longer even awakened to the clock tower's hourly ritual, especially not so late. The steady sequence of gongs drifted past like a lullaby, reassuring the city's sleeping inhabitants that all was well.

Big Ben fell silent again, and so did the streets.

Then a low rumble started deep underground, as if the convoluted sewers near the Thames suffered from indigestion.

In Moorgate Passage, a pair of dogs hungrily dug through garbage in search of edible scraps, as they did every night. They half-heartedly snarled at each other, too hungry to notice the mysterious sounds.

But the noise rose steadily in volume, like buried, restless thunder. The ominous trembling grew louder and louder, shaking forcefully until it rattled loose roof slates and chimney pots. . . .

One mutt lifted his head and pricked his ears. The second dog used the opportunity to seize a rank-smelling fish head from the trash heap and bounded away with his prize. Then he, too, paused, whining. His jaws opened and the moist fish head fell to the slick street. The rumble grew more ominous, a different sort of growl.

The two dogs snarled at the sound that seemed to come from everywhere beneath and around them, then they scuttled away in fear. The second mutt doubled back to snatch up the fish head, then sprang down the alley just as the sound reached an explosive roar.

A dark brick wall at the opposite end of the alley split and broke as something huge, black, and mechanical hammered its way up from beneath the streets, knocking bricks and timbers apart. Walls fell, brushed aside from the leviathan as if they were little more than dust and dry leaves.

2

Both dogs ran for their lives as the immense subterranean machine roared and clanked after them.

Though he had been deeply asleep, immersed in dreams of playing in the park with his father on a Sunday afternoon, Bartholomew Dunning sat up quickly in bed. The pallid six-year-old boy clutched an old woolen blanket and stared into the faint light that came through the window of his cellar bedroom. On a narrow brick windowsill above the bed, his tin toy horse and buggy shuddered and rattled, as if they had come alive.

The rumbling made the entire tenement shake. Dust sprinkled down from the ceiling, captured in the hazy moonlight that penetrated the fog.

Bartholomew wanted to call out for his father, but he knew Constable Dunning would be out walking the streets, keeping London safe, as he did every night . . . all night. But right now the boy wanted his father. He pulled the blanket up to his chin, hoping to hide. But the noise grew louder.

The toys jittered and wobbled, then finally tumbled off the windowsill. More dust sifted down from the tenement ceiling, and Bartholomew could hear shouts from the residents in the floors above.

Gathering his courage, thinking of his father in his fine policeman's uniform striding down dark alleys and arresting pickpockets and murderers, Bartholomew scurried out of bed as the monstrous noise came deafeningly close. Someone upstairs let out a loud yell.

Because his father worked every night, and slept most of the day, Bartholomew could spend time with him only on Sunday. But Constable Dunning put food on the table and coal in the grate for the boy and his two sisters; they had to care for themselves without a mother to watch over them. His sisters snored together in the inner room, not even awakened by the noise. It was up to the boy to see what was happening outside.

Shrill whistles pierced the growing noise, and he took comfort in knowing the police were rushing to the scene.

Bartholomew went to the window, stood on tiptoe, and used the flat of his hand to wipe fog from the pane. The glass remained blurry from the grime outside, but an immense shadow passed along the street. When he pressed his face close, the boy could see well enough that his eyes widened in fear.

Massive mechanical treads rolled past at street level, crushing cobblestones, clanking and clattering like the loudest factory line.

Bartholomew's windows splintered and fell in. He screamed, scrambling backward as the whole frame came crashing down. Part of the wall and ceiling slumped under the crushing passage of the huge vehicle. Broken bricks and crumbling mortar buried and destroyed his toy horse and buggy.

He crawled for shelter under his bed, a place usually reserved for nighttime monsters. Right now, though, the boy was only afraid of the very real and tangible beast outside.

Then the mechanical juggernaut surged past, smashing gutters and shouldering aside brick corners that got in its way.

As dust and rubble continued to patter all around him, Bartholomew peered out from his hiding place. Safe, for now.

But he knew his father was out in the streets, armed with little more than his whistle and truncheon. Even a stern constable in a clean uniform would be no match for that thing.

Tabard Row had been quiet all evening, and Constable Dunning paused in his rounds to smoke his pipe. He took a long draw on the tobacco, savoring the moment of bliss.

His children were home together, asleep. Their mother had died of consumption two years earlier, and the boy Bartholomew had been forced to grow up much faster than he should have. Once, he'd playfully tried on his father's constable cap, and it had nearly fallen down to his small shoulders. Bartholomew was the man of the house whenever his father left to patrol the night streets, and the boy took his responsibilities with admirable, heart-aching seriousness, though his father occasionally saw him playing with his toys. Just a little boy, no more than six years old.

At least he was safe tonight. . . .

Constable Dunning's peaceful feeling was suddenly shattered by the pitiful wailing of dogs. A moment later a monstrous rumble shook the ground, accompanied by breaking glass and shattering walls.

Dunning drew his baton and trotted toward the sound, by habit tapping his truncheon on the wall as he went, making a sound like rapid gunfire. Shrill whistles sounded the alarm from other officers heading in the same direction. Drawing a deep breath, he blew a long high-pitched note on his own whistle.

"It's down in Moorgate Passage!" one of the policemen

called, joining up with Dunning. They ran together, reacting out of instinct without stopping to worry about the nature of the threat. From the sound of it, this was more serious than a drunken brawl, a cutpurse, or a pair of whores trying to claw each others' eyes out.

The two constables sprinted onto Threadneedle Street, heading for Moorgate. Dunning stumbled and nearly sprawled on his face in a filthy gutter as he and his companion collided with a pair of utterly terrified dogs racing in the opposite direction, off into the night.

"Bleedin' ratbags! What's gotten into 'em?" said Dunning.

Then again, perhaps the mutts had the right idea.

Like a factory-made demon, a giant armor-plated machine careened around—and *through*—a corner of the narrow street, demolishing everything in its path.

"Good Christ!" Dunning's companion skittered to a halt, eyes wide. His truncheon drooped in his grip, laughably insignificant compared to the mechanized titan lurching toward them with a roar of engines and a belch of oily exhaust smoke.

It was a tank vehicle plated with thick iron sheets riveted into place on a body that rode on implacable paired tracks. Glaring headlamps shone forward like the baleful gaze of a dragon. Its reinforced bow slammed like a battering ram through the wall, knocking it down without pause. The heavy treads crushed fallen bricks into powder. Dunning couldn't even guess how many tons the vehicle must weigh.

Three other constables converged from their own beats, stopped in their tracks. "It's an infernal juggernaut!"

"Run!" Dunning's tone was urgent as he backed away. Not cowardly—just sensible. There would be no real protection against a mechanized leviathan that could plow through solid walls.

While three of the policemen staggered backward, Dunning's companion took an unexpected initiative. Swallowing hard, he raised his truncheon, stepped into the middle of the street, and blew his whistle again for good measure. He stood his ground in the glare of the behemoth's headlights, raised his hand, and said, "Halt! In the name of the Queen!"

"Get out of the way, you fool!" Dunning shouted.

When the land ironclad did not slow down, the man tried to dodge into a doorway, but the lumbering vehicle filled the narrow street. The young constable was caught between the treads and went down. His scream was cut short with a wet, squelching sound under the increasing roar of the demonic engines.

The tank moved onward, without pause.

Sickened and angry, Dunning ran to his comrade's aid, but he arrived too late. Courageously—though futilely—he beat the metal monster with his baton and his fists. He made barely a mark on the thick plating.

Ignoring him, the land ironclad rolled on down the street.

Dunning ran after the machine, not knowing how he might stop its inexorable progress. The street opened up, away from the crowded slums, grimy pubs, and dim opium dens. Ahead stood a particularly impressive building with an ornate multistoried facade of marble columns, graceful statues, and stately blocks of gray-white stone.

Dunning's stomach clenched as he glanced up at the deeply engraved words BANK OF ENGLAND on the lintel over the building's main entrance. "Not the Old Lady," he muttered, hardly able to conceive of such a violation.

The tank rolled toward it, picking up speed.

The privately owned bank, often referred to as the Old Lady of Threadneedle Street, had been established more than two centuries earlier. In the past two hundred years, the Bank of England had become more than simply a financial institution: The Old Lady was a symbol of England itself.

The juggernaut smashed into the bank's broad central door. Columns broke apart and tumbled down; the massive locked door collapsed inward.

And the mammoth machine kept moving forward all the way into the financial fortress, undeterred.

The tank's heavy treads, now bloodstained, clattered down a flight of marble steps that groaned and cracked under the immense weight. Picking up speed, the land ironclad ground its way across the polished marble floor of the lobby.

A night contingent of British soldiers guarding the bank drew their guns and opened fire. Like hail pattering on a tin roof, the bullets ricocheted ineffectually off the iron armor plates. The panicked soldiers leaped aside as the tank smashed through teller desks, back offices, records archives, private consultation rooms lined with security boxes—and finally into the vault room.

Constable Dunning came running after it, picking his way through the rubble of stone and splintered wood and glass. He was aghast at the sheer carnage all around him. The soldiers recovered themselves then yelled indignant threats after the rampaging machine. Scrambling together, they all raced toward the vault room.

As if stymied, the mechanical monster came to rest against the massive iron door of the vault.

Dust and debris settled in ominous silence as Dunning and the soldier guards crept purposefully into the vault room. "Hah!" Dunning called, a bit disoriented by the frantic activity going on around him. "That door's too solid even for a beast like that!"

Several other constables, panting hard from their long run, entered the bank and stared at all the destruction.

The tank just sat there, throbbing, pressed up against the thick vault door. It seemed to be defeated . . . or simply gathering its breath, preparing to strike again.

The shaken soldiers arose and, together with the constables, encircled the machine. Dunning edged closer, peering at one of the scraped plates on the front of the tank. "What is it doing?" he asked, not expecting an answer.

With a loud clang, a panel opened and two human eyes stared out through the narrow slot. Dunning sprang back with a yelp. The slot slammed shut. "There're men inside that thing!"

Clanking, winding, slotting sounds began to emanate from within the mechanical beast. A panel *thwack*ed open on top of the machine, and a fat cylinder extended, swiveled about in search of a target, then locked into place. It was aimed at the vault door.

Everyone there could recognize a cannon barrel when they saw it.

"Get back!" shouted Dunning. He clapped his hands over his ears, but many of the others didn't react quickly enough.

The weapon fired with a deafening sound as if all the heavens had cracked asunder. The shock wave in the enclosed vault room threw constables and soldiers to the ground. The merciless cannon fired again, and then a third time.

Finally, the massive, dented vault door teetered, slumped, and at last fell inward. It crashed to the stone floor with a sound as deafening as the artillery explosions.

The air inside the ruined bank was thick with choking dust. The men's ears were bleeding. Dunning shook his head to clear it; with the back of one hand, he wiped powder and sweat from his eyes.

A thick metal hatch opened high on the juggernaut's flank and a step ladder cantilevered down. Men wearing easily recognizeable German army uniforms emerged, led by a pale-eyed man who wore cruelty on his face as naturally as another man might wear a moustache. The uniformed men carried sleek, modern-looking snub-nosed firearms and boxy radio sets on their hips.

Constable Dunning had never seen anything like it. He had heard, though, the Kaiser had been stepping up his war effort, planning against the British Empire. And here was the proof!

The foremost invader turned back to the dark interior of the massive ironclad machine. He spoke in clipped German. "We are ready, Herr Fantom."

Only then did their leader step into the open, emerging from the infernal machine. Dramatically garbed in black clothes and a sweeping cape, the man cut a formidable presence. He wore gleaming black boots, crisp gloves—and a frightening silver mask that hid most of his features. Dunning caught only a partial glimpse of a terribly disfigured face.

Dunning stared, burning the Fantom's face into his memory. He had read something about a similar murderous villain who had terrorized the Paris Opera House, not many years ago. But that Fantom had supposedly been killed. . . .

Now the man in the metal mask gazed around the room, ignoring the astonished constables and soldiers as if they were no more relevant than insects.

"Ah, I love a night out in London," the leader said in German. "Leutnant Dante, instruct our men to go about their work. We have other appointments to keep."

The cruel-faced Dante dispatched a team of German soldiers who scrambled out of the land ironclad and into the vault. Others, brandishing their futuristic snub-nosed weapons, held the intimidated bank soldiers and constables at bay.

When the invaders marched brazenly into the ruins of the Bank of England vault, one of the British guards broke free. "Here now, you can't be—"

With a flourish, the Fantom pulled out a snub-nosed gun and callously shot the outspoken British guard between the eyes. As the guard crumpled, the masked leader tossed his gun to Lieutenant Dante. "Leave one of them alive to tell the tale. Only one. What you do with the rest . . . I leave to your vivid imagination."

Striding through the debris, his cape flowing behind him as if no dust would dare cling to his black clothes, the Fantom entered the vault, leaving Dante and the others to their given tasks.

As the ruthless executions began, Constable Dunning squeezed his eyes shut and thought of his children.

As the crack of gunfire and pleading screams resounded from outside the vault, the Fantom's Germans used crowbars and the butts of their weapons to break open security boxes of all sizes. The men spilled the contents onto the floor—bank notes, gold, jewelry, bonds—but they were searching for something in particular.

An eager henchman picked up a gold brick and could not help admiring it. "Such treasures."

"Treasure, yes," the Fantom agreed, hardly sparing a glance for the chunk of precious metal. "Some worth more than others."

With a gloved hand, the masked man snapped the latch of a mahogany plan-chest and reverently drew open the long drawer to reveal a sheaf of fragile parchment. He lifted one sheet, then another. Behind the metal mask his eyes darted back and forth.

The pages of age-yellowed paper bore hand-drawn architectural plans of a city on water, its deep foundations crumbling and cavernous. In spite of the faded ink, the detail was incredible, drawn by a genius centuries ago.

"Ah, here is the key to our labyrinth." The horribly scarred lips, barely visible beneath the silver mask, smiled. The Fantom snatched up the pages and swept out of the vault, ignoring the rest of the gold and treasure. "Time to go. We have what we need."

Outside, Constable Dunning huddled in horror and misery, his face spattered with blood. As relieved as he was to be alive, he felt a piercing guilt at being the only survivor among dozens of slaughtered policemen and

12

soldier guards. The German henchmen ignored him as they climbed back aboard the land ironclad.

The Fantom also vanished inside the vehicle, while his lieutenant spared a final glance for the surviving constable, who seemed oblivious to the departing soldiers. Dante said to him, "Count your blessings."

Then he swung the hatch shut, and the land ironclad roared back off the way it had come.

2

Like gigantic inflatable whales, six zeppelins floated inside a construction hangar that was large enough to swallow a small town. Spotlights shone on the graceful curved sides of the hydrogen-swollen dirigibles.

Atop the hangar, red wind socks extended parallel to snapping giant flags that displayed the colors of the German Empire. In the cool breezes that swept across the grassy lowlands off the Elbe River, the zeppelins strained against their tethers, as if restless.

Ferdinand Graf von Zeppelin had designed these huge airships, supported internally by a light skeletal framework and guided by rudders and propellers. Zeppelin himself had envisioned the military uses of these giant and silent craft after ascending in observation balloons with Union forces during the American Civil War. After retiring from military service, Zeppelin had spent most of his life's savings on independent aeronautics research—until finally the Kaiser himself had become interested enough in the work to provide much-needed financial backing.

In the past several years, Kaiser Wilhelm II had invested a fortune in the secret Valkyrie Zeppelin Works. The graceful, yet intimidating airships would be Germany's pride, drifting across the skies in fearsome formation. They looked silent and peaceful, like slumbering giants of the north.

The first gunshot rang out even before shouted orders launched the sneak attack. A German guard screamed as he died. Others scrambled for their weapons, taken completely by surprise. But no matter what they did, it was too late for them.

The Valkyrie Works were destined to fall this night.

"Forward, men! Tallyho! For Queen Victoria!" Heavily armed men wearing British military uniforms let out a simultaneous yell and rushed forward into the zeppelin factory.

Ratcheting sirens blared like prehistoric beasts in the cavernous construction hangar. Warning shouts rang out above the din, a mixture of German and English.

Straight-backed and grimly satisfied with how the operation had proceeded so far, Lieutenant Dante emerged from a workers' room. Tonight, for this second phase of the Fantom's plan, he was dressed as a British commander, even sporting a pencil-thin moustache. He directed squads of "British" soldiers as they roughly herded frightened German factory workers down iron steps from the catwalks and construction platforms above.

The radio box at Dante's hip squawked. He grabbed it, pressed it to his ear, and listened to the report from his scouts outside the factory perimeter. He scowled. "Fantom! We won't have the time we expected. The Germans are already arriving in force."

With his gleaming silver mask affixed to his mysteriously malformed face, the gaunt Fantom waited at the bottom of the metal stairs. "I expected the Kaiser to respond without delay."

Both of them spoke in richly accented English this time. The German workers—anyone who survived, that was—would hear him and remember who had attacked the extravagant new zeppelin factories in Hamburg. The Kaiser wasn't likely to be very forgiving of the British Empire.

Brandishing their modern snub-nosed weapons and shoving, the Fantom's men drove the other prisoners away. The sounds of fighting echoed intermittently through the hangar, screams, gunshots. Although the resistance was dwindling, the Kaiser's troops would arrive before long.

The Fantom turned, swirling his black cape. "But that is not relevant, Dante. Do we have the man we came for?"

The Fantom's lieutenant snapped his fingers, and one of the henchmen shoved a meek academic scientist forward. "As you requested, Fantom. This is Karl Draper, at your service, whether or not he bloody well likes it."

The Fantom regarded the cringing man before him. The German scientist wore spectacles and work overalls; from one pocket protruded a wad of cloth with which he had frequently mopped beads of perspiration from his forehead. Karl Draper looked into the bright, demonic eyes behind the silver mask; he swallowed hard at what he saw there.

"W-what do you want?" Draper asked in German, the tension of terror modulating his voice to a higher pitch.

"The *world*, Herr Draper. I want the world." Barely

visible beneath the lower curve of his mask, the Fantom's lips curled in a sinister smile. "And you will help give it to me."

The scientist looked as confused as he was frightened. "But . . . but I have no secret knowledge! I am just an architectural engineer."

The Fantom looked at Draper as if he were only a mildly interesting specimen in a very large collection. "Yes. I know."

Dante checked his boxy radio and frowned. "The Kaiser's troops have reached the gate, Fantom. They will be inside in a matter of moments, and they seem to be surprisingly well armed."

Below the mask, the Fantom's twisted lips smiled. "Yes, the Kaiser has been gearing up for war for many years now."

Dante stood, waiting for more detailed orders. "Should I tell the men to prepare for a pitched firefight?"

"Nothing so troublesome, Lieutenant. I'll provide a distraction to cover our exit. I think it will be rather impressive."

The Fantom glanced up to the hangar's next level and gestured to one of his loyal henchmen who stood on the iron steps above. The soldier tossed down a sleek and complicated rocket-launching weapon. The masked leader shrugged his cape out of the way, shouldered the weapon, and cocked the firing pin.

"Are you mad?" the German scientist cried upon seeing the rocket launcher. "This place is full of hydrogen gas!"

"Exactly." He turned to Dante. "Get Herr Draper to safety, please."

Shouting into his radio box, Dante sounded the retreat. Leaving the corralled factory prisoners waiting for rescue from the incensed German army, the invading soldiers in British uniforms beat an orderly withdrawal from the main work area.

The masked leader swung the weapon to bear on the space behind them, where the six enormous zeppelins hovered by the yawning open doors of the hangar. Shouting curses at the English, the Kaiser's reinforcements swarmed through the front doorway, demanding that the British troops surrender.

When the oncoming German soldiers were halfway across the hangar, running directly under the dirigibles, the Fantom fired the heavy rocket launcher.

"Nein!" Karl Draper shouted, his face filled with horror. Dante pushed him impatiently ahead.

Whistling, sputtering, and buzzing as it flew, the rocket trailed a control wire behind it. The Fantom studied the trajectory like an expert skeet shooter and adjusted his aim to put the nearest zeppelin in the crosshairs. He couldn't possibly miss.

The wire-controlled rocket angled up and tore through the side of the gas-filled airship, then detonated. Though a single spark would have been sufficient, the Fantom found this extravagant method more dramatic and satisfying.

Contained within baffled chambers of the huge lighter-than-air dirigible, the rich hydrogen gas erupted in incinerating flames. The explosion sent out shock waves powerful enough to knock the rushing German soldiers flat. Many of them caught fire, like living candles, screaming as they burned and fell to the hangar floor. The trapped factory workers and defeated guards tried to escape, but the flames rolled forward like fiery floodwaters from a burst dam.

A wave of flame spewed from the first dying zeppelin and ignited its nearest counterpart, triggering a catastrophic chain reaction that leaped from one zeppelin to the next. Soon, the entire Valkyrie Works were in flames.

The Fantom's silver mask caught and reflected the dazzling firestorm. He admired the holocaust he had triggered. Quite impressive.

Then he turned and followed his men, thoroughly satisfied with how well he had stirred the hornet's nest.

3

A dry savannah wind blew along dirt roads lined with single-level stores, huts, and merchant stalls. A few natives loudly hawked overripe fruits and vegetables from produce carts. The smell was thick with rot, manure, and sweat. It seemed inconceivable that a person might choose to live here unless he had absolutely no other options.

Sanderson Reed looked at his surroundings with disdain, waving his straw hat in front of his face as much to chase away the odors as to cool himself. He was a pallid bureaucrat in his late twenties; to him, traveling so far from home was an unpleasant chore instead of an adventure.

"Nairobi. The big city . . . according to the map of Kenya." He made a snorting sound.

According to the briefing M had given him, this was little more than a glorified, boggy watering hole for the Maasai people. Not exactly civilization. Reed wished he was back in London. For all its faults, at least that city had culture.

Hearing him mutter, the dark-skinned driver of the wagon turned to him. "Sorry, sir? Did you say something, sir?"

20

"Nothing worth repeating. So, where is the Britannia Club? Are we almost there?" The drive had been as interminable as it was unpleasant.

"Almost there, sir." The wagon creaked ahead down to the end of the dirt road, finally stopping beside several horses tethered to a hitching post. With a sad attempt at pride, the driver gestured. "Here it is, sir. The Britannia Club. Nairobi's finest, sir."

With a sigh of dread, Reed looked at the rundown building. "I was afraid you were going to say that." He shook his head.

The Club was certainly one of the largest and sturdiest stuctures in all of Nairobi—but that wasn't saying much. The grounds had gone to seed, making the weeds indistinguishable from the once-tended flower beds. Union Jacks drooped from poles like dead fish, engorged with humidity. The heat and flies and squalor seemed to sap the life from even the flag of the British Empire. He doubted M would have approved.

As the patient driver waited, Reed climbed gracelessly out of the wagon. "Don't wander off," he said.

"No, sir."

Stepping toward the Britannia Club, the bureaucrat wrinkled his nose as he glanced over at a rundown graveyard nearby. "Couldn't they have picked a better place to put a club? On another *continent*, perhaps?"

Reed climbed the porch steps and entered the open front door; as many flies seemed to be wandering out as venturing inside. Not a good sign. He took a moment to assess the surroundings, observing the details of the room with a sour frown.

The Britannia Club spoke of weary, faded glory, a

time when Cecil Rhodes and intrepid explorers had seen the dark continent as a treasure box to be unlocked. Allan Quartermain had personally done much to foster that impression on gullible English schoolboys who were hungry to read tales of adventure.

The walls were crowded with a hodgepodge of stuffed animals, tribal shields, stretched pelts of striped and spotted animals, and dusty portraits of forgotten English adventurers. Ivory tusks hung from the rafters.

The club was full of the empire's dregs, old men awash in gin and memories. They sat around at the tables snoring, playing cards or checkers, or endlessly repeating stories of their past escapades.

A black valet stepped up to meet him. "Good afternoon, sir. May I help you? A drink perhaps?"

"I'd prefer information." Reed explained who he was looking for, and the valet, showing no surprise at all, gestured in the direction of a red-faced fellow in his midsixties, who—from all appearances—probably spent more time drinking than adventuring.

Anxious to finish his assignment and catch the next steamer back to England, Reed briskly approached his target. A second man sat at the table, brooding and silent, probably drunk. Reed ignored the companion, now that he had found his mark.

"Excuse me, gentlemen?" He waited for them to look up at him with bleary eyes. "Do I have the pleasure of addressing Allan Quartermain?"

The red-faced man grinned at him with discolored teeth. "You do, sir. Indeed you do!" A breath heavy with the sour juniper of bad gin wafted up to him. "Only, it's *Quatermain*. Bloody press always misspells my name.

Never asked them to print my adventures anyway, and then they can't even spell my name right."

"You're not . . . at all what I expected," Reed said, disappointed. But then, so far everything about Africa, Kenya, Nairobi, and the Britannia Club had also been a disappointment. But M had been very specific about this man.

"I presume you're another traveler, got it into your head to sample the dark continent? And while you're at it, why not hunt down old Allan Quatermain and have him tell his adventures, eh? Well, I've heard that one before, and I certainly welcome the company." Jovially, the red-faced man nudged his quiet companion. "*He's* not much of a conversationalist."

The other man just grunted.

"Well, actually—" the pallid young bureaucrat said.

"Sit down, sit down. Fill a seat, fill my glass." Quatermain shouted to the bartender. "Bruce! A double!" He turned back to Reed, smiling. "And I shall regale you with how I found King Solomon's Mines. Or I could relate my exploit in Egypt when I met Ayesha, *Ayesha*, 'She who must be obeyed.'" As if they were old friends, Quatermain reached out to grasp Reed's elbow.

"Scintillating, I'm sure, but it is not your past that interests me," Reed said, peeling the man's moist hand off his sleeve. He refused to sit down.

"Not interested? That must surely be a first, sir." Bruce arrived with Quatermain's drink, which the old adventurer gladly accepted. The brooding man at the table glanced at the visitor with a faint flicker of interest.

23

"My name is Sanderson Reed. I am a representative from Her Majesty's British Government. Terrible things are happening, Mr. Quatermain, and the empire needs you." His words fell heavily on the humid air, and dropped like gassed flies.

Blinking his gin-reddened eyes, Quatermain was unsure of what to say. Fumbling, he looked over at his companion, full of unspoken questions. Then the quiet man leaned back to look Reed in the eye, his gaze sharp as a surgeon's scalpel.

Startled, Reed realized that he had been duped. As he looked more carefully at the other man, he understood that *this* must be the real Allan Quatermain. His past was written on his face, his visage etched with hard lines from a life on the veldt.

"But the question is, young man, do *I* need the empire?" said the real Quatermain. His voice was rough and rich, with a pleasant lilt.

"I—" Reed started, rummaging through his rehearsed lines to find one that might fit the situation.

The jovial imposter clutched his fresh drink, as if it were a prize that he would allow no one to pry from his hands. He looked crestfallen, as if his favorite game had been spoiled. "I'll toddle off then, shall I, Allan?"

"Yes, of course, Nigel. You toddle off." Quatermain turned back to Reed. "Nigel is useful for keeping the story-seekers at bay. I'm Quatermain. Now, either sit down or leave, but don't just stand there like another one of those tiresome stuffed hunting trophies."

Reed quickly took the seat that Nigel had vacated. "The empire is in peril," he said again, lamely. He had expected that phrase to be sufficient.

"I'm sure you're too young to know, Mr. Reed, but the empire is always in some kind of peril," the old adventurer answered. "It gets to be as tedious as Nigel's inflated stories of things I may or may not have done."

Reed remained insistent. "We need you to lead a team of uniquely skilled men, like yourself, to combat this threat."

Quatermain gestured for the bartender to refill his glass and pour a stiff drink for Reed, who by now felt he needed one. "Very well. Explain yourself, and please try to make it interesting."

The bureaucrat sniffed. "You may not be much aware of current events, since Nairobi is so . . . unfortunately isolated. Believe me, there is great unrest. Europe, the Orient, parts of Asia, and even here on the dark continent. Many countries are on the brink of war on an unprecedented scale." His voice finally found its fervor.

Quatermain raised his eyebrows. "This is 'news'? The natives realize that they don't need their Great White Father. It's about bloody time."

"You think this is just unrest among the British colonies? If it were that simple, we'd deal with it in a snap," Reed said. "The Queen's army has plenty of resources to deal with ordinary problems such as that."

The famous old hunter ignored his fresh drink as his indignation grew. "Oh, yes, I know the practice. Send in the troops, kill a few villagers, and peace is restored." He made a disgusted sound. "No. Request denied. I'm not going anywhere." He crossed his arms over his chest. "You may leave now."

Reed did not accept the rebuff, but pressed on as he

had been instructed to do. "Europe is a sticky place at the moment. Countries at each other's throats, baying for blood. It's a powder keg. The trouble of which I speak could set a match to the whole thing, extending far beyond the British Empire. War."

You keep saying that. But a war with whom exactly?" Quatermain said, irritation and curiosity coloring his tone.

"Everyone. A *world war.*"

Instead of reacting with shock, the old adventurer nodded slowly, digesting the information. "And that notion makes you sweat, Mr. Reed?"

"Heavens, man! Doesn't it you?"

"This is Africa, dear boy. Sweating is what we do." Quatermain turned from Reed and picked up a copy of *The Strand Magazine* lying beside a deck of worn playing cards on the adjacent table; the issue was several months old, featuring a new story by the imaginative young writer H. G. Wells. "It's been almost interesting talking with you, Mr. Reed. Good day. Have a nice trip back to England."

Reed just blinked at him in disbelief. "Where's your sense of patriotism, Quatermain? Even though this is godforsaken Kenya, we're in the *Britannia* Club, for heaven's sake."

Quatermain stood, snapped to comical attention, and turned to his fellow drinkers as he raised his glass. "God save the Queen!"

Everyone in the bar responded with automatic enthusiasm, like windup toys. "God save the Queen!" A moment later they fell back to their drinking and card games and snoozing.

"And that's about as patriotic as it gets around here, Mr. Reed," Quatermain said as he sat down.

At the front entrance to the Britannia Club, he noticed more new arrivals, one of them carrying a leather case. The valet stepped up to the four travelers, who asked him what was obviously a familiar question by now. The adventurer sighed and turned back to Reed, who remained oblivious.

The young bureaucrat insisted in a low voice to keep the man's secret. "But you're Allan Quatermain! Stories of your exploits have thrilled English boys for decades."

"That I know. Nigel does a grand job of reminding me."

Predictably, the four new travelers approached jovial Nigel, who sat up on the sagging leather couch where he had gone to rest. One of them carried a brown satchel, which he tucked under a small table near the bar before stepping in front of the red-faced "adventurer."

Smiling, Nigel prepared for another performance. Quatermain's stand-in had already finished the drink he'd ordered upon Reed's arrival; these new visitors would no doubt buy him a new one.

Quatermain sighed sadly. "With each of my past 'exploits' those English boys find so entertaining, Mr. Reed, I have lost friends. Dear friends, white men and black—and more besides. I am not the man I once claimed to be. Maybe I never was."

In the background, Nigel spoke now-familiar words, putting his heart into the act. "Yes, indeed. I'm Allan Quatermain. Sit down—fill a seat, fill my glass." He signaled the bartender for his usual. "Bruce—"

Suddenly, one of the travelers pulled a handgun from his vest. In a single smooth movement, he shot Nigel in the chest. The florid-faced stand-in adventurer slammed backward into the leather sofa, then he slumped down, seeping red from the deep wound. His empty gin glass clattered to the floor.

4

The Britannia Club

Time seemed to stand still. Quatermain stared as his friend Nigel slumped dead.

Then the Britannia Club erupted into utter chaos as the other three newcomers also drew weapons. The old dregs of the empire—men who hadn't moved with such speed for decades—now dove for safety behind chairs and under tables. Cards and checkers and magazines scattered in a flurry. One potbellied man cowered behind a stuffed water buffalo; a bald veteran yanked a Zulu war shield from the wall and held it in front of him.

Quatermain, though, did not hide. He pulled an old but well-oiled Webley revolver from his jacket, pulled back the hammer, and fired. A single shot to the head took out the first assassin before the other three had time to realize what was happening. The man fell dead on top of Nigel.

"Wrong Quatermain," the old adventurer said.

The other assassins turned to see Quatermain coolly recocking his Webley, then realized their mistake. "That's him!" They dove for cover, returning fire even as the famous hunter shot again.

The room became a hail of bullets that chewed the club's already-battered paneling to pieces. Bottles shattered, and stuffed animals exploded. Quatermain dashed over to take cover behind Nigel's sagging leather sofa, dragging Reed with him. As he ran, ducked low, he took perfect shots at his attackers. His aim was accurate from a lifetime of practice—but the bullets ricocheted off their chests.

"They're indestructible!" Reed stared in amazement from behind the sofa, until Quatermain pulled him back down. The assassins returned fire, and bullets tore through the upholstery, popping out coarse hemp stuffing near Reed's ear.

"No. Just armor-plated." Quatermain cautiously reached around the couch to check Nigel's nonexistent pulse. "Remember what I was saying about losing friends every time someone wants me to get involved in another adventure?" He sighed with utter world-weariness. "Nigel was one of the last friends I had."

As the young bureaucrat huddled against the continuing gunfire, Quatermain grabbed a handy wicker chair and heaved it over the back of the bullet-riddled sofa. Using the chair as a distraction, he leaped up and over the couch.

The three bulletproof assassins fired with new weapons now—fully automatic machine rifles, far more modern than Quatermain's Webley revolver. After the thrown wicker chair exploded into splinters and dust, the killers turned their noisy, deadly weapons at the new target.

Shocked to see the automatic machine rifles cause faster and more thorough carnage than he had ever imagined, Quatermain realized he was caught in the crossfire. He dove for cover so frantically that his trusted revolver went skittering across the debris-strewn floor of the club. He ducked a stuffed lion that was shot to pieces, then took cover next to an elderly hunter, who was clumsily loading his shotgun.

"What in God's name! Automatic rifles?" he said.

"Dashed unsporting, if you ask me," said the elderly hunter. "They're probably Belgian. Shouldn't be allowed in the Club." Indignant, the old man stood up and fired his shotgun, winging one of the assassins. Quatermain was glad to see that their armor protection did not extend to their arms as well.

A second assassin coolly shot the elderly hunter dead, using at least a dozen more bullets than was necessary and expending the last rounds in his automatic machine rifle.

Furious, Quatermain snatched up the elderly man's fallen shotgun and blasted with the second barrel. His shot sent the assassin diving for cover, then he waded in, his anger endowing him with more confidence than the bulletproof plating gave his attackers.

Recovering from the shock, the downed assassin crawled across the floor, clutching the flesh wound on his blood-soaked sleeve. The second killer struggled to reload his empty automatic rifle. The third assassin wrenched a thick paw from the ruined stuffed carcass of a lion; the taxidermist had extended the lion's claws to make the trophy look more ferocious. Using the stiff paw as a club, he slashed at Quatermain with the hooked claws.

But the old adventurer was faster. He smashed the

man with a liquor bottle he grabbed from the bar, shattering it over his unprotected head. "Wicked waste of good scotch."

Finally finished reloading his machine rifle, the second assassin raised his weapon to fire—but Quatermain crashed into him with a rattling tea trolley. He sprawled with a yelp, and the famous adventurer lifted the cart and broke it over the man's head. Cakes and china cups went flying in all directions.

The distinctive click of a gun being cocked made Quatermain whirl, ready. His heart pounded, his blood flowed, his muscles *worked*—just as they had in his younger days. But instead of another enemy, he saw pallid Sanderson Reed nervously aiming the old Webley, which he had retrieved from the floor.

"You're liable to hurt someone with that," Quatermain said.

"I—I just wanted to help—"

"Allan!" Bruce the bartender called out. "Heads up, man!"

Quatermain whirled and barely dodged a swarm of sharp silver throwing knives. With a staccato patter, the blades thunked like arrows up the face of a wooden pillar in the middle of the gathering room. The last few knives stapled Quatermain's collar to the mahogany.

The man who had been grazed by the elderly hunter's shotgun blast looked badly wounded, his right shirt sleeve soaked with blood. But he was still coming, and he could throw with his uninjured arm.

Quatermain grimaced. "Just my luck the bastard's left handed."

Bending awkwardly, he tried to pull the knives loose,

32

but the thick material of his sweat-damp shirt would not tear free. He succeeded only in slicing his callused hand.

Seeing his victim pinned like a moth to a specimen board, the wounded assassin brandished a big gutting knife. He smiled as he stabbed at Quatermain's head.

Though he had limited mobility, the old adventurer thrashed and evaded the wicked strikes. So the assassin gripped the big knife and tried for his victim's gut, using an underarm swing.

Amazed at his own resilience after being so long out of practice, Quatermain squirmed his hips and hauled his body up out of the way, just as the assassin's blade stuck deep into the wood, driven by all his force.

Coming down from his agile move, Quatermain whacked the man on the head. The assassin grunted, and his own weight finally succeeded in pulling the wedged blade free—just in time for him to fall onto the point of his own gutting knife.

Then, covered with cream and jam like a monster from a mad baker's nightmare, the last assassin broke free from beneath the tea trolley, where he had lain stunned. He lunged forward, frothing frosting, and snatched up his own gun.

Quatermain spun, now that he was free of the knives. With a roar, he hefted a table as a shield, scattering checkers. He charged the pastry-clotted killer at full speed, hitting the man hard and driving him back toward the trophy-covered wall.

The blow spiked the assassin on a curved rhino horn mounted for show over the fireplace. The man's eyes bulged and he coughed powdered sugar, then oozed a bright red that was definitely not raspberry jam.

The impact knocked loose a large British flag hanging overhead; it floated down, smartly shrouding the assassin in his final death throes.

"Rule Britannia," Quatermain said, standing back and lifting his chin in satisfaction. He wiped perspiration off his forehead, catching his breath.

Reed shook his head, amazed by what he had just seen. "Well, Mr. Quatermain, I believe that only verifies—"

Impatient and still angry, the adventurer looked around. "Wait. Wasn't there one more of these buggers? I don't think I lost count—"

The black valet gestured at the door, calling out in high-pitched alarm, "Mister Quatermain!"

He looked to see the last killer running for his life. He'd been wounded in the scuffle, but that hadn't slowed him in the least. The assassin had already left the Club grounds and sprinted some distance down the dirt street toward the milling villagers, vegetable stands, shacks, and rickety cattle corrals.

"Bloody jackrabbit," Quatermain said, and turned to the bartender. "Bruce, it's time for Matilda."

The barman reverently pulled an elephant gun from behind the bar. "Matilda, sir." He tossed the long weapon to Quatermain, who caught it in mid-stride on his way to the Club doorway.

Quatermain glanced down at a small leather case that he thought one of the four assassins had been carrying when they'd entered the room. He frowned, wondering why the killers would have tucked it under a small table by the bar—but he turned his attention to the immediate problem at hand. The last of the four assassins was getting away.

Eyes gleaming, Reed followed him through the doorway onto the shaded porch of the Club.

"Our bolter may have answers." Quatermain inspected and then shouldered the elephant gun.

"But he's so far away," Reed said. "You'll never hit him."

Quatermain ignored the remark, taking aim. He squinted, shook his head and lowered the gun.

"Yes, I thought he was—" Reed said, nodding with a trace of smugness.

But Quatermain wasn't finished. He took a pair of wire glasses from his shirt pocket. "God, I hate getting old." He put the glasses on, adjusted them, and took aim again. The elephant gun belched a roar like a cannon, and Reed flinched, squeezing his eyes shut and clapping his hands over his ears.

The bullet covered the distance to its target at incredible speed. The wounded assassin glanced back, thinking he'd gotten away—and the projectile slammed into his unprotected shoulder, shattering bone and flesh. He yelped and fell to the ground, sprawling on the trampled dirt of the road.

Quatermain lowered his gun and put his glasses away. He cracked his neck, surprised and exhilarated. "Well then, let us see what that fellow has to say for himself." He went to the hitching post and swiftly untied one of the waiting horses. He handed the reins of a second to Reed. "Nigel won't mind if you borrow his horse."

The two men approached the downed assassin, riding hard. Many locals had already left their market stalls and huts, gathering to stare at the bleeding killer, who was dressed as an Englishman.

Reed shook his head, his face paler than usual. "They must have learned I was coming for you. They wanted to kill you before you could offer to help."

"Obviously," said Quatermain.

They dismounted, striding forward like conquerors. The wounded assassin looked at them with fanatical determination, then used his one good arm to fumble desperately in his pockets. His other shoulder was a smashed and bloody ruin from the elephant gun.

"It's no use, man," Reed told him. "We'll get you to a doctor, and then to jail."

Finally, the assassin found a pill in his rumpled pocket and pulled it free with blood-spattered fingers.

Quatermain rushed forward. "Stop him! We need the information!"

He grabbed the man's wrist, but it was too late. The assassin bit down on the pill with a smug smile that instantly transformed into a pain-wracked grimace as he died.

Cursing, Quatermain dropped the man's wrist in disgust. The crowd looked at him in awe, but the old adventurer wanted no part of them.

After all that had happened, Reed did not forget his primary mission. He cleared his throat. "You may have no love for the empire, Mr. Quatermain, but I know you love Africa." He gestured around him, as if there might be something admirable to be found in Nairobi. "A war in Europe will spread to its colonies—"

Suddenly, behind them, the Britannia Club exploded.

Flames erupted through the door and roof; windows shattered. Splinters flew up into the air. The support beams toppled, and the whole structure groaned, then collapsed into an inferno.

Quatermain stared, his lips curled downward in a frown.

No longer interested in the assassin's motionless body, the crowd of natives turned their attention to the explosion. Shouting with excitement, they rushed toward the Brittania Club to help, or at least watch from up close.

Quatermain's eyes were steely as he watched his home burn.

"It appears the war has already arrived here," Reed finished. "You can't hide from it, Quatermain."

"All right. I'm in," the old adventurer said. "Damn . . ."

Reed smiled. "Excellent. Pack for an English summer."

With a smug look, the young bureaucrat strode away to the waiting buggy. The driver hadn't moved from his seat, watching all the excitement with bemused interest.

As he took two steps to follow, Quatermain hesitated, then looked back toward the African veldt, with its open skies and waving grasses. Thunderheads were gathering over the windswept plains.

Near the burning wreckage of the old Brittania Club, the forlorn, crumbling graveyard stood against the magnificent vista, and Quatermain thought of all the friends, acquaintances, lovers he had buried there.

It was time to leave.

5

Under torrential rain, a hansom cab drove north from Oxford Street. The driver tilted his derby, and cold water poured off the brim onto his already drenched lap. The rubberized fabric of his mackintosh was proof against the downpour, but the water found ways to creep between the folds of his coat and down his trouser legs into his shoes.

Nevertheless, the driver maintained his good cheer. His grin was sincere as he called down into the cab at his fare. "Nice day for doing, eh sir?" As if anyone could carry on a conversation with the din of the drumming rain and the clopping and splashing of the horse's hooves on the wet cobblestones.

"Yes . . . absolutely idyllic," said Quatermain. His voice was the only dry thing on the whole street.

The cab had as many leaks as it had uncomfortable lumps on the seat, and more than its share of groaning, creaking noises. He felt very far from home, and comfort. After his long journey from Africa, he had hoped to nap in these last few moments before attending the meeting that Sanderson Reed had arranged.

But as with so many others, those hopes had been dashed.

The hansom cab pulled up outside the stately Albion Museum in London, where Reed waited, holding an open black umbrella. Moving as if he was afraid of being attacked at any moment, the bureaucrat hurried forward into the rain. He opened the cab's door, and muddy water sloshed from the sideboard. "You made good time getting here, Mr. Quatermain."

"Not as good as Phileas Fogg." The old adventurer stepped out of the cab and stood in the rain, taller than Reed's umbrella. "Fellow went round the world in eighty days."

He had been in monsoon seasons before, and had spent many a night in swamps or huddling under baobab trees for shelter. Monsoons on the veldt had a purity, cleansing the air with fresh moisture; here, confined in the city, the downpour simply turned the grime into muck.

"No need to go around the world. Coming to London is sufficient, sir." Reed paid the driver, meticulously counting out the appropriate amount in coins and intentionally forgetting a tip. Then he took the umbrella's protection for himself, even if Quatermain didn't want it. "This way, please. Your contact is waiting."

Quatermain had the impression he was being watched, a sense he'd developed from long years as a hunter and explorer. A glance over his shoulder showed him a young man across the street who wore an overcoat and cap to keep the rain off him. The clothing also succeeded in hiding the young man's face, making him seem up to no good; he was clearly enduring a soaking just to catch a glimpse of Allan Quatermain.

Alas, he no longer had Nigel's playacting to cover him.

"If you please, Mr. Quatermain?" Reed said, urging him along.

They ascended the steps toward the museum. Passing between the museum's stone columns, under the ornate arches, and through the door into blessed dryness, the two men walked with echoing, squeaking footsteps on the polished floor. Reed snapped the umbrella shut and shook it. Rainwater running off their clothes made the marble tiles treacherously slippery.

Quatermain looked around the Albion's dim displays illuminated by gas lamps that had been lit early this afternoon because of the rain's gloom. He saw proudly displayed antiquities, statues, and assorted treasures. He felt a pang, reminded somewhat of the dreary trophies hanging in the Britannia Club.

Brisk and officious, Reed led him directly to a wooden doorway marked NO ADMITTANCE TO THE GENERAL PUBLIC. Fumbling with a fistfull of keys, he unlocked the door and swung it open on groaning hinges. "This way, please. It's down just a few levels."

The two men descended staircase after staircase into the bowels of the stodgy museum. It was like stumbling through the prison caves of Ayesha, and with each new level, Quatermain lost a bit more of his patience. "How deep are we going? Has one of your explorers found a passage to the center of the Earth?"

The winding stairs finally terminated in a low brick corridor that looked as if it had been modeled on the Paris sewers. A closed wooden door at the far end blocked the hall. "I have done my part, Mr. Quatermain, and I will take my leave of you now. Perhaps we will meet again." He motioned for the old adventurer to enter through the door. "My employer will explain the rest."

The old hunter felt a prickle of hairs on the back of his neck similar to what he experienced the times he'd entered the rank-smelling den of a lion. Perhaps he would find predators even here, though of a different sort. He hesitated, suddenly wary.

Reed stood at the door and waited, then cleared his throat impatiently. Quatermain finally stepped inside, and the bureaucrat closed the door, plunging the hidden private room into shadow.

To most men, this darkness would have disguised the room's secrets, but Allan Quatermain knew how to make full use of all his senses. He sniffed the air. "I've come a long way to be playing childrens' games. Who are you?"

The red dot of a glowing cigarette gave the smoker away on the far side of the room. His chuckle sounded like desiccated, rattling bones. "After Africa's dry and sunny veldts, London's weather isn't improving your mood, I see."

With the turn of one knob on a small panel, blue-orange gaslight flickered up close to a fiftyish man so gaunt that the shadows turned him into a skeleton. His head seemed overly large for his thin neck, his brow heavy and solid. His cigarette holder angled jauntily upward.

Quatermain was not impressed. "I asked for your name, not speculations on my mood."

Slim and self-assured, the man sucked on the black

end of his cigarette holder and blew a long, gray breath. "I am known by many names, Mr. Quatermain. My underlings call me sir. My superiors call me . . . M."

"M?"

"Just M."

"Not very adept at spelling, I suppose," Quatermain grumbled. "I hope your superiors don't boast diplomas from Oxford."

"Charming." M was neither particularly annoyed nor amused. "I must say, the delight is mine—meeting so notable a recruit to this newest generation of the League of Extraordinary Gentlemen. Thank you for joining us."

"League of . . . what?" Quatermain asked.

M turned more gas knobs, and the isolated chamber was fully illuminated in dramatic pools of flickering gaslight. A long table was surrounded by sumptuous leather chairs. "This is a most exclusive society, Mr. Quatermain. Membership is rather difficult to come by."

The old adventurer was not enamored with the honor. He had just left the destroyed Britannia Club and had wasted many days and nights in travel; he had no intention of coming all this way to London just to become part of another gentlemens' society. "I believe I've made a mistake in coming here."

"You will make a bigger mistake if you leave." M did not rise from his chair. "Come, look around. It will give me a chance to explain."

The meeting room of the League of Extraordinary Gentlemen was filled with exquisite sculptures, priceless paintings, the finest furniture. The paraphernalia seemed more mysterious and intriguing than the pompous relics in the main halls of the museum above.

"You see, Mr. Quatermain," M said, "there have been many times when a danger upon the world required the service of singular individuals." With a cadaverous smile, he gestured to group portraits of various adventurers from history lumped together in their approximate eras. Quatermain recognized many of them, and saw that he was in distinguished company indeed.

"The task has fallen to me to assemble another group of heroes for our modern age. I am pleased to count you among them."

"It's like a shrine," the adventurer said, not liking the idea. He looked up at a portrait of swarthy Richard Burton dressed as an Arab. "How very curious."

"In its main exhibit halls and here in the private chambers, this museum is full of the curious." M looked over Quatermain's shoulder, suddenly smiling as another man entered. "And the extraordinary. Allan Quatermain, please meet Captain Nemo."

Quatermain turned to see a thin and shadowy man quietly closing the door. He moved with the silent grace of a cat, and his face wore the hard expression of an age-wearied man, though he looked to be only about fifty years old. Nemo was very distinguished in a blue uniform that combined elements of naval captain and Indian nabob, with a sash tied at his waist. His skin was dark tan, and his full dark beard extended to his heart. The blue turban on his head further marked his Indian heritage.

"I know of Mr. Quatermain," Nemo said, without giving further details. His voice was deep and smooth, like cool molasses.

"And I know of you, Captain," Quatermain countered. "Rumor has it that you are a pirate."

Nemo turned a set of black eyes on him. He crossed his arms over his uniformed chest. "I'd prefer a less provocative title."

"I'm sure you would."

M watched the two men, bemused, as if he saw visible lines of tension in the air. He smiled.

"From one such as you, certainly, who stands as a symbol of the British Empire's domination of foreign lands—" Nemo began.

"I am neither a symbol, nor a slaver," Quatermain interrupted. His nostrils flared. He himself had seen the excesses of colonial oppression, downtrodden natives, cultures and societies railroaded into conformity "for their own good" by the White Man's Burden.

Nemo noted his reaction with approval and reconsidered his initial assessment. "Perhaps I have made a premature assumption. I have sufficient enemies in the world. I do not need to make more."

Quatermain backed off and turned his attention to another portrait. "I'm rather surprised, Nemo—knowing your history—that you agreed to this enterprise. You struck me as being an . . . independent sort."

"Independence? Yes. I seek my people's release from the British Empire."

From his overstuffed chair, M explained, "In return for Captain Nemo's aid, we'll open a dialogue with the Indian government."

"That is reason enough, I suppose," Quatermain said.

"*One* reason," corrected Nemo.

"And the other?" Quatermain asked.

"Is my concern." Nemo stood rigid, clearly not intending to volunteer any further information.

M stubbed out his cigarette in a terra-cotta ashtray. "Gentlemen, shall we get started?" He tossed a large manila folder in front of Quatermain. It slid across the polished table, and the adventurer picked it up, flipping through the papers. Inside were pictures and dossiers of three people.

"What did Reed tell you, Mr. Quatermain? How much do you know?"

"He spoke of unrest." The old hunter paced back and forth beneath the impressive portraits of his League predecessors as he perused the dossiers. "I recommended laudanum."

M folded his bony, long-fingered hands together. "This trouble can't be medicated, I'm afraid. Nations are striking at nations. England is on the brink of declaring war against the Kaiser. Germany has vowed revenge against the British Empire. France, Italy, Belgium, they all have swords drawn and armies rallied. The slightest spark will set them off. It will be like a street brawl on a global scale."

The dossier held intelligence illustrations of heavily armored land ironclads, streamlined cannons, rocket launchers, and countless other machines of war. Quatermain flipped through the pictures, his frown deepening.

M explained. "Many of the recent attacks were marked by the use of highly advanced weaponry, amazing technological breakthroughs that have caused unprecedented destruction. Each country denies its actions, despite clear evidence to the contrary and many witnesses that firmly place the blame on other governments." He cracked his bony knuckles with a sound like gunshots. "Europe is a tinderbox. A world at war is a genuine possibility." Then M calmly remembered his duties as host. "Sherry?"

"Always thought it a woman's drink," Quatermain said.

M poured himself a sherry, despite the other man's deprecations. "I'll alert the servants they should begin brewing gin in the bath for you, shall I?"

"One doesn't brew gin. One distills it," Quatermain muttered.

Captain Nemo stood straight and silent, watching and listening. M took the folder from Quatermain's hands and spread the pages on the table so they all could see. "Our boys abroad have been hard at work to obtain all this information."

"You mean your spies," Quatermain said.

"They've discovered that, despite the accounts of witnesses, these widely separated attacks are all the work of one man who calls himself the 'Fantom.' "

"Very operatic. Does he wear a mask? Have a scarred face?" Quatermain asked.

"As a matter of fact, he does."

The old adventurer's surprise and sarcasm deflated. He took one of the leather seats around the table. "What's in it for him?"

"Profit. Sheer profit." M pointed to the illustrations. "Those ingenious machines are the Fantom's creations, the work of experts he holds imprisoned. He has captured the greatest scientists and engineers from various countries, forcing them to develop new methods of absolute destruction—and his sham attacks may be little more than extravagant demonstrations of his wares.

"Worse, the Fantom's provocative strikes have every nation clamoring to acquire the very weapons that assail them. England demands to possess them before the Germans do. Portugal wants them before Spain. The French insist on having them before the British. An endless circle."

"Then it is a 'race for arms,' " said Quatermain.

"While millions perish," Nemo said with an angry, resigned sigh. "My struggle against War itself has accomplished little, after all these years."

"There's one last chance to avert war. The leaders of Europe will meet secretly in Venice. They will expose the Fantom's plans and reach an accord against him. This summit meeting must remain hidden from all the patriots and local warmongers who are ready to go to war. The greatest threat, though, comes from the Fantom himself."

"Then you believe this Fantom will attack the conference?" Quatermain said.

"If he can find it—and I would not doubt his ability to obtain such information. By striking the secret meeting and assassinating the leaders of the anxious nations, he will surely trigger the world-scale war he desires so much.

"The I-types don't trust us, gentlemen, so we can't send in conventional forces. We need a team to get to Venice and stop the Fantom." He closed the dossier. "You have four days."

"Four days to reach Venice? From London? Impossible!" Quatermain cried.

"Let me worry about that," Nemo said.

Quatermain glanced at Nemo's file and understood. "Well now, four days it is." He looked at the Indian captain with new respect. "Extraordinary gentlemen, indeed."

"And in that four days you must also assemble the rest of your team." M removed a pocket watch, flipped it open, and glanced at the time. "One of them is late: Harker, the chemist."

"Well, he'd better learn how to tell time," said an unseen man, a new voice that seemed to come from the air itself. "It's not so much to ask."

Quatermain looked about, mystified. The gaslight was bright, and he saw no convenient shadows or alcoves in which a man might hide. "My eyesight must be worse than I thought."

A new dossier dropped out of the air onto the others strewn across the tabletop. "Your eyesight's fine. Heh!"

"No games, M," Quatermain warned.

"I told you our members were extraordinary, Mr. Quatermain," M said. "A while ago a talented—albeit misguided—man of science discovered the means to become invisible. A Mr. Hawley Griffin. Perhaps you've heard of him, even in Kenya?"

"Yes, I recall the tale. But . . . didn't he die? Something about a mob reaction?"

The unseen man continued. "He died, but his invisibility process didn't. I stole the formula . . . and here I stand for all to see."

"Is this some parlor trick, M?" Quatermain, scowled, then abruptly flinched as something invisible slapped him in the head.

"Boo!" said the unseen man. "Believe it."

"Enough, Ghost," Nemo said.

"Oooh, he speaks!" the invisible man chortled. "I thought for a moment the nefarious captain had been stuffed. Pleased to meet you both. I'm Rodney Skinner, gentleman thief."

M frowned in the direction of the voice. "Skinner, make yourself presentable."

The invisible thief's coat, draped on the back of a chair, started to move by itself. It took shape as the man got dressed, tugging arms through the sleeves. Next, a pot of white greasepaint rose into the air.

Skinner continued to chat as he dressed. "You see, I thought invisibility would be a boon to my work, being a thief and all. Heh! You can imagine." His grease-painted lips blew out a sigh. "My undoing—once you're invisible, it's bloody hard to turn back."

The transparent hand continued to dab greasepaint on his face, distributing smears so that his physiognomy took shape eerily as he spoke. "And it's bloody hard to spend your money if no one can see you."

"In the end, we finally caught him," M said. "He'll be a valuable member of your team."

"And they'll provide the antidote if I'm a good boy," Skinner said, explaining the real reason for his cooperation.

"And are you a good boy?" Quatermain asked.

"I guess you'll find out, won't you?"

The door quickly opened again, and all eyes turned toward the voice. "Am I late?" A beautiful woman stood at the door, carefully pushing it shut.

Quatermain blinked at her stunning appearance. She was slender and fit-looking, dressed in a stylish but not gaudy dress. She appeared to be in her early thirties with startlingly green eyes and dark hair; a white silken scarf was chastely tied around her throat. Her skin was ivory pale, as perfect as milk.

"Why, being late is a woman's prerogative, Mrs. Harker." M showed no trace of annoyance at all.

Quatermain groaned quietly. This meeting had grown worse with each new revelation. "Please, M, tell me this is Harker's wife with a sick note."

Her green eyes flashed at him with a surprisingly feral light. " 'Sick' would be a mild understatement, sir. My husband's been dead for years. At the moment, I am perfectly capable of taking care of myself."

"Gentlemen, this is Mrs. Wilhelmina Harker," M said. "Please welcome her to our League."

"And you couldn't find a chemist with—" Quatermain began, remembering all the times and all the adventures where women had caused him trouble.

"With the right to vote? Alas, no," Mina said.

M was unruffled. He sucked on the end of his cigarette holder again. "In addition to her chemical abilities, Mina's . . . prior acquaintance with a reluctant team member may also be of use to us."

Mina grimaced slightly, as if she didn't look forward to meeting her "prior acquaintance" again.

"And that's it? Chemistry and an old friendship?" Quatermain raised his eyebrows. "Come on, I'm waiting to be impressed." Many lives would depend upon the abilities of the members of this team.

"Patience . . . is a virtue," Mina said, then added in a sultry, eerily hypnotic voice, "Are you virtuous?"

"The clock hands turn, gentlemen," said M, gathering

all the dossiers. "As I said earlier, we have very little time. You have other members to recruit before you depart for Venice."

"Kicking us out, already?" the now greasepainted Skinner asked. "A moment ago it was all sherry and giggles."

6

London

Still uneasy in their partnership, Quatermain, Mina, Nemo, and Skinner emerged from the museum onto the street, where it was still raining.

The invisible man wore a long coat, slouching hat, dark pince-nez, and full white makeup on his exposed skin. He opened an umbrella to shelter himself from the downpour. "Care to snuggle close?" he asked Mina. "Heh."

"I'd rather get drenched, thank you." She lifted her chin and turned away from his greasepainted leer.

"Come now, you're not still upset about that little incident at Miss Rosa Coote's Correctional Academy for Wayward Gentlewomen, are you?"

Mina turned to him. regarding his unreadable mask coolly. "That is only one of the many despicable things about you, Mr. Skinner. Getting girls pregnant by claiming to be the Holy Spirit—indeed! How am I to choose only one reason to avoid you?"

As they walked down the wet stone steps toward the street, Quatermain stopped in his tracks. Instead of a hansom cab, a strange vehicle waited for them at the curb, massive and six-wheeled with a brute engine under its expansive hood. "What in God's name is that?"

Mina Harker and the invisible man also looked surprised and puzzled, but Nemo simply strode forward. "It is mine."

"Good one, Nemo. It really helps when you're so bloody mysterious," Skinner said. "What *is* it?"

"The future, gentlemen. The future."

"I believe it is an unorthodox design of an automobile," Mina said. "I notice several fundamental similarities to the contraptions currently being marketed by Karl Benz in Germany and Henry Ford in America."

Nemo regarded this as somewhat of an affront. Although Karl Benz was indeed selling automobiles—and would probably become the most successful manufacturer of the vehicles within a year or two—Ford had yet to do more than build a prototype. If Ford didn't begin a marketing program soon, Nemo doubted the man's work would ever amount to anything.

The captain, a consummate designer and inventor in his own right, had researched the capabilities of every model in the world to date and found them all wanting, so he had created his own design. He was proud of the innovations his vehicle represented, but he did not intend to share them with other money-hungry industrialists.

Nemo stepped up to the side of the muscular automobile. Its steam exhaust vents and swirling lines were marked out in elegant Hindu style, functionality with a veneer of ornateness. Though spattered with the dirt and soot of London's streets, the metallic adornments showed gleaming gold, silver, and chrome over colorful alloy body plates. The vehicle's six wheels would allow it to drive overland as well as down the smoothest streets.

A tough-looking older man stepped away from the car and saluted Nemo. "Waiting for you, Captain. Ready to go." He opened the side hatch and bade them enter.

Nemo nodded politely to the man and introduced him. "This is my first mate."

"Call me Ishmael," said the old man.

Curious, Skinner clambered into the dry car then reached out his gloved hand to help Mina in, but she pointedly entered without his help. "I wouldn't want you to smear your makeup."

"What, Missy? You were intending to give me a little kiss? Aheh!"

"I meant to smear it with my knuckles, not my lips."

Nemo entered the car, and Quatermain came last, taking a final wary glance at the street. From the far corner, he once again saw the suspicious-looking young man lurking on a sheltered stoop, still watching them. Quatermain frowned, then ignored the observer who was so painfully obvious about being unobtrusive. "If the Fantom hires only amateurs like that, then we don't have much to worry about," he muttered.

The vehicle's engine rumbled loudly, then the six tires began to turn, moving them at increasing speed along the streets. "Our destination's not more'n a mile away," Ishmael said. "Hang on."

"What a cheerful fellow," said Skinner.

Uncomfortably silent, Quatermain, Nemo, and Mina sat in the car.

The invisible man turned to Quatermain. "So how did M get you?"

"It's none of your business. For a thief you certainly talk a lot. No wonder you were caught."

Skinner snickered. "Oh, I see! Found something to hold over you. Saucy daguerreotypes? I've heard that jaded travelers find the long-limbed boys of North Africa a delicious respite—"

"Do shut up."

Skinner turned back to Mina, grinning behind his face paint. "Ah, that's nothing compared to how the League got me, eh Ms. Harker? Heh! Aheh!"

"A sordid business theme is no need to relate, so as Mr. Quatermain said, do shut up." Her mouth formed a tight rosebud of annoyance. "I have no wish to revisit it."

Now the invisible man seemed to be pouting, though it was difficult to tell behind his greasepaint and dark glasses. "Just making conversation, Ma'am, and Quatermain. Hold onto your pith helmet. If we're all supposed to work together, and risk our lives together, what's wrong with a little healthy curiosity?"

Nemo brooded, looking at the others with intense dark eyes. "The thief's question was perfectly acceptable, Mr. Quatermain. Why are you here?"

"I have been pressed into service to resolve a situation in which you are all participants," Quatermain said, which answered nothing at all.

"A little testy, Mr. Q," said Mina.

"Please call me by my full name, Mrs. Harker. Let us leave the mysterious single letters to our friend M, all right? Besides, I doubt if a woman would measure danger the way that I do."

Mina retorted, "And I imagine you with quite the library, Mr. Quatermain. All those books you must have read—merely by looking at their covers . . . ?"

The confines of Nemo's car seemed to be oppressively close. Quatermain felt defensive. "It is not an assessment I make without basis. I've had women along on past exploits, and I've found them to be either a nuisance or outright trouble. At best, they are a distraction."

"Oh?" Mina said. "Do I distract you?"

"My dear girl, I've buried two wives and many lovers. And I'm in no hurry for more of either."

"Well, aheh, you can send them my way—" the invisible man said, leaning forward.

"Skinner, shut up," Quatermain and Mina rang out simultaneously.

Nemo sat stock-still, his back rigid in the seat, as if he heard nothing of the silly quarrels.

Ishmael brought the car to a gliding halt, and the engine puttered and hissed. "Here we are, Captain. Tiger Bay, East of Limehouse."

Only too happy to be out of the odd-looking car, and the company it contained, Quatermain fumbled with the latch and eventually figured out how to operate the door. He stepped out and took a deep breath of the damp air as mist rolled in after the rain. He could smell the mud of the river and fish from the markets. Warehouses large and small lined the Thames bank. Water lapped eerily against the nearby docks.

Nemo emerged and waited for Mina and Skinner to join him. They all stood together in the street.

"Shall I wait, Captain?" Ishmael called from the driver's compartment.

Nemo's eyes narrowed beneath his turban. "No, Ishmael. Bring my Lady to me."

The first mate nodded and drove away. The evening fog had already begun to thicken, and people were hurrying home for the night.

Ignoring the invisible thief, Mina primly touched her hair, regained her composure, and looked about at the buildings. "Yes, this is the place." She pointed a chalky pale hand toward an ominous house that spoke of ancient, moldering wealth.

As Thames fog rolled in, the building seemed to groan with menace and the weight of years of unforgiven sins. Mina looked far from happy.

"That's where we will find Mr. Dorian Gray."

7

The door of Dorian Gray's house was a massive wooden barricade with ornate panels and a heavy brass knocker. The invisible man hung back as the other League members approached, not out of fear but from lack of initiative; Mina Harker hesitated for an entirely different reason.

Quatermain looked at Nemo, but the dark captain simply stared implacably, as if the door would have the good sense to open by itself. It was left to the old adventurer to step up to the entrance, grasp the handle of the ostentatious knocker, and rap hard several times. It sounded like a hammer battering a piece of thick hull plating.

After the resounding echoes died away, Quatermain waited, staring at the door instead of his fellow recruits. Finally he heard soft, delicate footsteps padding like a lion approaching prey. The door opened to reveal a suave man shrouded in shadows and lingering sweet tobacco smoke. "Hello?"

Quatermain squared his shoulders, facing him. They were of the same height, but the other man seemed much more full of himself. "Gray? Mr. Dorian Gray?"

The man stepped forward into the light. He was a dashing fellow with unruly hair and a smile that seemed just the faintest degree away from an outright sneer. He wore a deep purple smoking jacket and exotic slippers. "I am indeed."

"We . . . came by way of M."

"Ah, M for mystery . . . or perhaps it's for melodrama . . . or mediocrity." Dorian Gray looked at the old adventurer on his doorstep as if he was nothing more than a speck. "Well, I told him and I'm telling you—whoever you are—I'm not interested."

He finally deigned to notice the odd company on his doorstep: Nemo in his outlandish semimilitaristic uniform and colorful turban, Skinner in his dark glasses and white face paint.

And Mina.

"Hello, Dorian," she said, seeing his eyes go wide with sudden recognition.

"Mina? Mina Harker! It's been ages . . . though perhaps not long enough—"

Without comment, she pushed past Quatermain, her skirts rustling, and entered Gray's front hall. The elegant man backed up to let her inside.

Before the other League members could follow her, she grasped the edge of the door and flung it shut in Quatermain's face, leaving them standing alone outside on the rain-damp step. He blinked, at a loss. "She who must be obeyed," Quatermain muttered under his breath. "I've heard that one before. And she already thinks she's our captain. Trouble. Plenty of trouble."

Skinner snickered. "I knew she was a sassy one. Aheh!"

Nemo had not moved. "Another demonstration of the much-vaunted British civility."

The three men stood there in uncomfortable silence, then the door opened again. Now Gray wore a more friendly expression, smiling so that his youthful face appeared ready to crack. "Please, gentlemen, excuse my bad manners. Come in." He extended a welcoming hand.

Mina stood in the foyer behind him, looking satisfied. "Mina tells me that an intelligent man, an open-minded and cultured person such as myself should do his guests the courtesy of *listening* to them—before turning down their request." He shot a sly look at Mina, whose green eyes reflected the challenge back at him.

Dorian Gray seemed full of life, but in the way a piece of spoiled fruit is full of flavor. His eyes were wide and bright, as if dazzled by harsh lights, despite the gloom of the day and the dimness of the foyer. His skin was vibrant, almost feverish, but when Quatermain shook his hand, Gray's grip felt dry and cool.

Strolling with unhurried grace after they had all made introductions, their host led them up a flight of creaking stairs. The wood of the rail was the most expensive mahogany, polished to a fine luster, no doubt by the sweat of many servants, though the house seemed quite silent. Gold-framed mirrors hung in prominent positions on the walls, implying that the man often liked to inspect his general appearance.

The walls were covered with portraits, all of them originals and no doubt quite valuable. The people featured on the canvases looked dark or oddly unhappy, possibly malformed in an indefinable way. Not being an art critic and unschooled in such things, Quatermain could not pinpoint exactly what was wrong with all these people. Perhaps the artist had been playing a malicious trick on his subjects, or perhaps he simply saw deeper to an inner rot in Dorian Gray's ancestors.

Farther along the wall, though, a single portrait was prominently missing. The vacant spot was like a shout.

"You seem to have lost a picture, Mr. Gray," Quatermain said.

"And you don't miss a thing, do you, Mr. Quatermain?" Gray walked along, running fingers through his thick hair as if admiring it; he didn't seem to feel that any additional answer was necessary.

"Maybe someone stole it," Skinner muttered under his breath.

They entered an impressive library, lined floor-to-ceiling with shelves and shelves of leatherbound books. Sliding ladders on rails ran up the walls, extending to even higher alcoves, and a spiral staircase led to a loft in the immense room. The chairs, vases, and furniture were all of the most stylish and expensive variety. Dorian Gray certainly enjoyed his material pleasures.

Removing his rain-wet hat and leaving a gaping emptiness where the top and back of his head should have been, Skinner zeroed in on the drinks trolley. "Scotch, anyone? Ah, an excellent double-malt. Pricey!"

"Yes. Please. Help yourself," said Gray.

Gaslight radiated through the invisible man's grease-paint mask. With gloved hands he poured a large tumbler of scotch and drank it in gulps. The fluid was visible as it poured down his throat and pooled in his stomach. "Ah, nice and smokey! Burns as it goes down. Care for a snort, Quatermain?"

"At least it isn't sherry."

Nemo watched the transparent thief's performance, but seemed more curious about Dorian Gray's complete lack of surprise. "You take Skinner's uniqueness in your stride."

Sounding bored, Gray led them to a sitting area where a roaring fire blazed. "Yes, well, I spent many years seeking new pleasures and unique experiences. And I did them all. By now, I've seen too much in my life to shock easily." He picked up a poker and stabbed at the burning logs like a hunter slaughtering his kill. Sparks flew from the grate as he turned to Mina, who stood behind a high-backed leather chair. "Although, I must say, I was surprised to see you again."

Mina answered with equal parts venom and sarcasm, "When our last parting was such sweet sorrow, Dorian?"

"Meow," Skinner said, dutifully handing a drink to Quatermain after pouring a second Scotch for himself. Both glasses were very full of the amber liquid.

Their host looked as if nothing in the world could penetrate his cool composure, or bother him in the least. "Ah, so you're merely meant as an enticement to me, Mina. M must be losing his touch."

Skinner said, "I read the papers, Mr. Gray. Wasn't there some sort of business with you and Oscar Wilde? Before his numerous . . . er, troubles with the press, eh?"

"Mr. Wilde and I are no longer on speaking terms, and I'm afraid it ended badly." Gray turned with a flicker of anger that made him look incalculably old, but the invisible man did not know when to stop.

"Was it his fondness for the highlife?"

Gray snapped at him. "I have no fear of hedonism. I

simply lost my tolerance for Mr. Wilde's immeasurable ego. Nothing about him warrants my further interest."

He seated himself in the comfortable chair in front of the fire and crossed a leg over his other knee, dangling his exotic slipper close to the flames. He looked up at the older adventurer, raising his eyebrows. "Nevertheless, *your* presence intrigues me, Mina. And Quatermain. They say you're indestructible. They say you've survived enough exploits to kill a hundred men."

"A bit of hyperbole." Embarrassed, Quatermain took another sip of his Scotch, noting that it was indeed quite good, far superior to anything Bruce at the lamented Britannia Club had ever served. "Well, a witch doctor did bless me once. . . . I saved his village. He said that Africa would never allow me to die."

"Ah, but you're not in Africa now," said Gray.

"No. Therefore, I'd best be careful."

Mina leaned over Gray's chair and looked down at his full head of hair. She ran her fingers lightly through it, seductively, as if she had a purpose. "So will you join us, Dorian?"

He sighed long and slow, staring into the flames. His expression was a mask of utter disinterest. "Ah, there was a time when my love of experience would have drawn me to this adventure. I would have enjoyed it, no doubt. A lark. But now I have other priorities. I seek to . . . tame my own demons. Therefore, I must decline. Sorry. I'm sure M can dredge someone else out of his extensive files."

Nemo turned from studying the spines of the extravagant books in the library. "Yes, M's files. I confess a curiosity as to what those files say about Mr. Gray. And why he is considered so important. We, all of us, have obvious traits useful in this endeavor. Quatermain is a hunter, and Mrs. Harker represents science. I myself am quite skilled with technology, and Mr. Skinner has stealth." Crossing his arms over his blue uniform, he scrutinized Dorian Gray. "What of you?"

"I have . . . experience," he answered with an undertone of great weariness. "A vast amount of experience."

Nemo looked at the man's boyish appearance, and his lips turned down in a skeptical frown. "How could one as young as yourself have experienced more than Quatermain or I?"

For the past several minutes, Quatermain had been staring at the man, ransacking his memory. Finally, the answer came to him, unlikely as it seemed. "Because Gray and I have met before. I didn't recall it at first, but I remember now. Many years ago at Eton College."

"A lecture, no doubt?" Mina said. "You the nation's hero, telling of your exploits in Africa, King Solomon's mines, the lost city of gold. Dorian the eager listening boy." She seemed amused.

"No, quite the reverse, Mrs. Harker." Quatermain seated himself in the second leather wingback by the fireplace, leaning closer to their host. The suave man in the other chair looked at him, secretly amused. "It was Gray visiting Eton, giving his lecture—and I was just a boy. Isn't that right, Mr. Gray?"

Their host pointed a finger at him. "Touché."

Quatermain shook his head, turning back to Mina and Nemo. "He hasn't changed a bit in all those years. Not a bit."

"Must be a healthy diet and virtuous living," the invisible man said snidely from the drink cart.

"Hardly," Gray said.

Skinner finished his Scotch with a slurp and poured a third, very full glass for himself. "Anyone?"

The others were still trying to make sense of Quatermain's remark when the old adventurer suddenly snapped to attention. He surveyed the room's upper levels, peering toward the high bookshelves, the railed alcoves above, the loft filled with shadows. Everyone felt his tension.

"What is it?" Mina whispered.

Without a word, Quatermain slowly rose from his chair. The old leather let out a rustling sigh, but when he held out a hand for silence, no one dared to ask what he sensed. The others stared into the shadows, noticing nothing. The tension grew, accompanied only by the crackle of the fire and the quiet breaths of the waiting companions.

Gray seemed to think he was overreacting. "Really, Mr. Quatermain. You must be on edge—"

Then they heard a creak, the faintest sound. Dust sifted downward from the loft ceiling. Mina instinctively crouched; she moved like a panther, despite the tight, confining bodice and voluminous skirts of her dress.

Quatermain reached inside his linen jacket and eased out his Webley revolver. It felt heavy but comforting in his grip.

Before he could cock the hammer, though, a flurry of marksmen appeared like a startled flock of birds from every shadow on every level. Long rifle barrels extended, ominously reflecting the gaslights and the library fire.

"Gray?" Quatermain growled. "What is this? Your own brand of home security?"

"They're not mine." Finally, a note of interest had crept into Gray's voice, altering his usual bored demeanor.

"They are mine." The voice was rough, powerful, and slightly muffled.

As one, the members of the League whirled. At the top of the library's spiral staircase, a thin man stepped forward dressed in a heavy overcoat and black gloves. His hair was wild, and a silver mask concealed his upper face and part of his cheeks, leaving only his chin and twisted lips exposed. Hideous scars covered the visible portions of his face, implying terrible disfigurement beneath the mask.

The Fantom looked even worse when he smiled, seeing them so helpless.

8

Dorian Gray's Residence

No one dared exhale. The Fantom took a step down the metal stair. He moved like a heavy shadow, powerful and completely confident in his control of the situation.

Quatermain took half a step forward. "First meetings usually warrant introductions." All the threatening rifles shifted slightly, tracking him. He ignored them, concentrating on the real enemy. "Do you have a name, or just a mask and a costume?"

"Fine. I am the Fantom. And you are the League of so-called Extraordinary Gentlemen." Firelight shimmered like quicksilver on his mask. "There, introductions made. Now we can be about our vital, and possibly deadly, business." He continued down the spiral staircase. "And while I may be scarred, Mr. Quatermain, I am not blind. Drop the gun."

Quatermain lifted his eyes to the numerous marksmen stationed all around the library. Reluctantly, he dropped his Webley revolver.

All of the Fantom's rifle bearers wore long leather coats, handkerchiefs tied across their faces, and wide steel hats that made them look like drones. The identical marksmen all had an anonymous quality, as if they had been stamped out of a factory line—all except for one young man on the upper level.

He wore the same helmet and leather coat, but the young man didn't seem to fit in with the other henchmen. Quatermain's hunter sense picked him out, and the mysterious marksman raised his head so that light fell on his determined blue eyes. His face was young, handsome, flushed with excitement. He had been trying to catch Quatermain's attention; noticing that he had finally succeeded, the marksman actually winked at him.

Suddenly, Quatermain recognized the suspicious-looking young man who had been ineptly following and watching them all afternoon, slouching on doorsteps and attempting nonchalance. He was not surprised to see the stranger among these enemies. But something wasn't right. What was the young man doing here?

The Fantom, reveling in the moment, continued his grand entrance. "Your mission is to stop me. That, of course, I cannot permit." He reached the bottom of the staircase and faced them in the library. "So I give to you all a one-time invitation. *Join me.*"

Not wanting to draw attention to what might be a potential ally, Quatermain did not look again at the mysterious young marksman. He met the Fantom's masked gaze. "Join you—or die? I'm familiar with that ultimatum. Not very original."

His revolver lay on the floor, but he would never be able to reach it before all the marksmen riddled him with bullets.

The Fantom raised his arms and spread his black-gloved hands. "And I am familiar with men such as you, Mr. Quatermain. You walk the knife-edge of law and disorder. An individual, not a blind soldier to march empty-headed into battle. What do you owe England? Come, undo the stuffy waistcoat of tyranny. Why remain loyal to an empire that uses you, but can barely abide you? Bring *me* your talents and I'll—"

"—add us to your collection of lackeys and kidnapped scientists?" Mina finished for him. "How appealing."

"Don't you see?" The Fantom stroked his silver mask, tantalizing them, threatening—or promising—to yank it off and reveal his horribly disfigured face. "We're all of us outcasts, society's dregs."

"Heh, he's not exactly wrong about that," said Skinner, still holding his full glass of Scotch, as if about to propose a toast.

"As much as I despise the conflicts of nations, you think we'll help you start a war that will consume the planet?" Nemo said. His stern face could barely contain the outpouring of disgust he felt for the suggestion.

"While you profit from your 'arms race'?" Quatermain added. "How noble."

The Fantom's laugh was like breaking glass. "I cannot deny that fortunes are made in war, gentlemen. Not the politicians or kings, not the hapless fighters—it is the businessmen and visionaries who profit from such a situation. Imagine the riches a world war will yield!"

Quatermain glanced up again at the odd young marksman, who seemed to be anxiously trying to get his attention. The imposter gestured slightly with his rifle barrel; from his own familiarity and expertise, Quatermain identified a customized Winchester with exotic aiming sight, decorated barrel, and carved stock. *Very interesting.* The mysterious young man seemed to be bidding him to act when the time was right.

None of his companions had noticed the misfit henchman above. Quatermain's mind raced, and he tried to stall for time. He stood up to the black-garbed Fantom. "I have held the treasure of King Solomon in my hands, sir. It taught me that happiness can't be found in mountains of gold, nor in visions of power."

From across the library, Skinner cleared his throat nervously. "Aheh! I, on the other hand, find gold to be a beautiful hue." He lifted his glass. "Like this Scotch."

When Quatermain's glance flicked down at his Webley lying on the floor, the Fantom noticed at once. "Remind me to play you at cards one day. Your face is like an open book." With his polished shoe, he kicked the revolver far away. It skittered and spun, coming to rest under the library ladders.

Impatient now, he squared his shoulders and raised his voice to address the League. "So what's it to be? Does Quatermain speak for all of you?"

"Your evil is palpable, sir," Mina said. "Even a so-called 'dreg' such as myself must maintain her standards. I have associated with vile men before"—she shot a quick glance at Dorian Gray, who had not even bothered to rise from his chair at the fireplace—"but I do have certain standards."

"Personally, I don't care for guns in my home." Gray sounded bored again. "And I don't recall extending an invitation to any of you."

"I, on the other hand, always side with superior force." The invisible man stepped forward. His white

70

face paint showed his grin. "Take me, Fantom. I'm yours."

Nemo was at his side so fast that Skinner barely had time to take another step. He placed a firm hand on the invisible man's shoulder, squeezing so hard that the thief winced and squirmed. "Skinner is with me. And I am with them."

The Fantom let out an exaggerated sigh. "Then I'm truly saddened. I had hoped you would take advantage of an obvious opportunity." He lifted a black-gloved hand. "Men!"

The marksmen aimed. With a loud click, the firing bolts of sophisticated breech-loading rifles were drawn back.

Just then, with a fierce yell, the young imposter turned his modified Winchester on his fellow marksmen. He blasted away, killing two of the unsuspecting henchmen, then dove for shelter.

The Fantom wheeled, surprised.

Everything happened in an instant. All the members of the League had tensed, looking for any last-chance opportunity, and they flew into action. Nemo and Mina leaped for cover.

Quatermain launched himself at the nearest library ladder, grabbing the rungs and running. He shoved it along its rail, smashing the marksmen's protruding rifles aside as it went. Several weapons, wrenched free, tumbled to the library floor.

The marksmen on the other side of the library did not hesitate to fire, though. Gunshots blasted out like a dozen firing squads, and the air filled with bullets. Dorian Gray's paintings, lamps, and ornaments shredded or

71

shattered. With muffled thuds, dozens of books exploded; some tumbled off the shelves, as if trying to escape the fusillade. Paper fragments filled the air with a parchment blizzard.

The dapper Dorian Gray, looking incongruously elegant in his purple smoking jacket, staggered and jittered from multiple impacts. His body was riddled with bulletholes, and his face wore an expression of surprised displeasure.

"Dorian!" Mina struggled to run to him, but Captain Nemo snagged her and pulled her behind a pillar. A bullet struck the pillar, sending a spray of wood splinters near their faces.

With a sharp yelp, Skinner ran the opposite direction. He tossed the full glass of Scotch onto his white-painted face, squeezing his eyes shut momentarily; the alcohol dissolved his makeup coating, making it easier for him to wipe away with a piece of cloth, and by the time he had thrown off his coat, the invisible man had completely vanished.

After reloading his Winchester, the young imposter advanced on the other marksmen, opening fire again. He cocked the customized weapon one-handed while yanking the bothersome handkerchief from his face. Then he blasted again. But, to his disbelief, his shots ricocheted off the Fantom's marksmen. These were wearing body armor, much like the assassins who had attacked Quatermain at the Britannia Club.

With remarkable strength and determination, Mina Harker struggled free of Nemo's grip. She took an urgent step away from the shelter of their hiding place—and gasped in a new sort of shock at what she saw: Gray stood in front of the fireplace, still on his feet and apparently unhurt. He snatched up a long cane resting beside the fireplace implements and pulled away its covering to reveal a thin, wickedly sharp sword. He stormed into the fray, showing no evidence of wounds, despite all the bullets that had struck him.

At this sudden turn of events, the Fantom turned and sprinted for the staircase that would take him to the house's exit and the street.

"Not one for a bit of a fight, are you, Fantom?" Quatermain called after the masked villain. In a blurred sequence of movement, he retrieved his revolver from where his opponent had kicked it, cocked the hammer, aimed, and fired. His shot passed directly through the bookcase, striking the Fantom squarely in the right shoulder. But the impact only spun him around. He hit a column, caromed off, and kept running, though in the opposite direction now. His black overcoat was torn, but no blood oozed from the wound.

"Damned body armor," Quatermain mutterered, then ran after him, heedless of the danger. As he zigzagged through the lethal gauntlet, he passed Dorian Gray coming the other way, furiously slashing right and left with his cane-sword.

From above, the mysterious young marksman covered Quatermain's pursuit, using his Winchester to pick enemy shooters from their high perches around the library.

Upon seeing Quatermain's insane act of bravery in charging after the Fantom, Captain Nemo stepped out of the shadows himself. He glared at one of the enemy henchmen and rushed toward him.

"No gun, darkie?" said one of the marksmen. "What's the matter?"

Nemo turned with slow poise, gathering his concentration and his energy. His voluminous black beard bristled as he smiled. A group of marksmen had drawn a bead on him, considering the unarmed captain an easy target. "No gun. I walk a different path."

Before they could open fire, Nemo exploded into astonishing action, using his entire body as a weapon. He became a blur of limbs, landing crushing blows with his hands, elbows, knees, and booted feet. His spinning kicks carried a lethal force against which body armor was no use. Caught in the hurricane of martial arts destruction, enemy marksmen fell and scattered like ninepins.

The Fantom reached a rickety stairway and scrambled up it with Quatermain in hot pursuit. Though panting, the old adventurer seemed intent on not letting his enemy escape. Hand over hand, clutching the rail, the Fantom climbed higher—until the stairs ended abruptly against a trapdoor.

His gloved hand grabbed at the handle of the trapdoor, but it was locked. Taking little pleasure but great satisfaction, Quatermain charged forward and was almost upon him—

When the Fantom's Lieutenant Dante dropped from nowhere and slammed into him. Quatermain staggered, losing his balance.

"Run, James!" Dante shouted.

The Fantom smashed at the trapdoor with his armored shoulder, broke it open, and hauled himself up to the next floor.

Recovering himself, Quatermain slammed a heavy fist into Dante's chin, and the lieutenant reciprocated with punches of his own. Finally, the old hunter, impatient to be after his true quarry, delivered a decisive head-butt, which sent Dante reeling. Quatermain shoved the other man aside and pushed forward, silently cursing Dorian Gray. "Why does one man require such a ridiculously large house?"

Bested for now, Dante stumbled into the shadows.

From across the upper level of the library, the imposter marksman saw the Fantom about to escape. He kicked an advancing marksman aside and dashed off to help Quatermain.

Reaching the edge of the upper level, he did not pause but took a flying leap over the railing of the alcove and landed on the same floor. Panting, and grinning, he joined in the pursuit of the Fantom.

Meanwhile, Nemo ducked, rolled, and leaped. He seemed untouchable, unshootable. He broke limbs without mercy. The marksmen had never seen anything like him. They could understand bullets and knives and clubs . . . but not this. The captain's face wore such an intense and merciless expression that the henchmen turned to run away in terror.

Instead, they ran into Dorian Gray and his wicked, slender sword.

The suave man stabbed and slashed, looking uninterested even as the henchmen fought back, howling. He was oblivious to the wounds that the men inflicted on him. "Ow," he said, though his tone of voice was less than convincing.

A skewered marksman fell to his knees before Gray and took a death grip on Gray's shirt beneath the smoking jacket. It tore open, affording the man a dying glimpse of Gray's wounds as they healed completely before his eyes.

"What are you?" the henchman gasped.

Gray pulled his long blade from the man's body and kicked him aside like a discarded pillow. "I'm . . . complicated."

Across the room, the invisible man had found a blade of his own and went to work. His hovering knife floated and swooped like a flying projectile. The nearest henchman didn't understand what he was seeing, until the blade swung down to slash his throat.

Leaving blood droplets dancing in the air, the invisibly wielded blade struck sideways beneath the marksman's raised left arm to exploit the opening in the bulletproof armor. The knife dealt a lethal blow to the man's heart.

Pulling ahead of Quatermain, the imposter marksman chased the Fantom up two more flights of decaying stairs. "I sure didn't think a man in such fancy duds could run like a greased pig!"

Cocking his Winchester one-handed again, he let loose another booming shot up through rotted floorboards. Splinters and dust flew from the blast, but the hoped-for cry of pain from the Fantom did not come.

The masked villain smashed through a thin barricade to reach the dim, topmost level of Dorian Gray's old dock house. Every window in the attic was bricked up, leaving no escape.

Face flushed, his rifle extended, the young imposter cornered the evil mastermind. The Fantom backed against the grimy wallboards, which had been weakened by age and decay.

The masked villain turned and with fearless resolve threw himself against the thin patch of wallboards. Engulfed in dust and cobwebs, he broke completely through the attic wall and plunged out into the night.

"Hey!" The imposter marksman cursed and raced for the broken opening. He peered through it, desperately trying to get a glimpse of the escaped man, but saw nothing.

A moment later, Quatermain reached a window on the floor beneath the attic. He threw open the sash and stuck his head out, hoping to catch sight of his quarry. He saw debris still falling, broken boards, loose shingles, dust, and shards of glass. Far below, there was only a fog-bound dock and empty streets.

And no sign of the Fantom at all.

9

In the aftermath of the fight, Nemo checked for survivors among the bodies strewn in the library. He moved methodically from man to man, ears cocked for a groan of pain—though it wasn't clear from the grim set of his face whether he intended to succor or execute any of the Fantom's men he found alive.

One severely wounded marksman looked up into Nemo's angry face and fierce black eyes and died with a sudden whimper, before the black-bearded captain could even check his injuries. Nemo was neither pleased nor disappointed.

Taking care of important business, Skinner finished applying fresh greasepaint over his features. He donned his dark-lensed pince-nez spectacles over the empty craters of his eyes, shrugged on his long-sleeved coat, then carefully tugged his hat over the hollow top and back of his head.

Though he was completely visible now, Skinner still managed to startle Dorian Gray out of his preoccupied thoughts. "Heh, Mr. Gray! And I thought I was special. You're invulnerable to harm."

"And also invulnerable to the sands of time, if indeed you're older than Quatermain," Nemo mused, looking up from another victim on the library floor. "As we were discussing before our unexpected interruption." The captain's implacable expression demanded answers, but their host was not forthcoming.

"I don't like to boast," Gray said dismissively. He frowned at the numerous punctures and bullet holes in his fine smoking jacket; he seemed unsettled, even disappointed. "By the way, what happened to Mina?"

A fuming Allan Quatermain returned with heavy footsteps to the main library chamber. Without a word, he tucked his revolver into his interior jacket pocket. "She's probably hip-deep in some kind of peril. Expecting us to rescue her, no doubt."

Mina reappeared, her auburn hair perfectly in place. She casually brushed at a few small blood spatters on the colorful fabric of her dress. "Oh, don't be such an old alarmist, Mr. Q. And my hips are none of your business."

She sensed someone behind her, but before she could turn, one of the last marksmen lurched out of an alcove. Although he knew he was outnumbered and trapped, all of his fellows slain, the Fantom gone, the marksman grabbed Mina with a powerful grip and held her before him as if she were a shield. He rammed a gleaming knife within a hair's breadth of her pale throat. The silk scarf she always wore would offer no protection from the sharpened steel.

Quatermain drew his revolver, and Nemo dropped into a fighting stance, while the invisible man froze in the process of pouring himself another drink. Faster than any of them, though, the mysterious young imposter leaped down from the upper levels of the library. His boots slammed on the floor with a crack like thunder. He aimed his flamboyant Winchester at the marksman's face. "Let 'er go, Mister, or I'll shoot ya!"

Cornered, the Fantom's marksman had nothing to lose. "Shoot! Go on! I'll kill her on reflex!" The hand that held the knife twitched against the hollow of Mina's throat, and she remained very still. Her head lolled forward, obscuring her face. Her hair fell into disarray.

In the frozen standoff, the young imposter lowered his Winchester. Nemo remained tense, but took a step backward to a safer, nonthreatening distance. Quatermain lowered his revolver with an angry sigh. "I told you from the beginning she'd be trouble."

The cornered marksman fairly crowed with triumph. "I guessed as much! They'd do anything to protect you." He cinched his muscular arm tight around her narrow waist.

"That's your biggest mistake, sir," Mina said in a quiet, threatening voice. "Thinking I need the likes of *them* to protect me." She turned on him, her eyes demonic red and pulsing now with an unearthly glow. She opened her mouth to show the long, ivory sabers of vampire fangs. Then she was upon him.

Though still holding the knife, the marksman gasped in terror and tried to squirm away, but she easily sank her extended fangs into his throat. He struggled, beating futilely at her. She bit deeper. Arterial blood sprayed.

Then, with a savage twist of her jaw, she ripped out his windpipe. His dagger slid harmlessly away from her throat, then clattered to the library floor.

At the drink cart, Skinner gulped down another Scotch.

As if she were discarding a dirty handkerchief, Mina let the dead marksman drop to the ground.

Quatermain looked at Nemo, stunned. "Extraordinary," the captain said.

Mina's features rapidly returned to her cold pale beauty. Dorian Gray watched her without surprise. She flicked open her vanity mirror, withdrew a soft white cloth from her pocket, and calmly dabbed blood from her mouth.

"Boy, they told me European women had funny ways," said the handsome young imposter, propping his modified Winchester at his side. "There, Ma'am, you missed a spot." In a gentlemanly fashion, he pointed out a drop of blood on her ivory-pale cheek.

"Excuse me . . . and you are?" Mina regarded him with piercing green eyes now. Quatermain also turned to the unexpected ally, waiting for the young man's answer.

"I'm Special Agent Tom Sawyer, Ma'am," he said proudly, "of the American Secret Service."

10

While the others in the library stared at the young man in surprised silence, a chuckle came from the invisible man. "So you're a . . . spy?" Skinner sounded slightly drunk. "I thought spies get shot."

"Not if they shoot first. Which I did," Sawyer said with exaggerated pride. "I followed you all. Knocked out a straggler and took his place." He rapped on his wide-brimmed metal helmet, then took it off. "Darned silly outfits."

Despite his frenetic exertions in the fight, Captain Nemo had not broken into a sweat. He adjusted his blue turban, seating it on his head, then looked in barely veiled dismay at the countless books that had been ruined in the recent battle. Paper and bindings lay scattered and mangled on the floor. When he noticed the subject matter of many of the volumes, however—detailed analyses of the Marquis de Sade, drawings and daguerrotypes of numerous people in bizarre and painful-looking sexual positions—he turned away with a frown, reassessing the magnitude of the loss.

Gauging Sawyer, Quatermain said, "So America's aware of the situation?"

Sawyer gave an emphatic nod. "War starts in Europe, how long until it's crossed the Atlantic? We already lost one good man trying to nail this maniac. The man who fell victim to the Fantom was another agent—and a darned good one, too. A close friend of mine. He believed in what he was doing." The young man seemed amazingly earnest, and optimistic. "And now I'm going to finish the job." His customized Winchester seemed to be all he needed.

Gray noticed Mina sizing up the handsome young American and clearly wasn't happy about it. He sniffed. "Very noble. But this is a private party. You're not invited."

Sawyer stubbornly squared his shoulders. "I intend to find the Fantom. So do you all."

Mina came closer to the young spy, smiling seductively. "Actually, since Dorian has already declined to join our little effort, we are one shy of a full deck."

Remembering the incident moments earlier in which she had used her fangs to rip out the throat of the last hapless marksman, Sawyer swallowed hard and flinched from her close attention. "Uh, Ma'am . . ."

Gray took up the challenge. "On the contrary, that unexpected battle was just the spur I needed. Very exciting, for a change, with the promise of more to come. And the thrill of an old, sweet friendship renewed."

Mina rolled her eyes.

Gray plucked at his smoking jacket, frowned again at all the bullet holes. "I will have to change my attire, however." He turned to Sawyer and made a shooing gesture. "So, as you can see, young man, you're not needed here."

While Sawyer glared at him, Quatermain came forward to inspect the American agent's customized rifle. "Winchester?"

"Modified, American style," Sawyer confirmed, proud to show off his piece and purposefully ignoring Dorian Gray.

Quatermain took it and sighted on the narrow spine of a book on a high shelf. "American style of shooting, too."

"Whatever it takes." Sawyer grinned at the old adventurer, nodded toward the Winchester. "Like it? I brought two of 'em."

"He's in," Quatermain said.

11

The Thames, London
Night

Leaving the bodies and wreckage behind, the League exited from Gray's opulent residence into the foggy streets. Dark river water lapped against the nearby docks, but a thick mist hid the Thames from view.

Tom Sawyer looked behind him. "I sure hate to leave such a mess in there. My Aunt Polly would give me a tongue-lashing I'd never forget."

"Leave it." Gray was not concerned. "My private staff has had considerable experience in dealing with messes that were far worse." He didn't explain further.

"We don't have time for house cleaning." Nemo led the way toward the unseen docks, striding ahead in his elaborate blue uniform. "We had best be about our business. According to M's instructions, the League has one final member to recruit before we can be off to Venice."

"Recruit? *Capture* is more the word. It will be quite a hunt," Quatermain said. "Though I prefer the open savannah to the streets of Paris."

"You make him sound like an animal," said Mina.

The old adventurer glanced at her with undisguised curiosity. "Speaking of which, Mrs. Harker—your con-

85

duct in there . . . let's just say the attacker wasn't the only one who had his breath taken away. Would you care to explain yourself?"

"Indeed, we're aquiver with curiosity," Skinner said, edging forward with a grin on his painted face. "After all, you have plenty of dirt on me, dear lady—as you are so keen to remind me over and over again. Heh!"

Mina looked at the men, each one a member of the odd team sworn to save the world from a devastating war. "Very well, in the spirit of cooperation." She touched the corner of her lip, possibly feeling a speck of dried blood still there.

"My husband was Jonathan Harker. Together with a professor named Van Helsing, we fought a dangerous evil. It had a name: Count Dracula. He was . . . Transylvanian." Mina lifted her delicate eyebrows, but saw no sign of recognition from her companions.

"European? One of those radical anarchists the newspapers love to report on?" Skinner said.

Mina pulled down her ever-present scarf, exposing two pale puncture marks that scarred her otherwise perfect throat. "I don't know, Mr. Skinner. Is the vampiric sucking of peoples' blood considered radical behavior?"

Tom Sawyer turned away with a mixture of embarrassment and horror. Quatermain studied the scars, trying to guess what kind of animal would have made such wounds. Dorian Gray simply seemed interested in admiring Mina's neck.

"In the course of battling Dracula, I was brought under his influence. Rather violently. That monster has been destroyed now, and I have recovered. Partially, at least. However, if I ever appear cold to you, it's because I am filled with enough of Dracula's essence that I fear where unbridled emotion would lead." She turned to Quatermain, as if implying that he had passed some sort of judgment on her. "Put that in your file." She tucked her white scarf back into place and strode purposefully after Nemo to the end of the dock.

"Enough stories," Nemo said. "We must be off on our journey."

Seeing nothing but the fog-shrouded pier and the murky Thames, Dorian Gray crossed his arms over his chest and frowned. "Now what?"

At that moment, the jetty started to rumble. Bubbles began to boil in the black waters, accompanied by a bright submerged glow and a loud throbbing like massive muffled engines.

Nemo walked to the edge of the jetty, as if he meant to leap into the river itself. Instead, he stood at the brink, waiting. "Our transportation is forthcoming." As the splashing, churning noise increased, he turned to look at them with a secretive smile. "We will be in Paris soon."

"Is it a boat?" asked Sawyer. "I've been on a big paddle-wheel steamer on the Mississippi."

"Not that sort of boat, Mr. Sawyer, though it goes on water, if that's what you mean," Nemo said, facing the gathered companions. "And beneath it as well."

Behind him, a huge black conning tower broke the surface like a breaching whale. Nemo didn't flinch. The plated vessel rose up, gushing water as it climbed higher and higher, until its shape loomed over them.

"Whoa," said Sawyer.

But the conning tower was just the tip of the iceberg. High and long with elegant seafaring lines, the submarine boat surfaced majestically, splitting the surface of the Thames. Like the scales of an aquatic dragon, it was plated with white ceramic derived from the shells of mysterious crustaceans and encrusted with golden statues of Vishnu, Ganesh, and Shiva.

While the invisible man hung back from the mammoth boat in nervous uncertainty, Quatermain and Sawyer stepped forward together, amazed. Dorian Gray did not seem impressed, but Captain Nemo showed obvious pride. "Behold, *Nautilus*. The Sword of the Ocean."

The members of the League stood together at the end of the dock and watched the amazing colossus ease against the jetty. Massive rudders worked with exact precision, guiding it perfectly into place.

Once it had come to rest, exhaust vents opened with a sigh, and the *Nautilus* let out a breath of air.

So did each member of the League.

12

The creature bounded across tiled roof slopes, eaves, and chimney pots. His broad, bare feet slapped on the slats, and he made an impossible leap over a deep alley to an adjacent building. His clawed hands grasped for a hold on the gutter, and then he hauled himself onto the angled rooftop. A beast's brutish shadow momentarily showed in the moonlight, eclipsing the Eiffel Tower, then it sprang onward.

Its breath was heavy and wet, its grunting halfway between a howl of rage and a roar of victory. But first it had to escape the hunters. Its every muscular movement expressed exuberance for the chase, the hot pursuit—even though *it* was the quarry.

"This way!" Quatermain called, refusing to slow down. "Don't let him out of your sights."

"I've got 'im!" Tom Sawyer said. The two men hurried through the streets of Paris, close behind the monster, trying to track its movements as it charged overhead from rooftop to rooftop. "But I still don't see why our team needs a big monkey."

Out of breath but keeping pace with the young American agent, Quatermain said, "That big monkey's been terrorizing the Rue Morgue for months. Imagine the mayhem he'll give the enemy—if we can manage to get him on our side, that is."

The American swung his Winchester, searching for a target, then ran onward. "Well, I still think Inspector Dupin could have offered a bigger reward if he was so keen on stopping this beast."

"We all suffer from budgetary constraints, Sawyer. Welcome to the modern world."

Up ahead they saw movement in the moonlight. Quatermain signaled, but Sawyer had already seen. A large, malformed shape sprang with a heavy grunt from one building to the next. He landed heavily, sending loose roof tiles clattering down into the alleys.

Quatermain fired two shots to the left of the monster, shattering a narrow, crooked chimney. The gunshot sent the monster darting to the right as it reacted with animal instinct.

Gripping their rifles, the two men sped after the brute, trying to keep up as the monster bounded along the length of the shadowy conjoined roofs. They followed the sounds, tracked the monster's silhouette. Sawyer aimed vaguely in the direction of the inhumanly muscled figure and fired five shots in rapid succession. All to no effect.

Quatermain chided the young man for wasting ammunition. "If you can't do it with one bullet, lad, don't do it at all."

As if to prove his point, the old hunter fired at the monster. A section of roof decoration exploded in the beast-man's face, spraying tile shards and making the creature spin about and leap awkwardly to another rooftop across the street.

"He's doubled back!"

"Precisely. He doesn't know where we want him to go," Quatermain said. "Come on! We'll wrap this up soon."

Sawyer ran ahead of the older man around a left corner just as a stone angel came tumbling down from high above. "Look out!" Quatermain snatched the young man's arm and dragged him back as the statue smashed on the cobblestones, missing them by inches. "That was naughty of him."

"Thanks," Sawyer said. "Who does he think he is, Quasimodo?"

"Keep your eyes open, boy! This isn't a coon hunt, and I can't protect you all the time." Quatermain sniffed the air. "Ah, but he's afraid. It won't be long now, mark my words."

"I can't smell anything." Sawyer drew an exaggerated sniff. "Just the gutters."

"Shhh." Quatermain put his ear up against the moist brick wall and listened for vibrations. He waited for a moment, then stepped out of cover, aimed upward, and fired a series of perfect shots, driving the monster out of the shadows. The beast roared a challenge, lifting clawed hands, but Quatermain fired again, once more barely missing.

Each well-aimed shot was about a hair away from the beast, and each impact sent plaster and brick exploding around its misshapen head. The monster had no choice but to back away, trying to dodge the attack. Each bullet drove the creature closer and closer to a steeply tiled roof that sloped into a cul-de-sac. A carefully orchestrated trap.

Finally, predictably, the beast leaped and landed with broad bare feet on the dew-slick tiles of the steep roof. His thick, blunt toenails were like spatulas carved out of horn.

As the monster scrambled for purchase, Quatermain paused below and lifted his trusty elephant gun Matilda. He aimed and fired the perfect coup de grâce—not at the cornered brute, but at a sagging gutter upon which all the tiles depended.

With a thunderous, shattering clatter, the tiles slid off en masse, like an avalanche. High above, the howling monster tried to scramble up. His clawed hands tried to get a hold on the sliding surface. Finally, he snatched at a chimney pot with long clawed fingers and strained with iron-cable sinews—but the pot itself broke free with a groan. Airborne, the monster tumbled into the cul-de-sac.

"Perfect," Quatermain said. He pulled out a flare gun and launched a blooming phosphorus flower high into the night sky of Paris. "Now we've got him."

The light of the flare illuminated the stunned monster as he sprawled grunting and twitching on the hard ground. With an inhuman groan, the beast lifted its head up, cradling its temples from the pain of the impact.

"We've got to get there before it moves!" Sawyer said.

"Not to worry for now. Captain Nemo rigged up a little surprise."

As it tried to regain its feet, the huge, man-shaped thing began to realize it had fallen on top of a thin mesh of wire and rope—a hidden net that suddenly activated. With a sound like an overstressed spring breaking loose, the net shot upward, engulfing and lifting its prey.

Once the trap was triggered, a central cable drew the corners of the mesh tight and then began to drag the snarling package down the cul-de-sac at incredible speed. Helpless, the captive monster jostled and bounced in the net that rapidly pulled him—roaring all the while—to a slipway on the Seine river.

Gleaming and enormous in the moonlight, the *Nautilus* waited at the end of the cable, engines humming as it reeled in the trapped beast. The tough cable led straight into an open hatch. Turbines and spindles whirled, pulling the netted creature through the hatch and into the submarine boat.

The heavy metal door slammed shut as Quatermain and Sawyer bounded back to the underwater vessel, satisfied with their night's hunting.

"There we are," the old adventurer said. "Our team is complete. Now, off to Venice."

13

The Nautilus

Aboard the underwater war vessel, Nemo's loyal crewmen went about their duties. Their captain had issued his orders, and the submarine craft was under way, heading for their important rendezvous in Venice.

When two of the sailors cast uneasy glances at each other with each roaring howl from the lower chamber, the salty first mate Ishmael scolded them. "Never mind that. You've got work to do."

The men studiously paid no attention to the thunderous violent pounding and roars emanating from the vessel's bowels. The scraping of hard claws sounded like sharp fingernails on a slate board, the snarling like that of a trapped animal. The hammering came like a blacksmith's sledge against a sturdy anvil. Some of the inhuman snarls began to sound like threats, English words forming colorful and creative curses.

The *Nautilus* crewmen hurried down the corridors. Ishmael frowned and went back to his post. . . .

Inside the cabin Nemo had assigned to her, Mina Harker continued unpacking for the voyage. Her narrow shelves, the top of the bureau, the sink, even her narrow bunk were already cluttered with the tools of chemistry, the apparatus of her expertise: vials, rubber tubing, glass pipettes, atomizers, and test tubes.

As she unpacked more equipment, Mina muttered to herself, bothered by Allan Quatermain's annoyingly quaint and old-fashioned objections to her participation in the mission. She mimicked his voice, though no one could hear her. "This hunt's too dangerous for a woman. Even one such as you. Leave it to me, the incredibly brave and strong *male*."

Then a thunderous bang shook the walls, as if the *Nautilus* had rammed into an iceberg. As her cabin shelves shook, a rack of Mina's test tubes crashed to the deck, and she let out a long and definitely unladylike string of curses. . . .

Inside his private cabin down the narrow corridor, Dorian Gray plucked his eyebrows with a fine pair of tweezers. The pounding and howling was quite a distraction, and the mirror rattled so much that Gray couldn't finish his task. Annoyed, he tossed the tweezers down onto his vanity surface and went to investigate.

He wasn't the only one incensed. He converged with Mina Harker and the grossly made-up Skinner at an intersection of corridors. "Heh! The Great White Hunter must have bagged his prize," said the invisible man. "Maybe we can all get together for tea. I think he must be just your sort of man, Mrs. Harker."

"I think not," both Gray and Mina said simultaneously.

They hurried toward the escalating sound of chaos. Up ahead, one of Nemo's uniformed crewmen flew out of the ice room doorway, struck the bulkhead wall, and lay groaning on the floor.

"Perhaps instead the prize bagged our hunter," Gray said with a superior smile.

"Boys and their adventures," Mina said.

The trio entered the thick-walled ice room and stopped at the hatchway, gaping, as the gigantic, hairy creature—some sort of hybrid between man and primate—hurled himself against the thick shackles that bound his hands and neck to the wall of the chamber. The manacles attached to the chains were already bloodied from the beast's unceasing exertions.

Oddly enough, the captive monster's swollen and inhuman form was clad in the tatters of prim gentleman's clothing: trousers, a waistcoat, a starched-collared shirt which was now split apart at his tree-trunk neck.

Quatermain, Sawyer, and Nemo stood at a safe distance, clearly not knowing what to do next. "Henry, you've got to calm yourself," Quatermain said, trying to be reasonable with the monster. "Think pleasant—"

"I'm *Edward Hyde!*" the beast roared, spraying spittle and sending out waves of foul breath. "Not that worm Jekyll!" The chains clanked again, rivets groaning on the wall. But the shackles seemed secure enough, for now.

Gray, Skinner, and Mina approached with varying degrees of trepidation.

"Stay back if you value your life." Quatermain held out a cautionary hand.

Hyde lunged at them and was brought to an abrupt halt by the manacles and the cuff around his thick neck. With bloodshot eyes, he leered brazenly at Mina. She merely cocked a brow at him.

Skinner was startled, and he stumbled. With no more politeness than if he was picking up a scrap of litter, Dorian Gray grabbed the invisible man.

"Ow, you scratched me," Skinner whined.

"Better me than him," Gray said, letting go of the thief's sleeve. "Look at those claws." He studied the captive monster and said sarcastically, "Well, this is nice."

"I was about to suggest music," Mina said. "Soothing the savage beast and all that."

"Debussy," said the beast-man. The League reacted with surprise to the cultured suggestion, all except Quatermain, who seemed to have expected it. Hyde continued, "That is, if you want to get on my good side. Debussy usually works, though Jekyll prefers Mozart. Sissy music."

"I could play my mouth harp," Sawyer suggested.

Quatermain stepped up and looked Hyde square in the bloodshot eyes. The creature's swollen red lips could barely cover his crooked teeth. "Mr. Edward Hyde, you've done terrible things in England. So terrible that you were forced to flee the country."

Hyde laughed wickedly, proudly.

Quatermain continued, relaying the message M had given him at the outset. "I'm ashamed to say that Her Majesty's Government is willing to offer you amnesty in return for your services on this particular mission. Would you like to go home?"

"Home is where the heart is, that's what they say. I've ripped out a few hearts in my time. Tough to chew." His lips worked, but a mistiness came to his eyes. "Ah, the stink of the Thames, all the people coughing with tuberculosis, the hopelessness, the desperate poor. And they never did catch the Ripper, did they? Outdid even my best work—must have come straight from Hell, and then gone back there."

Hyde shifted about like a caged tiger, brooding. "I have been missing London after all. Its sorrow is as sweet to me as rare wine." He offered the League members a Cheshire cat smile and slumped cooperatively against the metal wall. The chains fell slack. "I'm yours." He turned to Mina. "By the by, call me a beast again, Miss. Please? I'm liable to become overly affectionate." He smiled slyly to everyone. "Aww, don't be scared."

"Hey, who said we're scared?" Tom Sawyer said.

"You do!" Playfully, it seemed, Hyde lunged, pulling a chain clean out of the wall, as if he could have done it at any time. He lashed it through the air, and Sawyer and Quatermain ducked to avoid it. The *Nautilus* crewmen shouted, scrambling to grab their weapons. Nemo crouched, ready to fight with his bare hands.

Hyde didn't advance on them, though. He sniffed the air, then let out a guffaw like breaking rocks. "You *stink* of fear."

"Quite the parlor trick," said Gray, unnerved but still pretending to be uninterested.

Suddenly the monstrously muscled Hyde winced as if he had swallowed acid. The pain immediately escalated, rippling through his chest and shoulders. "You call it a parlor trick?" He gasped for breath, his throat convulsing. "Wait until you see my next one." Hyde clutched his stomach and doubled over. "Abracadabra."

He thrashed against his remaining chains, screaming and howling as his hairy body distorted. His muscles contracted, his skin tightened, tissues distended. Bones cracked and reshaped as his body transformed.

He slammed against the chamber wall, back and forth, shrieking and howling, agonized as the metamorphosis wracked his body. The band around his neck snapped clean off, and he broke the remaining shackle on his left wrist. But escape was the last thing on his mind at the moment.

Hyde fell to the floor, still flailing in his fearsome seizure. None of the others approached him, wary for their lives.

Little by little Edward Hyde shrank into a smaller person. His coarse, unruly hair and thick black nails receded until finally, the beast was entirely gone. Another man lay there on the deck, awash in the monster's sour sweat.

"At least he fits those clothes better now," the invisible man pointed out, unhelpfully.

Shaking with weakness and personal misery, the scrawny stranger arose, blinking his nervous, saucer-wide eyes. He was a slight man who easily slipped his entire hand out of Hyde's wrist shackles, leaving the torn chains on the floor. His ashen face reflected his ordeal. His large Adam's apple bobbed up and down as he gulped.

"Henry Jekyll, at your service. And I would very much like to earn my pardon and return to London." He swallowed hard. "May I have a glass of water, please?"

"So the League is set," Quatermain said when the seven members gathered later inside the plush parlor of the submarine boat. Nemo had offered them all yellowish homemade cigars fashioned from a rare nicotine-containing seaweed. Quatermain drew a long puff, expecting to dislike the cigar, but found it rather pleasant. "Now we can finally be about our work."

Hearing a chatter of machinery, Nemo went to tear an incoming ticker tape from a wall unit. He skimmed down the punched words. "And so is the time and precise location for the conference. We have three days."

"Three days to get all the way to Italy? Goodness!" said Tom Sawyer. "Can this canoe do it?"

"Do not underestimate the *Nautilus*." Nemo went to stare out at the swirling undersea view. The ship cut through the waters at incredible speed, her long, lean lines demonstrating the accuracy of her nickname, Sword of the Ocean.

14

The *Nautilus*

The League gathered in the amazing vessel's conning tower as the submarine boat cruised the surface of the Atlantic off the coast of Portugal. A white wake curled from the bow as the beautifully ornamented vessel glided ahead. The salty air was as refreshing as the bright daylight.

"This is a whole lot different from riding a paddleboat," Tom Sawyer said.

Beside him, the famous hunter cleaned his big elephant gun in silence. Sawyer watched him, unable to keep silent. "So, you named your gun, Mr. Quatermain?"

"Matilda."

"Who's Matilda?" The young agent seemed eager for conversation. "Somebody special?"

"My gun." The old hunter sighted the gun out to sea, past where Mina Harker and Dorian Gray stood together on the far side of the *Nautilus*'s deck.

Gray smiled curiously as he looked at the woman in her formal blue dress, white scarf, and long gloves, all of which were certainly inappropriate for standing outside on the open deck of a submarine vessel racing across the water. He had witnessed the terrible changes in her, knew the demonic creature that lurked half-hidden beneath her perfect exterior. Just like himself. He edged closer. "Mina—rediscovering you . . . Ah, the mullahs of Arabia would call it kismet."

Mina did not find the moment quite so magical. "Don't get any ideas, Dorian. Our past is just and only that."

"Did I hurt you so?" His thin patrician lips formed a pained expression, which had no effect on the pale, beautiful woman.

"Don't flatter yourself. Until M mentioned your name, I'd all but forgotten you existed." She sniffed. "You were always strange, Dorian. Until the incident in your library, watching you riddled with bullets and remaining completely unaffected . . . I just didn't realize *how* strange."

"Strange? I prefer 'timeless.' "

"At least your appearance finally makes sense to me. Quatermain knew you as a grown man when he was just a boy? Even before, when we were together, I wasn't naïve enough to think that your 'youth' was due to clean living. You haven't aged a day."

"It's an overrated practice. And you yourself don't appear a moment older."

"I have an excuse."

"So do I."

As she turned away from Gray and started toward the conning tower's hatch, Sawyer watched the beautiful woman with obvious admiration.

Quatermain continued to study his elephant gun, gazing through the sight and never taking his eyes away, but still he sensed Sawyer's fascination with Mina Harker. "She's out of your league, boy."

With good-natured American cockiness, Sawyer said, "Fortune rewards the bold, Mr. Quatermain." He stepped forward with his disarming grin, intending to be a gentleman and open the hatch for Mina. "If you require any help during the voyage, Mrs. Harker, let me know."

Mina let him work the heavy hatch. "Help? I'm curious as to how you think you could assist me, Agent Sawyer."

The young man struggled with the wheel, still grinning. "Oh, heavy lifting. Light banter. Whatever you need. I'm a useful guy."

"Not to me," Mina said as he finally hauled open the hatch. "You're sweet and young, Mr. Sawyer. Neither of which are traits I hold in high regard."

Sawyer managed to keep a straight face as Mina descended into the confines of the *Nautilus*. "Well, you're sure to the point, Ma'am. I'll give you that."

Gray followed a moment later with a smug smirk, enjoying a moment of amusement at the young agent's expense. Sawyer stayed outside on the upper deck, not sure what to do next.

As he stared across the open, peaceful waves, Captain Nemo received a message from Ishmael. He called to the others still on the conning tower. "We will be diving in a moment. Please come back inside."

"Good," said Sawyer, humiliated. He glanced back at Quatermain, who remained farthest from the hatchway.

Their eyes locked as the old hunter cracked open the gun and ejected shells.

Only a few minutes later, the *Nautilus* dove beneath the waves, slowly descending like a leviathan. Turbines churned, propellers cut the water, and a great belch of ballast bubbles boiled upward.

The golden statues on the conning tower and the bow stood against the brine, as if resisting the depths to the last moment, and then they too sank deep beneath the waves.

15

The Bridge of the *Nautilus*
Night

Nemo sat in his scrolled captain's chair, using nautical logs of his own design to plot their best course to the northeastern coast of Italy. Lead scribing pencils and protractors lay spread out on the chart table.

Outside, schools of silver fish swirled about, attracted by the submarine's dazzling running lights, but fleeing from the swift approach of the armor-plated vessel.

So far they had traveled down the Thames and out of London, across the English Channel and along the French coast to the Seine, which they had followed to Paris. They had navigated back out to the Atlantic, keeping to the deep waters around the Iberian Peninsula, and passed through the Strait of Gibraltar into the calm, blue Mediterranean on their way to Italy.

Not bad for little more than a day's sailing.

When a low whistle signal sounded from the galley, Nemo looked at the ticking enclosed clock in its alcove on the bridge. He rose from his labors, stretched, and turned to the apparently unoccupied room. "Dinner is imminent, Mr. Skinner. Put some clothes on, there's a good fellow."

He walked off the bridge, leaving it empty, save for the silent invisible man. Skinner coughed, as if disappointed that the captain had remembered his presence there. . . .

Hearing Nemo approach, Quatermain stepped quickly out of his cabin, nearly bumping into the *Nautilus* captain as he passed by. "Dinner is served, Quatermain. I can offer you a jacket, if you require one."

"Thank you, no. I've lived in Africa too long to stand on stuffy old ceremony like that." The adventurer paused, wrestling with words that weighed heavily on his mind, while Nemo looked at him, waiting. "I wanted to thank you for your contribution so far, Captain. I may have been overly rude earlier when I called you a . . . pirate."

Nemo responded with the merest hint of a smile. "And I may have been overly charitable when I said I wasn't one." He stroked his thick black beard. "In my philosophy I try to live in the 'now'—where the ghosts of old wrongs do not abide. I have plenty of scars, and memories, but I would accomplish little if I allowed myself to be shackled by them. What of you?"

"I don't believe in ghosts. Although I've seen my share of them."

"Your past haunts you," Nemo observed.

"Vanity. Pride. Mistakes that cost me someone dear. It's an old story."

"So now you throw yourself in harm's way?"

Quatermain tried to think of an analogy the submarine captain might understand. "Old tigers, sensing the end, are at their most fierce. They go down fighting."

Bounding out of his cabin, Agent Tom Sawyer appeared, oblivious to the conversation. "Say, where's your dining room, Nemo?" He rubbed his stomach. "I could eat a mule."

When they reached the submarine's richly appointed room, however, they saw a server removing plates from the table, under the somber watchful eye of First Mate Ishmael.

The table had been laid extravagantly, with gold-trimmed china, finely woven napkins, and a startling centerpiece made from a shark's head ringed with frilly kelp and colorful shells. From a side serving table, a savory, fishy aroma wafted up from a tureen of chowder. Plates of iced shellfish were waiting to be served.

In spite of these elaborate preparations, a server took away many of the place settings that had been set out for the members of the League.

"Where are the others?" Nemo frowned, affronted. "Did they not receive the summons to dine?"

"I checked with them personally, Captain," Ishmael said, scratching his cheek. He did not look pleased. "They all asked to eat in their cabins."

"We may be a League, but we're sure not a team." Sawyer, at least, seemed extremely interested in the mouth-watering smells of the food. "My Aunt Polly always said the best efforts of gluing a family together were usually done at the dinner table."

"Team or not, there's work to be done," Quatermain said angrily. "Maybe the others are being particularly dedicated to their preparations."

"Or just not very sociable," Sawyer said.

Nemo regarded them. "If you two gentlemen would

care to join me in my cabin, we can look at certain plans in my possession. It will help us formulate our next move."

"As long as we can eat while we do it." Sawyer's stomach rumbled audibly. "Say, are those oysters?"

Nemo nodded silent instructions to Ishmael, then led the other two men to his cabin.

16

The *Nautilus*

While Nemo and Quatermain paid little attention to their meals, intent on the plans and discussions for their arrival in Venice, Tom Sawyer finished off two bowls of chowder, a dozen oysters—"Just like the ones I used to eat back home in Missouri!"—and a grilled shark steak. He munched on salted fried sardines fresh from the sea, then licked his fingers. He was careful not to get grease on the fragile papers the turbaned captain was displaying for them.

In the bright light of his cabin, Nemo gently leafed through a large book of aged drawings until he came to the particular page he had wanted to show them. "The plans the Fantom stole from the Bank of England. These are copies . . . to my knowledge, possibly the only ones in existence."

"What are they?" Sawyer asked. "Looks like a maze—sewers, maybe? Looks as bad as Injun Joe's cave." He brightened. "Say, didn't the Fantom have some sort of hideout in the sewers of Paris, under the Opera House?"

"If it is the same man." Nemo glanced at the young American. "These, Agent Sawyer, are Leonardo da

Vinci's blueprints of Venice, notably its foundations and waterways."

Quatermain studied the drawings. "It's a key, a complete and secret route for the Fantom to reach the secure place where the conference of world leaders is being held. He'll slip inside, and nobody can stop him. Except us."

"So you reckon he'll attack by sea?" Sawyer said.

Quatermain turned to Nemo. "What do you think, Captain?"

As usual, Nemo did not give a straightforward answer. "I think there is still much we do not know about this Fantom."

Since the others had not bothered to gather for dinner, Quatermain sought them out in their cabins. There was little time to decide upon a course of action, or to decipher the Fantom's true scheme. No one suggested that the masked man had been defeated by the shoot-out at Dorian Gray's house. His plans would not have been so easily thwarted.

Quatermain went first to Gray's cabin, where he found the elegant, youthful man's insouciance irritating.

"I have a question for you, Mr. Gray. An appeal to all the 'experience' you bring to our group."

Ever urbane, Gray raised his eyebrows. "Indeed? Ask away."

"According to M, the Fantom's been abducting scientists from various nations. All of them are versed in creating weapons of war—all except one."

He held up a cardboard photographic print of Karl Draper taken from the files provided by M. The bald,

110

bespectacled man looked mousy, somewhat startled by the flare of the photographer's flash powder.

"So? Why bring him to me?" Gray's bored, disinterested attitude had returned.

"Surely time has taught you to see beyond the obvious," Quatermain said. "Consider the question. What is so special about this man? Why is he important to the Fantom? Do you even know who he is?"

Gray grudgingly took the picture and noted the man's name on the back of it. "Karl Draper."

"He's a structural engineer. An architect, not a weapons designer. Why would the Fantom want him?"

"To build a new summer home, perhaps? Someplace without mirrors, so that he can take off his mask and relax on the weekends?"

"That's about as funny as a toothache," Quatermain growled, walking out in disgust. Why had M insisted on including the self-centered sophisticate in their number? For the life of him, Quatermain couldn't imagine that Gray would ever be of any practical use to the League.

It was a busy, restless night, as they all bided their time, faced their fears, and prepared for what was likely to be an unpleasant encounter in Venice. Deep under the sea, it was difficult to tell the hour, day or night; Quatermain followed his own rhythms. He paced the narrow corridors of the *Nautilus,* deep in thought, a sheaf of files and books under his arm.

A wide-eyed and fidgety Henry Jekyll peered out from his cabin door. "Mr. Quatermain? I'd like to help, if I could. Is there . . . um, something you would like me to do?"

"Nothing for now, Jekyll," he said, passing by. Then, to reassure the nervous little man, he added, "Don't worry, though. Mr. Hyde will have ample opportunity to get his hands dirty."

The distaste on Jekyll's face showed that this wasn't necessarily what he'd wanted to hear. He looked as if he had swallowed something particularly unpleasant . . . such as one of the oysters Tom Sawyer had enjoyed so much.

"But try to make sure we don't see Hyde until we actually need him." Quatermain turned a corner and passed Nemo's cabin again. Sawyer had already gone to bed, stuffed from his large meal, but the captain's door was ajar. Nemo knelt before a large, many-armed statue of Kali, muttering in prayerful devotion. He bowed low and touched his turbaned head to the feet of the idol, unaware of the other man's curiosity.

"That's Kali, the Goddess of Death," said Mina's voice in a whisper. She had crept up on the hunter with absolute, unnerving stealth. "Nemo worships death. Can we trust him?"

Quatermain looked over his shoulder at the vampire-woman, embarrassed to be caught observing the man's private devotions. "He's not the one I'm worried about." He walked away, clutching his papers under his arm.

Mina looked back into Nemo's cabin, intent on learning what she could about him. But the dark and mysterious captain rose, went to the door—obviously aware she had been eavesdropping all along—and closed it coldly in her face.

Weary and troubled, very unsure about how well the members of this group would manage together, Quatermain returned to his cabin and sat down. By the light of a single lamp, he began once again to study his files and papers.

His research ranged far from the specific dossiers of the League members to the activities of the Fantom. He perused Scotland Yard criminal reports and several copies of *The Strand Magazine*. He compared information from an illustrated article in one issue of the periodical, and made a note in his crime files. He saw connections, albeit faint ones, everywhere.

Suddenly, Quatermain sensed something nearby: a breath, a presence. In an instant he turned off his light and, with a single fluid motion, lunged from his chair.

In the pitch black cabin, they were on equal footing. He heard movement, touched skin, and caught a handful of hair. Quatermain struck out, responding to a frantic struggle, and landed several blows, which resulted in a very rewarding series of whimpers.

He reached the cabin door and flung it open, flooding the room with a shaft of light from the hall. Quatermain stood there, glaring. "I want you dressed at all times, Mr. Skinner—or it's my boot up your arse. Now get out!"

Without an apology, the invisible man hurried out. His bare footsteps hurried down the corridor, and the door to his own cabin opened, seemingly by itself.

Satisfied that he was truly alone again, Quatermain slammed the door shut and went to bed.

17

Ancient stuccoed buildings loomed on either side of Venice's famous, sluggish canals. The smell of floating garbage, wet stone, and old moss suffused the night mists that crept along the pilings. Overhead, windows were shuttered for the night, most of them dark; only a few denizens of the darkest hours remained awake.

The following night there would be a spectacular Carnival, with dancing and celebrations, music and drinking. Tonight, the people rested, content with anticipation.

But the Fantom did not rest.

In the odorous, gently lapping water that rose and fell like the sleeping breaths of the ocean, several dead fish floated belly-up, far from the reach of the feral cats prowling the alleys. A rank of unoccupied gondolas, moored to brightly striped poles near a boathouse, creaked and knocked against each other. The black-painted, curved hulls were slender and graceful, resembling dark crescent moons; the single, long oar for each boat had been stored for the night under a patched canvas covering.

114

The uneasy night silence only made the pained groans and gasps louder by comparison as they drifted down to the water from the boathouse. The sound of an open hand striking flesh was like that of a chef tenderizing a veal cutlet.

Inside the building, behind closed doors and barricaded windows, the Fantom paced in front of the bespectacled German structural engineer. Karl Draper writhed in misery, though he was drugged and only semicoherent. He didn't seem to know where he was, only that he wanted to crawl away.

Beside the Fantom, Dante watched the captive as if the man were nothing more than a smear of something unpleasant he had scraped off the bottom of his shoe.

The Fantom turned his back, holding a wide-barreled syringe with a dauntingly long, thick needle. "My truth serum isn't fully developed, Herr Draper, or I'd know everything by now." In the lamplight that illuminated the boathouse, a final droplet of greenish liquid glistened like a tear at the sharp end. "It has had sufficient time to work."

In disgust, the Fantom dropped the empty syringe to the boathouse floor and ground it to glass dust under his black heel. He slapped Karl Draper to consciousness, aiming his blows at the bright red welts that already covered the man's cheek. "Still, despite its deficiencies, I'm sure the serum doesn't feel very pleasant coursing through your veins."

Dante unrolled a sheaf of thick, yellowed sheets of paper on a worktable made of rough planks. Judging by the sticky stains and clumped flakes of silver scales, the table had recently been used to gut and clean fish.

"Look at the plans and tell me what I need to know," the Fantom insisted. His voice was low and quiet now, and much more threatening.

"No," the engineer croaked out in German. "I can resist your serum. Nothing will make me tell."

With another backhand, the Fantom knocked Draper's spectacles loose. Dante dutifully retrieved them, holding the glasses a bit too tightly, as if he wanted to clench his fists and twist the frames. Instead, he gave them back to the Fantom.

"You force me to rely on more proven methods," said the Fantom, swirling his black cape. "Fortunately, they are just as effective." He turned to Dante, gave a meaningful glare, and the lieutenant nodded.

Around them in the drafty boathouse room, the Fantom's henchmen worked diligently on their tasks. Each man had his assignment, and they knew better than to debate their master's orders. They worked quietly, muffling any suspicious sounds that might attract too much attention in the still night. The city of Venice would have no advance warning of its doom, and their party tomorrow night would be much different from what they expected.

Two henchmen taped and waterproofed a set of wooden barrels while another group of the Fantom's followers outfitted themselves in thick diving gear: oiled leather suits, rubber-coated gloves, and heavy helmets with glass windows. They strung weights around their waists to help them reach the foundations of the centuries-old buildings and remain in place long enough to complete their tasks.

The boathouse's back rooms and stalls held the Fantom's other prisoners, bound and gagged. The captives crowded together like animals in pens, forced to wait while the evil genius competed his preparations. So far, two of them had died trying to escape; the Fantom had tossed the horribly mutilated bodies back in among the prisoners as "an appropriate lesson." Since then, no one else had made an attempt to break free.

Now, wearing a determined expression, Dante retrieved the German prisoner the Fantom had chosen as his first bargaining chip. The lieutenant brandished his weapon and pulled the man away from his comrades, who shrank back, praying they would not be noticed themselves. Dante shoved the prisoner out of the holding pen and dragged him into the main room. The man stood cringing, barely able to remain on his feet.

The Fantom regarded the man, dismissed him as an inadequate specimen, then returned his attention to Karl Draper. Like a stern mother, he replaced the structural engineer's spectacles on his face, then let him blink at the hapless prisoner until recognition clearly showed on his face.

"Herr Muller you know. I believe you worked together at the Valkyrie Zeppelin Works? Were you friends?"

Predictably, Draper shook his head. The Fantom did not believe him. His scarred lower lip curled. "Of course not. Muller's specialty is motors." He turned his masked face toward the shaking prisoner. Muller swallowed hard, but could say nothing through his gag. "Unfortunately for him, I have all the motors I need. He is perfectly expendable."

The Fantom reached into his dark coat and removed a

heavy handgun with a strange, fat cylinder appended to its barrel. Muller's eyes went wide with panic.

Draper, though, struggled to remain calm through the bleary effects of the abortive truth serum. "You will not fire a gunshot here, Herr Fantom. The Venice Polizia will hear you and come to investigate. The people in the buildings will wake, and they will call for help."

The Fantom fingered the device at the end of the gun barrel. "Don't underestimate my imagination, Herr Draper. My lab rats dreamed up this new modification. It uses compressed air to silence the blast. No one will hear a gunshot—or anything at all."

"Impossible," Draper said.

The Fantom aimed the pistol and silently shot Muller in the center of the forehead before the motor specialist could flinch. His head snapped back, and his body drooped to the floor.

Shocked, despite the last vestiges of the drug's effects, the architect wailed and struggled to lurch out of his chair, but muscular Dante held him down. Muller twitched once more, then went completely still.

The Fantom swirled his black cape and leaned close, towering in all his monstrous deformity over the structural engineer. "The new twentieth century will be a time when the word 'impossible' no longer has any meaning." His scars looked like lumpy candle wax, his eyes behind the silver mask filled with demon fire.

"Now, then—I have many more of your colleagues from the zeppelin factory, if we are required to use them for further encouragement."

Hopeless and desperate, Draper struggled to lunge at his tormentor, but the masked villain easily stepped out of the way. When Dante had the mousy architect under control again, the Fantom opened a small closet door behind him. With a theatrical flourish, he revealed a girl held inside, bound and gagged, and isolated from the other captives.

"Or perhaps it would be best to use someone closer to you? Your daughter is so very beautiful, Herr Draper. Eva? Is that her name?" He dragged her out into the open, making her stand not far from the body of the slaughtered motor expert. "I haven't had time to fully . . . interrogate her yet."

Draper crumbled, tears flooding his eyes. "All right, I'll tell you what you want." His shaking voice could not contain the fullness of his misery.

Returning to the worktable, the Fantom tapped his fingers meaningfully on the old parchment pages spread out before the structural engineer: the original da Vinci blueprints of Venice stolen from the vault of the Bank of England.

"Of course you will," said the Fantom. "Now study these and give me your expert advice."

Trembling, Draper adjusted his spectacles and bent to peer at the faded original drawings, which showed the precise details of Venice's hidden foundations. And all their vulnerabilities.

The engineer had a difficult time concentrating while the Fantom continued to smile cruelly at his terrified daughter, Eva.

18

The Nautilus

Making good time as it rounded the boot of Italy and cruised up the eastern coast, the *Nautilus* ran at full power under a magnificent sky. Flying fish swarmed in the churning white wake.

Below the conning tower, in the submarine vessel's control room, sunlight penetrated the sea-splashed windows of the bridge. Wearing a deep frown and scratching his stubbly chin, First Mate Ishmael examined the complex controls and dials. Nemo stood next to him, curious, as Ishmael tapped the crystal plates that covered compasses and heading gauges.

"They're not 'ow I left them, Cap'n. S'all I'm saying."

Nemo glanced down at the deck, then silently crouched to examine something.

"You think it might be sabotage? We ain't that far off course—I caught it in time," Ishmael said. "Still, there's too many strangers aboard this boat, if y'ask me."

"Please don't refer to my Lady as a mere 'boat,' Ishmael."

Nemo brushed at the floor and dabbed some of the residue onto his fingertips, then sniffed them. "Powder. I don't recognize the smell. Perhaps Mrs. Harker will be able to—" Suddenly, he felt an unexpected movement in the air, a faint stirring in the control room. Nemo's dark eyebrows knitted together. "Mr. Skinner? Are you here skulking about?"

The silence that followed gave him no answer. He and Ishmael heard nothing more than the thrumming of the *Nautilus*'s engines and the rushing sound of the waves against the hull.

Around the corner, Tom Sawyer sauntered up to the bridge, eager to go outside to enjoy some fresh air and sunshine. He thought he heard quick, feathery footsteps, someone passing unseen? For a moment he was tempted to thrust out a foot to see if he could trip the invisible man, but he couldn't be sure he had actually heard anything. There wasn't much room in the narrow corridor for Skinner to go by, no matter how sneaky the thief might be.

A loud gunshot came from outside, above the bridge, and Sawyer started running.

Already on edge, Nemo and Ishmael went to the observation windows, looking around in alarm as another gunshot rang out from the deck overhead.

But Sawyer was grinning as he started to climb the conning tower. "He said he wouldn't start without me!"

With a slap and a hum, the launcher shot its buoyant target. The colorful shape sailed ahead through the air and landed with a splash far from the racing *Nautilus*.

At the edge of the foredeck, Quatermain adjusted his spectacles and squinted out at the water. He drew a deep breath, shouldered the stock, sighted along the line, and calmly aimed Matilda. The target bobbed in the water, and Quatermain tracked it, aiming . . . aiming . . . aiming. Then, as the colorful floater drifted past, he pulled the trigger.

The elephant gun made a sound like a crack of thunder, and the hunter braced himself against the recoil that punched into his shoulder bone. The target blew out of the waves, bright pieces flying up with a spray of water. Good enough for practice. He called out again in Hindi, "Pull!"

One of Nemo's turbaned crewmen ratcheted back the firing mechanism and launched another target.

When he reached the top of the conning tower, Sawyer blinked in the Mediterranean sunlight and kept watching Quatermain instead of the flying target. The object soared through the air and then splashed down.

The young American didn't venture closer, not wanting to disturb the old adventurer's aim. They stood apart, separated by the wide deck. As he aimed carefully, his eyes never leaving the floating target, Quatermain sensed the young man's presence. "Do you want something?"

"No, not really."

Quatermain fired again, another perfect shot, another target destroyed. He didn't bother to show any satisfaction at his prowess.

Sawyer was extremely impressed, though, and ventured closer. "Well, I guess I was just wondering why you signed up for all of this."

Quatermain didn't look at him. The turbaned crewman positioned another target in the launcher.

The young American pressed. "Cap'n Nemo told me

that you hate the British Empire. So it doesn't really make a whole lot of sense, you joining in."

"They called. I answered." Quatermain cracked the gun and reloaded.

Sawyer thrust his hands in his pockets. "Well, that isn't all of it, though. Is it?"

"Pull!" Quatermain said, and another target soared. Clearly there was to be no more conversation. He sighted it, following the target as if he was tracking a flight of geese. This time, he wanted to shoot the object out of the sky instead of waiting for it to strike the waves.

"I'm sorry for asking," Sawyer said, turning away.

Quatermain lowered his gun without firing and looked at the young American. He wrestled with words, dredging up memories he no longer wanted to think about. "Years ago . . . the British approached me with a mission for Queen and Country. They appealed to my patriotism. They promised thrills, adventure. . . ." He let out a long, lonely sigh.

"That's like the morning ride to work for you, I'd imagine." Sawyer looked at the old hunter with hopeful eyes.

Quatermain's gaze was distant, though—seeing farther than the hazy coastline of Italy. "I signed up without hesitation. I even took my son along, promised to watch him. I led, and my son followed."

He sighed. The *Nautilus* continued, surging past the floating target out on the waves. Quatermain leaned on his elephant gun, making no attempt to take the shot.

He didn't look at Sawyer as he continued. "The boy died in my arms. After that, I washed my hands of England, the Empire . . . and the legend of Allan bloody Quatermain."

The young American chose to see the other man's strength instead of his misery. "So if you succeed this time, then your son's memory will be honored."

"No. It doesn't work that way." Quatermain eyed the American agent who was so full of optimism and guileless honesty. He changed the subject abruptly, as if out of self-defense. "Now, would you like to learn how to shoot, lad?"

"I can already," said Sawyer, propping one hand on his hip.

"Yes, I saw you in Gray's library. Very American. Just fire enough bullets and hope that some of them will hit the target. No finesse. No skill."

The young agent frowned as if suspecting that he'd just been insulted. "I reckon a good many of the Fantom's marksmen would beg to differ."

The old adventurer wrinkled his brow. "Sawyer, I'm talking about pipping the ace at nine hundred yards." He offered the gun to the American. "Try."

Sawyer was surprised, but took the big weapon with eager hands. Holding it by the stock and barrel, hefting its weight, he let out a low, appreciative whistle. He squinted one eye and looked down the long barrel of the elephant gun.

"Steady on," Quatermain said. To the turbaned crewman, he called out, "Pull!"

The launcher flapped, and a fresh target soared high. The old hunter leaned in so they sighted the gun together, man and boy, as the colorful object tumbled and then splashed down.

"Now . . . aim," Quatermain said, focusing on the shot with all his concentration.

"Aww, that's easy."

"Allow for wind and target movement."

"That's easy, too," Sawyer said.

"It's the next part that's not. You've got to feel the shot."

Sawyer concentrated, aimed, tried to do exactly as Quatermain said. But the submarine vessel picked up speed, and a rooster tail of spray kicked up from the bow. The bobbing target was racing past.

"Take your time with it."

Sawyer swallowed. "It's moving pretty fast."

"Take your time. You have all the time you need. Anybody can hit it with ten shots. But take only one. Hit it the first time."

The target was getting closer. Sawyer was itching to fire. The elephant gun twitched in his hands.

"All . . . the time . . . in the world," said Quatermain.

The target passed, almost out of range. "Take . . . your . . ."

Sawyer fired—and missed the target by a fraction of an inch. The large-caliber bullet made a splash like a leaping fish.

"—time."

"Darn it!" Sawyer shaded his eyes and looked forlornly at the floating target as it drifted away.

But Quatermain was impressed. "Too soon, but that was bloody close, and at five hundred yards, too. Try again."

Sawyer shouldered the gun once more, grinning. "Pull!"

Though Sawyer didn't speak Hindi, the *Nautilus* crewman understood. The target soared.

With his confidence brimming, Sawyer said, "Did you teach your son to shoot like this?"

At that, Quatermain gently pushed the muzzle down and took the gun back. The moment between them was suddenly gone. "Lesson's over."

The old adventurer walked away, leaving Sawyer standing there alone on the deck, uncomfortably aware that he had said too much.

19

The Nautilus

Mina Harker worked at her intricate chemistry setup, tinkering with vials and retorts. She removed a test tube from an atomizer and examined it with sharp green eyes.

Her cabin door was ajar, and Dorian Gray pushed it farther open. "Brewing tea, Mina? Or something stronger?"

She looked up at him, but showed no pleasure at his arrival. "I'm identifying a powder that Nemo found in the control room. Residue of magnesium phosphorus." From his bored expression, she saw that the chemical meant nothing to him. She explained. "Photographers use it to create a flash."

"A camera?" Gray said. "Why would someone carry a clunky old camera aboard a submarine, much less use it?"

"It appears that someone wishes to capture this vessel's secrets." Mina went back to her work.

Gray hovered close to her—*too* close. He drew a deep breath to inhale her scent. "I thought you should know. I told those who've asked that I'm an old friend of your family."

"To spare me embarrassment? I'm above what others think. We were lovers once upon a time. Our love died. Many things die."

"Many things don't."

Mina finally looked up from her chemistry work to meet his gaze. "I was surprised that you ultimately agreed to join the League, Dorian. You are a selfish man. This task requires heroes . . . not vain hedonists."

"Perhaps I mean to undo the flaws in my character through selfless action. Maybe I want to face my demons."

Mina scoffed, turning away. Foul odors bubbled from a flask over a Bunsen burner. "What do you know of demons?"

"Maybe more than you know." He remained maddeningly close to her, even as she tried to work. "Do you recall the space on the wall of my home, Mina? Where a picture was missing?"

"Yes. It was glaringly obvious. What of it?"

Gray drew a long breath. "It's time—long past time, actually—that I tell you a story."

Outside in the corridor, Henry Jekyll paced back and forth, looking and listening to the sounds of the ship and the secret tales told between passengers. Mina's door was open, and chemical smells and soft voices wafted out into the passageway. He came close enough that his shadow barely fell on the edge of the door, then he cringed and backed away.

Yes, Henry—look, but don't touch. Don't risk anything. Don't get your fingers dirty. That's your way.

He hated the mocking voice. Jekyll hurried away

shame-faced, but in the mirror-bright shine of the *Nautilus*'s corridor fittings the brutish taunting reflection of Edward Hyde followed him.

"Shut your mouth," Jekyll said, just loud enough to answer the voice in his head.

Did I just hear a mouse squeak? Or was it just a worm stirring? Certainly nothing of any consequence.

"I won't be tricked again."

Tricked? You've known what I was about each time you drank the formula. I know about it, Henry. I know you. Hyde's deep voice ended in a gruff chuckle. *You like it.*

"Liar! I'm a good man." Jekyll whimpered. "I am a good man."

Who's lying now? Repeat it to yourself, keep saying the same thing . . . but it still won't be true.

"I make my own decisions."

So make your decision. You know which one I mean. You want it, Henry. Even more than you want . . . her.

Jekyll quailed, stumbled into the curved metal wall. Hyde chuckled again with a note that sounded like triumph. *You can't shut me out forever. Drink the elixir.*

"No."

She barely even looks at you, Hyde taunted. *She wants a big, strong, decisive man. Not a little weakling.*

"Be quiet!" Jekyll said.

She'd look at me!

Hyde appeared large in front of the doctor's eyes, rising up like a nightmarish simian demon. He loomed into reality, and with a powerful, blunt-fingered hand he grabbed Jekyll's throat, ready to wring it like a chicken. Drool trickled between crooked, broken teeth; his yellow eyes were bloodshot with thin scarlet lava flows.

In voice as hard and firm as an iron anvil, Captain Nemo said from behind him, "Contain your evil, Doctor."

Jekyll spun with a yelp, his knees weak. The feverish apparition of Hyde vanished like smoke in a cold wind.

Nemo stepped forward, and Jekyll seemed to fear the *Nautilus* captain as much as he trembled from his inner demons. "I'll not have that brute free upon my ship. Must I take drastic steps and keep you confined?"

"I'm . . . in control." Jekyll's teeth chattered together. He wiped a clammy hand through the perspiration on his forehead and smeared back his lank hair.

"In control, sir? I doubt that very much," Nemo said. "Even the strongest of men know evil's allure."

Flustered and reddening, Jekyll gathered his courage. "Your talk is all well and good, sir—but your own past is far from laudable!" He immediately regretted his outburst. "I—I'm sorry, Captain." He started to slink away, shamed and tortured.

"Has Hyde ever killed?" Nemo asked, crossing his arms over his blue-uniformed chest. "Has he actually broken a neck or torn out a throat with his bare hands?"

Jekyll looked back wearily and nodded. "He's done all the evils a man could do. And it is my terrible curse that I . . . recall every one of his actions, even though I could not stop them." He let out a low moan of misery.

"I sympathize. It is my curse that I recall my own."

Jekyll scampered away without looking back. Nemo watched him go. A shadow larger than normal followed him as he retreated down the *Nautilus* corridor. . . .

Before Nemo could return to the control bridge, he heard low voices through the partially open door of

Mina's cabin. He hesitated, normally a man who respected privacy and a person's right to keep their dark secrets . . . but Mina Harker had also spied on him while he'd made his prayers to Kali in his own cabin.

Intent on the woman in front of him, Dorian Gray continued his explanation. "So although the picture is my portrait, I doubt you'd recognize the face upon it."

"How so? I'm quite familiar with your features—and they haven't changed a bit in all the time I've known you."

His thin smile seemed self-satisfied. "For each year that passes, my *portrait* ages instead of me. I'm sure that my every dark, selfish, shameful act is there, too, in the way that men wear their pasts about them. And I have committed plenty of such acts. . . ."

"When did you last see the portrait?" Mina asked.

"I dare not look upon it myself, or the magic of the painting will be undone," Gray said. "I have taken it from my wall, leaving an empty space. I have hidden it, kept it safe. . . ."

Nemo turned silently on his heel, not wishing to hear any more. He understood science and invention, and he had studied Eastern philosophies, trained his body to become a machine that he controlled. He had cruised the seas in his armored submarine boat—but those things were comprehensible, explained by a strict set of laws and rules.

The sorcery and superstition of which Dorian Gray spoke—that was not part of Nemo's universe.

He marched back to the bridge to see if Ishmael had learned anything more about whoever had tampered with the controls.

*   *   *

In Jekyll's cabin, the thin and fidgety doctor sat on the edge of his bunk, wringing his hands.

Let me play, Henry. Come on, let me play. Hyde's noxious, whining voice whispered in his head. *I'll win. I always win.*

Jekyll rubbed his eyes, tempted.

Why fight it? Enjoy me, Henry. Enjoy me. . . .

He glanced over at the small medical case on his desk. Just one dose, a gulp of the elixir that would change him, free him, give him the strength to follow Hyde's—and his—every desire.

Let me out, Hyde urged.

But Jekyll stared at the case, shocked. The clasp had been undone while he was away.

"If I didn't know better, I'd swear I already had," Jekyll said, shaking his head. He looked at his fretful hands, expecting to see his nails blacken and coarse hair sprout from his knuckles. But they remained his pale, damp, weak hands and fingers. . . .

He looked inside the case, afraid it might snap shut and bite his wrist. He stared in surprise, then rooted around among the small glass bottles and cylinders.

Jekyll looked sharply at his cabin door, expecting to see someone there. The door was closed, and he was safe. But someone had been here.

One of the vials of his elixir was missing.

20

The Nautilus

In Mina's cabin at night, Gray produced a flask and a pair of delicate glass cups. He poured a shot of the rich, tan liquid for Mina, then one for himself. "Nightcap? It's the finest Spanish amontillado, very old. I found it inside a walled-up cellar in an old villa."

"I'm not much of a drinker," Mina said. She licked the corner of her lips. *Unless it's hot and fresh and red. . . .*

She remembered strolling with Dorian Gray after dusk through the streets of London, long, long ago. Her husband Jonathan had been dead for five years already, slain while defeating the evil Dracula. Her own life had been filled with shadows since then, her days of dazzling sunshine and carefree laughter gone—

Dorian had seemed so suave, so self-assured . . . so full of himself. They had walked through the gardens, playfully hiding and seeking in a convoluted shrubbery maze, but Mina had had an unfair advantage over him, an animal instinct that always allowed her to track her prey.

Dorian had quickly lost interest in the activity, and next they had gone to the zoo after dark. Very few other visitors walked the paths, and the animals themselves dozed, either overfed or simply resigned to their fates. But as he and Mina strolled along, the caged beasts grew restless. Tigers growled and paced, gorillas snorted and hooted, an ibex and a wildebeest withdrew skittishly to the far corners of their pens.

At the time Mina had thought it was her scent, the cloying air of death around her, the dark aura of vampirism . . . but perhaps the animals had been just as nervous about Dorian Gray.

The two of them had gone to the opera very late, dressed in their finest clothes. Dorian had a private box, one of the plushest and most expensive in the opera house. Mina had felt everyone staring at them, then turning away. She knew of Mr. Gray's numerous dalliances with exotic women of all kinds, from dark Abyssinian princesses, to beauties from China or Sumatra, to veiled Arabic women who exuded tantalizing perfumes. By comparison, Mina Harker must have looked terribly plain and mundane.

If she had shown her fangs, though, she supposed she might have been sufficiently exotic.

Dorian had sensed the intriguing, special quality within her. Mina doubted he knew the truth about her; but even if he had, she didn't think he would have shown fear or loathing—only amused fascination.

They had eaten a large dinner at a very late hour, the darkest and most comfortable time before dawn. Two thick steaks, rare and dripping—exactly the way Mina liked them, since her change.

Afterward, Dorian had poured them each a glass from an ancient squat bottle coated with dust from the deepest alcove of his cellar. The port wine was deep crimson, thick and sweet. Like the blood of a nobleman . . .

Now, in her cabin aboard the *Nautilus*, he offered her another drink. "Just a small one, then." He passed the glass to Mina, and she took it, absently clenching her powerful, alabaster hand. The fine glass broke, spilling the amontillado and cutting open her palm.

"How clumsy of me." Her green eyes flashed as she looked at the open wound.

Gray took her soft hand and dabbed it with his handkerchief. "We don't want blood everywhere." He pressed the cloth hard against the cut.

"No," Mina said, her voice growing hoarse. "Not blood." She pulled away the reddened handkerchief and looked at her own bloody hand, which quickly healed itself. Her pulse began to race, her cold skin flushed, as if from some inner fever. Her mouth was very dry.

Then Mina looked up at Gray with clear intent. Their eyes met.

She let the red-stained handkerchief fall to the floor, her wound already gone. They kissed passionately as they bumped the table, rattling but not breaking her chemistry paraphernalia.

Seeking a safer place, they fell together to the narrow cabin bed.

21

The Nautilus

While the engines hummed and an enclosed clock ticked on the curved metal wall, Quatermain and Sawyer worked in the *Nautilus* library, digging through the extensive reference material Captain Nemo had compiled in his many voyages.

Sawyer scratched his head and tried to concentrate on the files, open books, and hand-drawn maps he had retrieved from the submarine's shelves and cabinets. He had laid out everything that seemed remotely relevant to the Fantom, to Venice, and to the secret meeting of the world leaders. In spite of staring at it all for the better part of an hour, however, he still hadn't figured out how everything connected.

Quatermain paced and drank a brandy, meditating on the problem at hand. "I rarely have the opportunity to *ponder* a problem. In my day, I was usually too busy either running or shooting or grabbing up treasure."

The young man had not touched again on the sensitive subject of Quatermain's dead son, but he worked quietly and diligently. He was also a member of the American Secret Service, and he had an important mission. The old adventurer appreciated his assistance, but did not open the doors of friendship more than a crack.

"You know, Mr. Quatermain, when I was younger I served time as a detective, solving crimes, unraveling mysteries." He flipped pages, but saw no revelations there.

"Impressive," Quatermain raised his eyebrows. "Especially if you were just a boy then."

Quatermain sipped from his brandy, then returned to the files M had provided, as well as Nemo's extra material. "I'm sure solving our little mystery here is well within your means." He bent over copies of the da Vinci plans, pondering what possible advantage the Fantom could gain from knowing the details of the submerged foundations. And what part did the kidnapped structural engineer Karl Draper play?

Sawyer did not seem overly flattered by the adventurer's confidence. "I prefer to think of myself as a man of action, Mr. Quatermain. Book learnin' was never my especial skill."

Quatermain sighed and set down his empty brandy glass. "Ah, yes, a man of action. Adventure. I remember the lure, when all the mysteries of Africa were impossible to resist. King Solomon's mines, the Lost City of Gold, the holy flower, the treasure of the lake, and most especially Ayesha . . ." His voice trailed off. "She was beautiful, immortal, insidious. Her followers called her She-Who-Must-Be-Obeyed. Reminds me a bit of Mrs. Harker, in a way."

He paused, and Tom Sawyer looked at him with wide eyes. "I don't reckon Mina would be too happy with the comparison."

"No, I suppose not. And then there was my Zulu

friend and companion Umslopogaas. Never met a braver, more loyal man in the face of outright danger, whether it be lions or sorcery . . ."

He blinked shining eyes and suddenly brought himself back to the present. "Sorry, lad—long ago I made up my mind to let Nigel tell all the stories. I don't want to think about them anymore . . . and now Nigel is dead at the start of this whole nasty business. I just want to bring it to an end."

Captain Nemo entered the library, bringing the conversation to a halt. Beneath his blue turban, his eyebrows had drawn together in grim realization. "We have been thinking along the wrong lines, gentlemen." He went to the book of da Vinci drawings, pointing out key junctures. "The world leaders themselves are mere pawns, not at all the target of this terrible scheme."

He quickly explained what he had realized, while Quatermain and Sawyer bent over the plans, following the captain's rationale. Quatermain looked up gravely. "So the Fantom doesn't intend to attack the secret talks at all."

"Not precisely." Nemo closed the book of plans with finality. "With da Vinci's blueprints and Karl Draper's knowledge, he can set a bomb to blow Venice's foundations to rubble."

"The Fantom's going to sink the whole city!" Sawyer cried. "He'll knock it under the water."

"Yes, and thereby spark his world war," said Quatermain. "That's what he really wants." His sinewy fist clenched. "With the most vital leaders gathered there trying to reach an accord, there can be no other outcome."

The young American blurted the obvious. "Well, that's a lot worse than simply shaking up a dull old meeting any day!"

The news didn't get any better as Jekyll appeared in the doorway. His voice was shaky, his face flushed, his brow dotted with perspiration. "That isn't the sum of our problems." He swallowed hard and ran a hand through his limp hair. "Skinner has taken a vial of my formula!"

Tom Sawyer set his jaw. "I never trusted that invisible man."

"Are you sure it was him?" Quatermain said.

Jekyll's eyes darted from side to side. "Who else? You've seen how the sneaky blackguard operates." His reedy voice rose, as if he'd caught just a flicker of Hyde's personality.

A wall unit on the side of the *Nautilus* library chattered, and a ticker-tape message reeled out of a thin slot. Nemo tore it off and scanned the text. "Mr. Skinner's crimes will have to wait for the time being. Duty calls—we have arrived at our destination."

22

Venetia, a picturesque city built on 118 islands in a lagoon on Italy's Adriatic coast, boasted more than a hundred and fifty canals and four hundred bridges. The proud history of the area stretched back more than fourteen centuries, spawning world-renowned artisans, including the glassmakers of Murano and the lace makers of Burano.

Tonight, the looming facades seemed to haunt the sluggish canals of green-black water. Even the festive lamps and flower boxes overhead could not dispel the ghostly, brooding impression. In the narrow, time-worn architecture, specters seemed to hide in every shadow.

The distant music of Carnival throbbed from stages and plazas deeper in the city, but the revelry didn't reach this eerie quarter of calm waters and fetid smells. The *Nautilus* slid silently into the labyrinth of Venetian canals, following a shadow of menace and urgency.

A potbellied gondolier, dozing beneath the meager shelter of his boat's caponera, hardly stirred as the huge vessel passed him like a deep prehistoric sea monster. The submarine boat left no sign of its passage other than a ripple and a languid splash. The gondolier snorted, sat forward and blinked his eyes blearily, then spat into the canal before settling back into his slumber.

The *Nautilus* dropped deeper underwater, to the sodden base of the canals built many centuries before. The propellers turned, driving the armored vessel past Venice's cavernous foundations, the same monolithic structures that had been shown neatly in da Vinci's blueprints. Over the years, the caverns and thick supports had become crusted with algae, silt, barnacles.

Looking strikingly fresh and shiny in the murk, a huge bomb had been bolted to one of the largest stone blocks, its location precisely chosen according to the da Vinci drawings and the calculations of Karl Draper. Here, it would cause the most damage.

The device was wrapped in sheets of thick rubber that kept the deadly explosives dry. Wires extended upward to the surface. A faint trail of tiny silver bubbles rose through the murky water. . . .

At the street level, deeper in the city, noisy Carnival celebrations ranged from villa to villa. The crowds roared and laughed; many of the people didn't know the reason for the particular festival, celebrating which saint or holy day or medieval tradition. They simply drank and sang and enjoyed themselves.

Revelers crossed vine-strewn bridges, strumming musical instruments, drinking from bottles of wine, singing slurred songs. Torches and banners were carried aloft. Tumblers and minstrels evoked laughter from gathered spectators. Streetlights shone around them, casting a bright glow over the all-night celebrations.

Inside one of the impressive stone structures, though, the lights were dimmer, the mood serious and somber. Wearing Carnival costumes to hide their identities, a group of important ambassadors and world leaders entered according to the secret agenda. Alert guards showed them to a secure conference room, which was lit by large candelabras.

Suspicious of each other despite the reassurances of diplomacy, the men removed their feathered hats and sequined domino masks. Outside, they had not been noticed; the meeting would be completely discreet.

Three street-level windows had been shuttered for privacy. The room had been a third-floor chamber when the villa was built, but now because of the waterlogged city's sinking, it was at the level of the canals and the raised cobblestone street. The lower rooms had already drowned, and the air smelled of rot and mildew.

The important delegates representing France, England, Germany, Spain, Portugal, Italy, and Russia, exchanged subdued greetings. Many of the men spoke several languages; they had kept the number of interpreters to a minimum, to help assure secrecy.

"Now, gentlemen," said the British representative when they were all seated, "each one of us knows that the fate of the world may very well hang in the balance this night."

The expressions around the room remained grave. The German ambassador said, "All of our countries are counting on us to resolve our differences, to address accusations, and to make mutual resolutions regarding this arms race."

"We have evidence that the hostilities attributed to

France in recent months have in fact been the work of a . . . savage provocateur," said the French leader. "Our people have had enough war and bloodshed for one century, due to our own social strife, as well as foreign aggression." He glanced pointedly at the German representative, who snorted.

"Your complaint is with Chancellor Bismarck. He left power a decade ago. The German Empire seeks to strengthen itself internally, not annex worthless French territory."

"Worthless—!"

"Gentlemen!" The Russian pounded a beefy hand on the table. "This is going nowhere. We must establish peace terms and resolutions. All of our countries are tinderboxes."

"Well said, well said," the British diplomat interjected. "Let us not offer any excuse to light a political match. Now then, since we all have the same fundamental objective, shall we begin? The rest of the world does not know we are here. Therefore, it should be a simple matter to address our issues and formulate simple, binding resolutions."

"Provided we are not interrupted," the Frenchman said.

"This meeting has been established with the utmost security," the German pointed out. "What could possibly interrupt us?"

On the bridge of the *Nautilus,* Ishmael said in drawling Hindi, "Helm three feet to port. Steady. Two feet. Decrease prop a half knot." The members of the League crowded in the control room, ready to begin their work.

As his crew guided the armored vessel, Captain Nemo peered into his periscope. Through the eyepiece, he could see the far-off revelers, the celebratory torches, the feasts and flowers in the streets of Venice. "The Carnival is quite the affair."

"I love a party," said Gray. "Perhaps we should all join them. After all, Nemo's already wearing his own costume."

"I tend to avoid large gatherings and all that noise," the captain said.

As the canal narrowed, the stone walls closed together like a slow and deadly trap. The *Nautilus* eased cautiously forward like a big mechanical shark in the shadows of this dingy section of the drowning city. Ishmael's expert guidance kept the alloy armor plates from being scratched against the slimy walls, only inches away.

"We can go no farther, Captain," Ishmael said, before the undersea vessel could get stuck.

"All ahead stop!" Nemo said.

"Reverse engines!" Ishmael shouted.

The big brass propellers reversed, sloshing a backwash as they dampened the vessel's headlong inertia. The high prow snagged a clothesline, stretching it almost to snapping before the majestic boat came to a final stop beneath a high, vine-covered bridge that arched overhead.

On the metal deck in front of the conning tower, Nemo's crewmen jumped onto the canal towpath, tossing ropes. On either side of the narrow, mossy walkway, the men affixed the cable moorings, lashing them tight. One man glanced up at the curved bridge as four boisterous Carnival participants raced from one building to another, laughing with the drunken chase, and disappeared into the opposite villa. None of them glanced down at the water or the huge ship floating below.

Like metal tongues, three gangplanks extended from the ship's side hull and settled on the towpath. Captain Nemo and Allan Quatermain led the way as a large group of *Nautilus* crewmen marched out of the ship, including men suited up as divers. Their footsteps made muffled bangs on the gangplank, then crunched on the brick and gravel walkway. The rest of the League followed them out into the streets of Venice.

They exchanged orders like rapid-fire gunshots. "Break into squads and begin to sweep the city," Nemo said.

"One flare per five-man team," Ishmael said.

"Look for any hint of the Fantom," Quatermain said. "Signal at the first sign of suspicious activity."

"But this is a vast city of masks and mystery—" Mina said.

"Then you will be very much in your element," Quatermain said, and signaled her to hurry along.

"What about Skinner?" Tom Sawyer asked in a whisper, looking behind him. No one had been able to find the invisible man since Quatermain had chased him out of his cabin. Now that the *Nautilus* had arrived in Venice and their mission was to begin, Skinner had abandoned them. He could be anywhere.

The American, and most of the others, were convinced he had intended to cause trouble all along. "I bet he's working for the Fantom."

"Just be alert for his treachery, young man," said Dorian Gray with a distasteful curl of his lip. "We all will. He's still hereabouts, somewhere, probably spying on us all. No telling what sort of mischief he still has in mind."

145

Suddenly, blazing light and thunderous explosions filled the sky. The sounds were like cannons, echoing off the water and ricocheting between the rows of buildings that lined the canals. Flowerpots and windows rattled. A another flash of light and accompanying bangs shot across the night sky.

Nemo's crewmen looked around and grabbed for their weapons. Most of the League members were horrified, but Tom Sawyer chuckled. "Shucks, it's just fireworks, the finale of the Carnival." Under the bright flashes and colored smoke, they could hear the revelers cheering.

"I feared the worst!" Mina said. "I thought we were too late, that the Fantom had already—"

"Don't worry, Ma'am. We still have a chance," Sawyer said.

The next explosion, however, was definitely not part of the Carnival.

With a ripping crash, an incredible eruption rocked the ground. Quatermain reeled, and Sawyer reached out to steady him. Mina Harker maintained her balance with feral grace, but Jekyll fell to his knees, clutching the solid ground. All around them, the ancient buildings shook. Windows shattered.

Two of Nemo's crewmen stumbled off the towpath and fell into the water.

Belches of escaping air and silt churned up from the canals. Jagged cracks ran up the building walls and along the length of the narrow towpath, widening as they watched. Flowerpots tumbled from high sills and bridges, splashing into the water.

Jekyll covered his head. Inside him, even the vestige of Edward Hyde was intimidated.

23

Another explosion.

Exhausted and inebriated revelers fled screaming in all directions, stumbling into each other, falling to the paving stones, calling for help as they were buried under rubble. At Canzelli Tower, the center of the main detonation, smoke billowed up from cracked walkways. Water spouted from the old foundations like arterial blood.

The Fantom's carefully positioned blast had dealt a death blow to the ancient landmark. Weaving like a dizzy ox, the tower collapsed and sank, taking down neighboring structures. People wailed and tried to escape as the streets convulsed, broke apart, and opened up to the hungry influx of water.

The shock wave spread through the surrounding piazza. Adjacent buildings slumped like failed soufflés, streets collapsed, and a tidal wave rose up to engulf the piazza, like the sinking of legendary Atlantis.

The world leaders in the secret conference room looked at each other in confusion and dismay. Guards drew their handguns and stood alert.

One guard raced to a window, flung open the shutters, and thrust his head and shoulders outside to look up. "It is terrible! The end of the world!" Before he could move, a heavy block of stone fell away from an upper floor, striking him a crushing blow; without so much as an outcry, he fell dead.

"Assassins!" bellowed the Russian. The tile floor split and rattled as the detonations continued. "Anarchists!"

The French ambassador ducked under the heavy table as the stuccoed ceiling overhead began to crack and flake. "We have been discovered. Betrayed! Someone is trying to kill us all."

"English treachery," snarled the German. "This meeting was no more than a ploy to bring us together so we could all be murdered in a single stroke!"

"Bloody German paranoia." The British representative was the only one who hadn't jumped out of his chair. "And I believe every man here will agree that it's a well-known Prussian technique to level a whole city just to kill a few gentlemen."

"I agree," the ambassador from France cried from under the heavy table. "After what the Prussians did to poor Paris and Emperor Napoleon III!"

A louder, resounding rumble made the tiled floor shudder. An ornate silver candelabra rattled, then fell over with a crash, scattering its lit candles in all directions. One of the guards, seeing a minor emergency within his means to handle, hurried forward to stamp out the small flames.

"My Venetia!" The Italian wailed and scrambled over to the guards who stood in the trembling doorways. Shouting a flow of incomprehensible words, he commanded them to hold up the walls and arches with their bare hands. The guards attempted to obey. A large terracotta planter fell from a shelf and shattered.

The lead ambassadors of both Spain and Portugal, usually rivals, joined the Frenchman under the table. Luckily, they had each rescued a bottle of wine that was intended as a celebratory toast after the successful conclusion of their deliberations. Agreeing on this, at least, the ambassadors decided to drink it now.

All around them, the destruction of Venice continued.

24

Venice

"The Fantom didn't wait for us," Tom Sawyer said. "Darn his itchy trigger finger."

Before the League members had even lost sight of the *Nautilus* in the tight confines of the canal, the buildings around them rumbled and shook. Crashing sounds and further explosions built upon each other, one at a time, like an urban avalanche.

Shrill Carnival celebrants raced across the trembling walkway, screaming. Ancient bricks flaked away and fell pattering into the water or, with louder clangs, on the submarine's hull.

Mina gazed up at the cracking arched bridge overhead. "We're too late. What can we do now?" She didn't sound panicked; she was simply getting down to business to solve the problem.

Everyone looked at Quatermain.

The old adventurer dashed to a corner where the canal widened and he could look toward the middle of the densely packed city. Staring forward, he saw the wave of destruction spreading spontaneously from the epicenter of the piazza. In crumbling slow motion, tall, ornate buildings tottered and sank, block by block. One structure toppled into another, and another, as the chain reaction proceeded inexorably toward a prominent avenue of buildings.

Behind them, a ratcheting sound came from the *Nautilus*, gears and chains clattering, metal segments extending and clicking into place. Nemo's marvelous vessel was full of surprises: A separate crow's nest elevated, raising on hydraulics to lift a grizzled Ishmael above the connecting bridge and the tiled rooftops of the nearby villas so that he could see what was happening.

"I wish I knew where Mr. Skinner disappeared to," Sawyer grumbled, thinking of all the help they could get.

The first mate's face reflected his certainty of impending doom even before he shouted down to them. "The buildings are falling like dominos, Cap'n! Bang, bang, bang! The Calle del Luna is next!"

Keeping his balance on the crumbling towpath, Quatermain spun, eyes wide with an idea. "Nemo! What sort of weapons does that ship of yours carry? You must remove a domino!"

The dark captain's brow furrowed as his mind raced through calculations and possibilities. He instantly reached the same conclusion. "Yes! Get ahead of the collapse and destroy the next building." He looked at the structures, calculating trajectories. His thin, dark lips narrowed in a grim smile. "My *Nautilus* can do it. I could launch a rocket."

"We'll interrupt the chain of destruction," Sawyer said. "That's it!" With that, the young American agent bolted back down the towpath, sprinted up the gangplank, and ducked into the ship's hold.

Quatermain looked after him, wondering if Sawyer had an actual plan, or if he was just moving frenetically in order to be *doing* something.

Though rubble and broken glass continued to rain down all around him, Dorian Gray looked unimpressed. "Ridiculous!" He frowned at a smear of brick dust on his fine jacket; a piece of rubble fell into the canal nearby and splashed water on his shoe.

Jekyll panicked. "What're you talking about, Nemo? Quatermain, are you mad? Gray's right. It's too late to concoct a Plan B!" The shuddering buildings, the continued echoes of ever-increasing destruction, closed in on him. He looked like a cornered rabbit, trying to find a place to dash for shelter. But there was no bolt hole in sight. "We should get back aboard the *Nautilus* and escape. It's our only chance."

"And leave all these people?" Mina asked with a hint of scorn in her voice. "Rather an ineffective first mission for us, if we allow all of Venice to be destroyed."

"And allow a world-scale war to be triggered," Nemo said. "I refuse to simply surrender and flee." He glared at Jekyll, who cringed, more afraid of the dark captain than of the explosions and collapsing buildings.

The conversation had proceeded rapid-fire, in only a few seconds, but now amid all the destruction, Dorian Gray actually rolled his eyes. "Oh yes, M would be soooo disappointed in us. But what can we hope to achieve? This is more than any of us could imagine."

"Then it's time for swift action," Quatermain said. "Not more conversation. I'm not a bloody politician."

"And *I'm* an immortal, not a gazelle," Gray said. He coolly regarded the shaking city as if it held only mini-

152

mal interest for him. "How can we outrun this devastation?"

At that moment, the door of the *Nautilus* hold slammed open with a metal bang. Prefaced by the roar of an engine, Nemo's amazing six-wheeled car burst out and hurtled down the gangplank, pulled into a screeching skid, and fishtailed to a perfect halt on the widening walkway that led up into the Venetian streets.

Tom Sawyer poked his head out, grinning from behind the controls. "Care for a spin?"

25

Venice

Mina leaped into the back of the vehicle. "I'd love it!"

Quatermain jumped in the front, taking the seat next to Sawyer. He looked at the young American with an appreciative smile. "Good idea. Wish I'd thought of it."

"I was watching you all in the car back at the London museum," Sawyer said, revving the engine. "Made up my mind back then that I wanted to take 'er for a drive."

As Dorian Gray climbed in beside Mina, she primly shifted her skirts away from him. Quatermain shouted at the cringing, uncertain doctor still on the towpath. "Jekyll, hurry man! Get in!" But the man froze, as if every alternative were equally miserable.

Captain Nemo stepped up to the driver's compartment and spoke to Quatermain as Tom Sawyer impatiently shifted the controls, anxious to be off. "I will need specific coordinates to launch my rocket. Our targeting must be absolutely precise, or we will cause even more damage than we hope to prevent."

"Can you track this thing?" said Quatermain, rapping on the side of the unusual car.

"Of course. I planned for all contingencies when I drew up my designs."

Quatermain pulled his flare gun. "Then launch when you see the flare! We'll lead you right to the bull's-eye."

With each passing minute, more Venetian buildings groaned and collapsed, continuing the devastating ripple of the chain reaction. The captain hurried off to the gangplank into the *Nautilus*. "Ishmael and I will make the preparations immediately."

Quatermain turned to Sawyer, slapping his palm on the control board. "Full power!"

The young man floored the gas—and the engine promptly died, causing a moment of stunned shock. From the rear, Gray let out a quiet, disbelieving snort. Sawyer desperately tried to restart the engine, blushing and hiding his sheepish expression. "I, uh, think I killed it."

At the rear of the car, two of Nemo's uniformed crewmen tried to push the car forward, hoping the engine would turn over. Sawyer struggled with the controls, and the car's flooded engine coughed but refused to catch.

Quatermain realized that the last member of their team had not yet climbed into the car. "Jekyll! What are you doing? Come on!"

But the mousy doctor stood immobile, terrified of setting free his brutish alter ego. "I—I . . ."

With a new, violent blast, another building collapsed, this one nearer. Overhead, the stone bridge spanning the canal wrenched and cracked, but still clung together. Debris fell all around, pelting the hull of the *Nautilus*.

"We'll need Hyde!" Quatermain insisted. "Look around you."

Finally, the car's engine roared to life again, and Sawyer beamed in triumph, ready to go. But Jekyll remained helplessly frozen on the towpath. "No! Hyde will never use me again. I swear—"

"But without him, my dear doctor, what use are you?" Gray said with a taunting lilt in his voice. "Do you plan to apply bandages and iodine to our scrapes once we're all finished?"

"Just go," Quatermain said in disgust to Sawyer. "A damned inconvenient time for the man to have second thoughts about his purpose here."

The young American put Nemo's car into gear and they raced away, leaving Henry Jekyll alone with his fear, and Skinner—literally—nowhere in sight. . . .

The car raced along up the narrow street, inches from the crumbling walls on one side and the canal edge on the other. Its six wheels held their traction, in spite of the rubble that continued to fall onto the roadway.

"All right!" Sawyer said, then whooped as they careened over a particularly large bump. "So . . . where am I going?"

Quatermain pulled out the map of Venice that Nemo had provided before dispatching the team. He squinted in the dim light as the car lurched and bounced, then he drew out his eyeglasses again. After adjusting them, the old adventurer could finally read the fine lines and letters on the map. "Right ahead, then a left turn."

"No, go right after the canal forks." Mina leaned forward from the back.

"—a left turn that will lead us into the Calle del Luna—" Quatermain continued, ignoring her.

"It's not the best way," Mina insisted. "I've spent some time in this city. That counts for more than any map."

"Good thing we're all on the same team," Sawyer muttered, then decided to listen to Mina after all. He hauled the car hard right at the fork, missing the center divider by a hairbreadth.

"Caution, boy!" Quatermain yelled.

Suddenly, bullets spanged off the car's hood, leaving silver starbursts of impact. Sawyer wrestled with the steering, screeched the car to a halt.

On the villa roof's edge overhead, a sniper sprinted away, grasping a long rifle. The silhouettes of other snipers rose up, materializing from behind nearby statues in the streets. They fired a hailstorm of bullets at the car.

Looking uncharacteristically furious, Gray kicked open the door to the car and leaped out. "Damn Skinner! He must've told them we were coming." Heroically, he pulled his cane-sword, slashing the thin silver blade in a menacing arc, and launched himself into the fray as the air filled with projectiles. "Just go!"

"Dorian, it's no use —" Mina shouted.

"Keep driving, lad!" Quatermain said.

Sawyer gunned the engine and swerved under the partial cover of a narrow colonnade, smashed through a column, bounced off a wall, and kept going. He let out another whoop, as if he was actually enjoying this.

Glancing back through the rear car window, Mina caught a last fleeting image of Dorian Gray savagely fighting the snipers man-to-man. His cane-sword was already slick and red with blood.

Quatermain tried to aim the modified Winchester

that Sawyer had given him, but the passing stone columns broke his line of sight. "I can't get a clear shot."

Sawyer, wild with the moment, pulled two pistols of his own. "Then take the wheel!" He stood up, leaned out the door, and fired wildly as the unguided vehicle lurched along.

Quatermain grabbed the wheel, but with far less than his usual confidence. "Sit down, you buffoon! I don't know how to drive this thing." The car swerved, barely under control. Up ahead, though the end of the colonnade was approaching too swiftly, Sawyer hadn't slowed at all.

"Save your bullets, both of you—these men are mine!" Mina said with vengeance in her voice.

As Nemo's fabulous car emerged from the colonnade, bouncing and scraping, Mina sprang from the racing vehicle with superhuman agility. She flew briefly through the air and landed on a nearby wall, where she clung like a bat.

Setting his hot pistols beside him, Sawyer sat back down behind the wheel, looking even more enamored with the mysterious pale woman. "Did you see that? Did you see what she did?"

Left behind, Mina scrambled up the wall, finding tiny finger- and toeholds, moving with creepy agility. It was unbelievable.

"Keep your eyes on the bloody road," Quatermain said. "We've got our own part to do."

26

Venice

Inside the *Nautilus*'s brightly lit rocket room, huge machinery moved a rocket from its pallet to a firing tube. Diligent crewmen did their work without panic, accustomed to drills and having had plenty of experience in previous adventures.

Nemo barked orders at Ishmael. "Tune the tracer to the car's frequency. The rocket must be ready to fire as soon as we see their flare."

The first mate activated the tracer unit on the rocket room's wall, adjusting it until a sequence of lights shone green. The tracing device began to plot the car's position as an ink trail on a cylindrical map roll. "There he is, Cap'n."

The fresh line zigzagged and jittered, showing Tom Sawyer's weaving path through the streets of Venice.

Impacts rang on the hull in an echoing sequence of booms, as if an army was trying to batter its way into the floating *Nautilus*. Two of Nemo's crewmen dashed out, ready to fight against the Fantom's minions—but there was no enemy other than the surrounding structures, breaking apart and raining chunks of masonry onto the vessel. The crewmen ducked, shielding their heads.

More debris pelted the exterior of the submarine vessel. The polished gold trim and white ceramic plates were scraped, scuffed, stained. The arched bridge overhead groaned and splintered, ready to fall entirely at any moment.

"The buildings are coming down! We must away!" shouted a terrified crewman.

Nemo scrambled into the crow's nest, rising high to where he could view the city through a complicated binocular instrument. He watched as the sinking of Venice progressed. "No, we will stay, and we will do our job."

Yet he still saw no sign of Quatermain's flare.

A ceiling had collapsed, and fresh rubble blocked the door of the secret conference room. Three of the guards had already been killed, and the world leaders clung together like frightened children beneath the heavy table.

When the floor cracked and greenish-brown water began oozing up from between the tiles, they realized they were trapped.

"The building! She is sinking!" the Italian said.

Leaving their empty bottles of wine on the floor, the representatives scrambled out and sloshed through the deepening pools toward the exit. The German climbed onto the heavy table and stood there like the commander of a navy ship.

"We can't get out." The British ambassador stood with water rising past his ankles. "Bloody hell."

The bearlike Russian joined the German on the table. Since it was the only dry and sturdy place, the other representatives joined them. "We are lucky this table is well built and strong, like Mother Russia!"

The wood groaned in protest and wobbled as the last of the world leaders pulled themselves onto it.

While the water deepened on the floor, empty wine bottles floated like defective glass fishing boats; they slowly filled, then sank with a gurgle.

"Perhaps this would be a good time to resolve our differences," the Spanish ambassador suggested.

Leaving the colonnade and the tangled canals behind, the six-wheeled car screeched onto a wide street.

"There, ahead," Quatermain said, gesturing out his side of the car. "It's a straight shot from here."

On villa rooftops on both sides of the cobblestoned street, a swarm of the Fantom's snipers rose ominously, took their positions, readied their deadly rifles.

"Straight shot for them, maybe," Sawyer said, "a gauntlet for us."

But the snipers weren't the only figures visible. A liquid shadow, Mina Harker raced along in eerie silence above their heads, finding impossible perches, clinging to the walls like a nimble spider as she moved.

Quatermain pointed, nodding with unexpected admiration. "Not at all. The vampire has us covered."

Sawyer set his jaw, grasped the controls, then roared forward into the deadly targeting zone. Nemo's amazing car entered the gauntlet just as Mina attacked the snipers.

She took them completely by surprise, a blurry wraith of dark, jittery motion. Gunshots rang out, most of them fired in desperation and terror. The vampire woman pounced from man to man along the roof's edge, slashing and ripping. One moment she was airborne, the next skittering to another victim. Her claws and teeth flashed in the moonlight and the growing fires of explosions and destruction. For all her beauty and grace, she no longer looked remotely human.

At breakneck speed, Sawyer lurched the car along the exposed street, picking up speed past the deadly snipers. The vehicle would have been a clear target for a rain of gunfire—if one set of the Fantom's killers hadn't been so suddenly preoccupied with their own survival.

But the snipers on the opposite side of the street took aim and opened fire on the racing car, shattering cobblestones, puncturing the metal sidewalls and roof.

From the villa's high rooftop, Mina lifted her delicate chin, opened her bloodied mouth, and keened a bone-chilling note. Her piercing cry shot through the night sky, audible even above the loud explosions and roars of collapsing buildings.

From the darkness, a shadowy swarm answered her summons.

A huge flock of black-winged bats swooped through the night like a cloud of angry hornets. In a squeaking storm, hundreds and hundreds of bats descended in a flurry to engulf the snipers on the opposite roofline.

Mina continued the slaughter on her side of the street, while her winged pets savaged the overconfident snipers on the other side. It all happened so shockingly fast that the Fantom's men were not even aware of their danger until each screamed and wheeled around in turn, their throats torn open, eyes slashed, faces cut.

Three frantic men screamed and flailed, trying to drive away the flood of ravenous bats. They stumbled and fell from their high perches to strike the street far below with a wet, cracking sound. . . .

Holding on for dear life in the shuddering car, Quatermain peered through the bullet-pocked front windscreen to a wide canal at his right—and was astonished to spy the Fantom himself.

Helmeted henchmen were escorting the masked man toward a creaking dock. An armored gunboat floated in the canal beneath the walkway. The Fantom turned his silver-covered face to take in a last glance of the fires and continuing destruction he had brought about, then with a swirl of his black cape, he stepped onto the pier.

The old adventurer meaningfully placed his flare gun on the dashboard. "Sawyer, remember the flare! You know when to launch it." He snapped open the door of the racing vehicle. "I'm counting on you."

"Wha—?" the young agent said, taking his eyes from the obstacle course he was driving.

"I can't protect you this time, boy. I'm off." Quatermain clenched his jaw and braced himself. "This enemy's mine."

Then he was out of the car, taking the landing with a roll, while Sawyer careened onward at full speed. Before he could feel the pain of bruises and torn skin, Quatermain climbed to his feet and set off at a run toward the canal and the Fantom's gunboat.

Sawyer cursed and looked ahead. In just a matter of moments, Dorian Gray, Mina Harker, and now Allan Quatermain had all deserted him. running off to their own adventures. He glanced at the thick-barreled flare gun. "Heck, I wasn't even supposed to be part of this group."

Then his eyes suddenly filled with fear. Just ahead, the sequence of collapsing buildings had started to cross the path he drove. The buildings directly in front of him began to slump and sink.

Tom Sawyer let out a loud whoop, then gunned the gas and raced into the jaws of the beast.

Ishmael stood in the rocket room of the *Nautilus,* watching as the tracer pen plotted Sawyer's position. The car wove through the streets of Venice, heading to the center of the spreading waves of destruction.

High atop the crow's nest, Nemo lowered his binocular device, grabbed a voice tube that was connected to the extended metal framework, and yelled down into the rocket room, "I believe he's almost there. Be ready to launch!"

Ishmael rested a callused, oil-stained finger on the red firing button.

Just then, the damaged bridge spanning the canal above the submarine collapsed. Support beams and chunks of stone crashed down in a landslide of rubble onto the vessel's plated hull. The first mate stayed at his post in spite of the electrical panels that sparked and exploded in the rocket room.

"We'll be smashed apart!" cried a crewman. Other men rushed in to shut down live circuits and douse the fires before they could spread.

"If the Cap'n says we stay, then we stay," Ishmael said, glowering.

27

Venice

Running at full speed, ignoring the large-scale mayhem around him, Quatermain leaped over the edge of a raised street and stormed down onto the gunboat's dock, while the Fantom took a set of wooden stairs.

At the boat, the old adventurer attacked the villain's henchmen before they knew what was happening. With a rapid one-handed pump and click, he cocked the borrowed Winchester and shot one of the Fantom's men who was bent over a rope that lashed the gunboat to the side of the canal. Quatermain turned and fired his second barrel at another henchman; the blast hurled the man over the edge of the dock and into the canal.

When his Winchester clicked empty, the hunter didn't hesitate a moment—he hurled the long rifle like a tomahawk at the third henchman while still racing forward. The Fantom's man dutifully looked up at the proper moment, and the hard wood stock of the rifle cracked him between the eyes.

Quatermain punched a fourth henchman unconscious; his knuckles smashed into the man's face with the satisfying crunch of breaking teeth and nose. Unstoppable, he nailed the fifth man and simultaneously bent down to retrieve his rifle just as it clattered to the dock planks, all in a perfectly fluid movement. No doubt, Tom Sawyer would want the gun back.

At the other end of the dock, the Fantom froze, suddenly seeing himself unprotected. Trapped, he eyed his fallen henchmen, then the waiting gunboat, but it was too far away for him to leap on board.

And Quatermain stood in his way.

"Stand down, sir," the Fantom said in a hard, perfectly reasonable voice. "The die has already been cast, and you can do nothing about it. We'll both be killed if we linger here."

All around them, the tall buildings continued to sink. The dock itself cracked, shivering against the rusty iron anchors that held it to the side of the canal. Huge chunks of masonry smashed down on the gunboat.

Quatermain kept an eye on the enemy as he calmly reloaded the Winchester. "You're destroying Venice. It's fitting the city should destroy you, in turn." He stood like an implacable guard dog, preventing the Fantom from stepping aboard.

"But you'll die, too!" Now the villain's voice had a ragged edge of desperation, though the metal mask obscured his expression.

"I've faced death before. Perhaps it's my time."

Now the whole dock started to fall away into the canal. The gunboat broke free of its last remaining mooring rope. Quatermain stumbled, trying to keep his balance as the dock boards separated.

The Fantom gave up on his gunboat escape and turned to race back up the stairs. He ran for his life in the opposite direction, back into the crumbling streets of Venice.

Quatermain tucked the loaded Winchester under his arm and set off in hot pursuit.

The Calle del Luna was falling apart all around him.

Tom Sawyer remembered how Mississippi River floods had washed away shantytowns and fishing piers along the banks by St. Petersburg. The narrow, sluggish canals of Venice bore little resemblance to the mighty Mississippi, of course. But these buildings were much larger and older . . . and they were tumbling down toward him.

Pushing Nemo's car to its limits, Sawyer drove desperately, trying to outrace a wave of sinking buildings that collapsed only a hairbreadth behind him. Villas, museums, cathedrals all went down like piles of toy blocks. Graceful, centuries-old bridges across the canals tumbled away, crashing with huge splashes into the water.

Carnival merrymakers in garish costumes ran about in the streets, dodging out of the way. With buildings toppling all around them, the people had no safe place to go.

When Sawyer finally approached the Calle del Luna, masonry chunks smashed either side of the car as he gunned for the final bridge. Then the roadway dropped away ahead of him, as if a powerful prankster had pulled down a trapdoor. Wide, jagged cracks raced to overtake the car's back tires.

So he accelerated.

Beyond the bridge was a decrepit-looking, abandoned old theater. It appeared to have been falling apart for a long time now, even without the assistance of the Fantom's bombs.

Steering with his left hand, Sawyer snatched the flare gun from where Quatermain had set it, wrapping his right hand around the pistol grip. When the car hit the suddenly uneven slope of the dropping road, all six tires left the ground.

Sawyer had taken an exciting balloon ride once, with Becky Thatcher. This was much faster. In that eternal moment, the American agent pointed the pistol out the window and fired the flare.

Nemo's car landed on the other side of the collapsing bridge with a jolt that slammed Sawyer into the vehicle's controls. Still moving at full speed, the car punched through the crumbling columns and rotten doors of a dilapidated old theater, where it was swallowed up into the lobby of the building.

The blazing flare streaked up into the air and soared high above the city, like a meteor.

In the secret conference room, the representatives of powerful countries tried to stay safe and dry on the heavy table. Unfortunately, the weight of such disparate political views was too much for even the sturdy structure. With a loud crack and splinter, the joints gave way and one of the wooden legs buckled.

Shouting at each other, the ambassadors and leaders slid into the water that flooded the room of the sinking building. Already the street-level window had vanished beneath the inrushing flow from the canals. The cold water was only waist high, but rising quickly.

The Russian stood stoically, ruminating on what he

should do, while the Frenchman attempted to swim. The German and the Englishman tried to scramble onto the floating remains of the table, though both were already soaked.

The body of one of the guards drifted by, facedown; the Italian host tried to rouse him, but the guard did not respond. The water kept rising.

From the crow's nest, Nemo shaded his eyes and finally spotted the streaking flash of the flare climbing into the sky. He grabbed the voice tube and shouted, "Launch! They are in position."

"Aye, Cap'n." Below, Ishmael pressed the firing button.

A hatch cover in the top deck slid aside with a sharp clang. The rocket hissed and spat as it rode the launch tube upward and soared away like a much larger version of the sputtering flare.

Homing in on the tracer.

Quatermain chased the Fantom through the collapsing streets, sprinting toward a concentration of frantic crowds. The costumed revelers had congregated in an open piazza, pushing together in a breathless mob: Nobles and common folk all in disguise. Food vendors abandoned their trays, balloons drifted loose, banners were trampled underfoot.

The Fantom plunged into the shifting mass of frightened Venetians, elbowing women aside, tripping a young, black-haired man who was too drunk even to notice the city falling apart all around him.

Quatermain pounded after the villain, panting hard.

Like a cheetah running down its prey, he kept his eye on the fleeing enemy—but the Fantom was only one more silver mask amid a sea of masks.

The whistling flare soared overhead, then began its graceful descent. Some of the people cheered, as if it betokened an impending rescue. Seeing it, Quatermain knew that Tom Sawyer had succeeded. He paused for just a moment. "Bravo, lad, bravo."

The Fantom, though, looked up in dismay when he saw Nemo's rocket in flight, much larger than the small signal fireball. The rocket hurtled straight down toward the city.

Sawyer, dazed, sat in the car, glancing at the gaping hole he had smashed through the theater entrance. The car had come to a rest inside, hissing and groaning. A ceiling timber fell in a shower of plaster dust.

He shook his head, rubbing a hand across his forehead, ignoring the spot of blood he found from a small cut there. The windshield had shattered. He began to pick his way out of the battered vehicle. His ears were ringing.

But at least he had launched the flare.

Sawyer saw the last building on the avenue sinking. Then, next in line, the whole facade of the dilapidated theater started to come down, showering rubble across the opening the car had blasted through it.

Suddenly, screeching with its accelerated descent, Nemo's explosives-packed rocket followed the tracer to its target. Its nose plunged into the old theater's high roof.

With a yelp, Sawyer leaped from the car and scrambled for the nearest window. He dove headfirst into the street as the rocket struck, and the theater exploded all around him.

From the crow's nest of the *Nautilus*, Nemo observed the explosion in the distance and crossed his arms over his blue uniform with satisfaction.

Now, if only his companions had survived.

28

In the wake of the rocket's explosion, the costumed crowd in the piazza saw a bright fire. A loud shock wave reverberated through the surrounding area, bringing down an old theater at the edge of the collapsing buildings.

The explosion removed the key domino from the cascading collapse. The marching destruction lost its power, like a forest fire blocked by a firebreak. With a grinding rumble, the avalanche of buildings faltered against the empty spot and came to an end.

In the moment Quatermain took to stare, worried that Tom Sawyer might have been hurt in the rocket's explosion, the Fantom fled through the crowd.

Cursing, the old hunter surged across the piazza, elbowing cheering survivors out of the way. He caught a glimpse of the Fantom's dark form and swirling cape as he ducked down another street, into the shadows.

Quatermain left the giddy celebration behind and tried to follow his nemesis, who flowed like oil into the darkness. He paused at the scrolled cast-iron gate that marked the entrance to an overgrown, walled cemetery.

172

Inside, was a shadowy maze of trees and mausoleum structures, crypts, vaults, tombstones, statues. The iron gate stood ajar, the tall weeds trampled.

The Fantom had gone inside to hide.

Quatermain listened, using his hunter senses. Behind him, the shaking of the great, wounded city subsided. Venice groaned and moaned as its bones resettled. Silence descended, save for distant shouts.

The Fantom could be anywhere inside. Quatermain entered the cemetery, the cast-iron gate making a dismayingly loud screech as he pushed it open. He stepped forward, crouching, stalking. He noted a broken branch, sniffed it, and found that it was still moist. He tried to peer into the quietly rustling shadows, searching for any sign of the scarred man in black.

After a moment, he'd had enough of stealth. The enemy knew he had entered the cemetery. So he raised his voice loud enough to startle a pair of doves into flight, counting on the villain's pride to make him reveal himself. "You've failed, Fantom! Venice stands."

Lurking within the cemetery, the Fantom backed deeper into the shrouding darkness, out of sight. "I applaud your persistence, Mr. Quatermain." The evil voice reverberated from every direction.

The Fantom moved through the darkness, avoiding the old hunter.

"Oh, you'll be clapping all right, when I get my hands on you." Peering around, Quatermain pressed on through the shadows, continuing the hunt.

But the hidden Fantom easily avoided the adventurer. His goading voice came disembodied from among the leaning tombstones and monuments. "But like a dog smelling blood, you can't see the true picture."

"I see that you've failed. It's obvious enough."

"This was merely one objective," said the Fantom.

Out of the corner of his eye, Quatermain saw a flitting shadow as the Fantom continued his taunting. "Other schemes proceed as planned. There's nothing you can do to stop them."

Quatermain spun, aimed his Winchester—but could see nothing. "I know your big secret." The hunter's shadow passed over thick foliage, like a cloud across the moon. For a moment, he thought he saw a glint of silver metal—the Fantom's mask drawing deeper into hiding? He couldn't tell. "I know all about your spy among us."

The Fantom's voice carried no surprise, only a condescending lilt. "Ah, do you?"

Quatermain took a shot toward the voice. He thought for a moment he had hit the Fantom, but the shotgun pellets merely sprayed chipped white marble from the statue of a sorrowful stone angel.

The hunt continued, and the Fantom moved noiselessly through his domain of darkness, dressed all in black. He chose when to speak, casting his voice like a ventriloquist. "You see yourself as the brave John Bull— but I know you're a coward, Quatermain. Hiding from the memory of your son's death."

As the hunter desperately searched for another target to shoot, the Fantom laughed, taunting. "You should have trained him better. I am not the only failure here, Allan Quatermain. Your mistake was much larger, wasn't it? You may have as well put the gun to the lad's head and pulled the trigger yourself."

Quatermain started to react, then stopped and gritted his teeth. He refused to open fire indiscriminately. He waited for a good shot, the right target.

"Oh, yes. I know all about you—" Then the Fantom froze as his black shoe stepped on a dry branch, cracking it. The sound echoed through the cemetery, as loud as a gunshot.

Quatermain searched for where it came from. "It's you who fears the mirror, sir—and not, I think, because of scars."

His eye caught another flicker of movement off to his right. Quatermain whirled, but saw that the movement was merely a swaying branch. He did however see a subtle flash of motion to his left, vanishing behind a tree. He eased forward, rifle extended. "It's because you are neither extraordinary—"

Quatermain lunged around the trunk. " —nor a gentleman!"

The shadow leaped back, and Quatermain drove in for the kill. The Fantom lashed out, knocking the gun aside. Quatermain shot, a fraction too late. The Winchester's blast rang out, sending debris flying.

The Fantom collided with Quatermain, a long silver stiletto flashing in the moonlight. The blade came down like a cobra striking, and he stabbed Quatermain deep in the shoulder.

With a roar, the old adventurer backhanded the villain and landed a blow that should have felled a water buffalo. The Fantom reeled away, and his mask went skittering across the ground. Quatermain glimpsed the hidden visage, expecting to see a disfigured horror. Instead, it was a shockingly familiar face.

The Fantom was M!

Quatermain's blow had scraped loose some of the half-hidden "scars" on the Fantom's face—merely lumps of wax and flesh-colored paste. Stage show makeup now hung half off the face.

"You? What the hell!"

"You don't know the half of it," M said. "Fool."

He spun with catlike agility, and kicked Quatermain's legs out from under him. As the old hunter fell against a hard block of stone, the knife injury in his back pulsing with agony, M grabbed his fallen silver mask from the ground and scrambled away.

Despite the deep stab wound, Quatermain was quick to recover. He ripped the stiletto from his shoulder, ignoring the hot gush of blood. Out of reflex and long years of practice, he hurled the knife at the receding villain.

The blade flew true and found its mark. The point sank into M's back as he fled. He howled, staggered, then sprinted away into the darkness. He must have been wearing the same damned body armor his henchmen used.

Quatermain collapsed on the cemetary grounds—quite an appropriate place after all, he thought—as the strength flowed out of him. . . .

29

The Ruins of Venice

The world leaders looked like drowned rats, expecting to die trapped within the sinking chamber. They clung together on the drifting tabletop as if it were a life raft. The air smelled of fish and mud and far less pleasant things.

As the shuddering explosions rattled into silence and the buildings stopped falling all around them, the representatives of the most powerful countries of Europe sat in silence and wonder.

"Someone has stopped the disaster!" the representative from Italy said proudly. "No doubt it was one of our brilliant Italian engineers."

"Perhaps your engineers should have designed a better escape route for us in the first place," the Spanish ambassador grumbled. "Or a city that wouldn't fall apart so easily."

"Venetia is over a thousand years old, signore! She has survived a hundred armies—"

"We will live," the German interrupted. "Now we must find a way to get out of here."

"I wish we had kept some of that wine." The Frenchman drew his skinny knees up to his chest and looked miserable.

The Portuguese ambassador vomited over the edge of the swaying table.

"Perhaps we should simply swim under the water and out through the halls." The British representative cracked his knuckles and practiced keeping a stiff upper lip. "I was on the swim team back at Oxford—"

Like a walrus diving off an iceberg, the Russian plunged into the water and began to stroke with surprising grace and power. He spat foul water out of his mouth. "Tastes like a sewer."

"Those, signore, are our canals," the Italian answered indignantly. He felt as if he was being insulted from all sides.

But the gathered men understood that they were safe now, and it would be only a matter of time before they were rescued. "I say, perhaps we should finish our discussions and come to an agreement?" the Englishman suggested. "That way, in the end, we'll be able to call this little gathering an unqualified success."

Inside the *Nautilus* rocket room, Ishmael and the crew cleaned up the aftermath of the destruction. The air smelled of smoke from burned circuits and control panels. Puddles of water lay on the deck where they had splashed. A few small trickles had made their way through stressed hull plates, like trails of teardrops, but the loyal first mate and his men had already fixed the most vital problems.

Ishmael sighed and continued his inspection, marking necessary repairs on a clipboard. The *Nautilus* could still move, but she was a far cry from being "as good as new." The falling bridge had caused the most damage, much of it merely cosmetic on the beautiful exterior of the Sword of the Ocean.

The two crewmen assisting him were covered with soot and grease. One man climbed back out of the rocket launcher. "All secure, Ishmael."

The first mate nodded and blew out a long sigh. "Let me handle the rest from here, men. Go report to Captain Nemo and then check the engine room. I want to be away from here as soon as our comrades return."

The two men departed, closing the bulkhead door and leaving Ishmael to sigh over all the work that remained to be done. "She hasn't been battered so badly since our bout with that giant squid."

An outside hatch opened, and Dorian Gray entered from the night. He looked uncharacteristically battered and bedraggled.

"Mister Gray!" The first mate stared in shock at his condition. "What happened to you?"

Though he showed no sign of physical injury, Gray's clothes were riddled with bullet holes and deep slashes from his battles against the Fantom's henchmen. Self-satisfied and struggling to retain his shreds of dignity, he slipped his sticky cane-sword back into its case. "Mere misadventure. It was somewhat amusing, actually." Gray brushed dust and blood from his jacket. He looked around, seeing Ishmael alone in the mess of the rocket room. "Have the others returned?"

"You're the first, sir, but hopefully not the last." Ishmael turned back to work. He picked up a wrench and began to remove a cover plate from one of the consoles.

"All this because of a damned traitor. That invisible bastard has a lot to answer for."

"Skinner? No," Gray said, smiling gently. "Not Skinner."

The first mate glanced up, confused by his comment. Dorian Gray had drawn a pistol from his tattered jacket. "Me," he said, and fired.

Ishmael fell, clutching the mortal wound on his chest.

30

The Ruins of Venice

Over the next hour, the League members returned from the streets one at a time, picking their way through the rubble, finding a safe path along ruined towpaths and raised walkways. The *Nautilus* rested among flotsam, her ceramic shell woefully scarred and cracked in many places.

The buildings tilted drunkenly; large walls had fractured or slumped. The ruins of the fallen bridge filled part of the narrow canal ahead of the submarine vessel. She would have to reverse and back out of the channel.

Nemo's medics helped the wounded crewmen, assisted by Mina Harker and Henry Jekyll, both of whom had some surgical experience. The turbaned captain directed operations while several crew members in wet suits cleared debris from around the shell of the vessel.

Quatermain finally staggered back, clutching a blood-soaked rag against the stiletto wound in his shoulder. Mina saw him and shouted, but the old adventurer called directly to Nemo in a hoarse voice, "Mobilize your men, Captain. The hunt's still on."

"You've found the Fantom?" Mina's lip twitched, as if she could hardly restrain herself from baring her fangs.

"Worse. The Fantom . . . is *M himself.*" Quatermain slumped down on a pile of rubble and took a hip flask of whiskey from his grimy jacket. He unscrewed the cap with his teeth, then tilted the flask to pour the alcohol on his shoulder injury, wincing as he did so.

"M? What . . . what are you saying?" Jekyll said. The mousy doctor handed him a long strip of cloth, and the hunter expertly field-dressed his own wound.

Nemo and Mina both moved closer. Quatermain explained. "M—the very man who recruited us to fight the Fantom. We'll get our answers later." He looked all around. "Where are the others?"

"Dorian is missing in action," Mina said, "and that invisible bastard must have fled when he realized we knew about him."

"No one has seen Mr. Skinner since we arrived in Venice. He and M were probably working together." Nemo stroked his long beard. "Actually, no one has ever seen him, for that matter. Who knows who the man could have been, originally?"

"And what about . . . Tom Sawyer?" Quatermain asked, trying not to show any special interest.

The young agent called from out of sight in a happy, American-accented drawl. "Aww, he'll live to fight another day." He stepped out of the shadows between damaged buildings, bloodied but triumphant. "And I sure do intend to."

Quatermain nodded his approval, while gritting his teeth against the throbbing pain. "We will see that you get the chance. As soon as possible."

Mina went to Sawyer, but the American hesitated as she paid altogether too much attention to the fresh blood of his wounds. She chuckled at his discomfiture. "Don't worry. I've had my fill of throats for tonight."

"Cap'n . . . Cap—" Ishmael lurched to one of the hatches, clutching the frame with a bloody hand and standing there weakly. Crimson soaked his chest, and he drew on the last of his life's strength just to remain upright.

Quatermain and Mina ran toward the first mate, but Nemo arrived first, taking Ishmael's shoulders just as his knees turned to water. "It was Gray. . . ."

Ishmael collapsed, and Nemo took his old friend in his arms. Blood stained the captain's impeccable blue uniform, but he didn't care. "Rest now, Ishmael." He glared up at the cringing English doctor on the dock. "Jekyll—tend to him! Now!"

Jekyll scurried forward, but the first mate refused to let himself be doctored. He had kept himself alive through the urgent need to explain the treachery to his captain. "Not . . . Skinner. *Gray.*" He clutched at Nemo's uniform blouse, and the captain took his hand, squeezing it, as his eyebrows drew together and his dark eyes kindled with angry flames.

"Gray's . . . tricked us all, Cap'n." His mission complete, Ishmael died from the terrible gunshot wound.

"Another fallen friend, another lost soul." Nemo's voice sounded hollow and deeply forlorn. "After all the amazing exploits we shared, under the polar icecaps, through the Suez Canal, finding Atlantis, and undersea volcanoes . . . we have just shared our last."

Ignoring the pain in his wounded shoulder, Quatermain held Jekyll back, allowing Nemo a moment to grieve. "I understand, Captain."

Mina stared disbelieving at the dead first mate. "But Dorian . . . ? How could—"

Suddenly, from within the submarine vessel, they heard the thrumming sound of machinery grinding away, small engines shuddering to life. Angered, Nemo stood and looked around at his crewmen, but none of his workers were operating any of the *Nautilus's* systems.

"What is it?" Sawyer said. "All that noise?" The aquatic vessel shuddered.

"That is the sound of treachery!" Nemo rushed up the gangplank with the others at his heels. The crewmen shouted, calling themselves to arms. Together, the League members dashed across the *Nautilus's* hold, following the captain.

When they reached the far side of the vessel, Nemo leaned out of an observation hatch.

From the aft, a massive section of the vessel's hull separated from the rest of the submarine. A hemispherical craft detached itself from the main vessel, lifted up, and floated free after uncoupling from the *Nautilus*.

Nemo's face held a storm of fury and vengeance, but he could do nothing about the situation. The small craft was unreachable from where they stood. Quatermain pressed closer to him.

"But . . . what is that thing?" Sawyer asked. "You've sure got a lot tricks up your sleeve, Captain."

"It is my exploration pod," Nemo said. "I call it a nautiloid."

Then, its propellers churning, the smaller craft spun around in the canal, and they could see the suave man sitting at its controls. He locked eyes with the League members who were staring back at him, and raised a hand to them in scornful dismissal.

"Dorian," Mina said. "Why—?"

But Gray didn't seem interested in her at all. He looked back at them coldly as the nautiloid retreated down the narrow channel. Nemo shouted for all his crewmen, but the *Nautilus* was not in any condition to depart.

As the nautiloid continued to withdraw down the canal, two men dashed down the narrow streets to intercept it. Quatermain saw them, recognized them, and could barely contain his own anger. M, still wearing his Fantom clothes, and his lieutenant Dante jumped from a crumbling bridge over the widening waterway and dropped onto the smaller vessel. Dorian Gray opened an upper hatch, and the other two villains climbed into the safety of the vessel.

Quatermain clenched his fists. "Nemo, can you track that? Like you tracked the car?"

"Track it?" Nemo was furious. Ishmael's bloodstains still shone brightly on his uniformed chest. "More than that, Mr. Quatermain. I intend to catch it!"

31

The *Nautilus*

The *Nautilus*'s engines thundered to life, and the propellers churned sediment from the canals. At the urgent steam whistle that signaled imminent departure, Nemo's crewmen jumped back aboard, ready to go. They ran across the decks, scrambled down metal rungs into the hold, sealed the hatches overhead.

With every moment, the Fantom drew farther away.

Captain Nemo went to the control room, which seemed ominously empty without his first mate, and stood directing the operations. "Enough. We must be off." His voice was cold and flat, diamond hard, with deliberate determination.

Clattering and straining under heavy gear-turnings, the cable moorings retracted automatically, tearing the towpath stanchions from their mounts in a shower of old brick and rusted anchor-spikes. Creating a foaming wake, the undersea ship backed away through the narrow canal, working itself around debris from the collapsed bridge.

"Check all systems," Nemo said into his voice tube. "Verify our repairs. I need this ship running and ready to submerge as soon as we are away from Venice."

The uniformed men worked together in a grim blur, calling readings to each other, running through test results, patching a last few leaks. They checked vital systems and rerouted to secondary equipment where necessary to keep the *Nautilus* alive and increase its speed. The ship cruised like a plump crocodile though reeds as it navigated out of the maze of narrow canals.

Daylight began to tinge the sky, illuminating the shaken Carnival revelers who were still abroad in the streets. Some of them watched the armored hulk churn along, dragging the torn stanchions like trolling fishhooks behind them. The engines increased their output, and the vessel stirred up a thunderous foaming wake, as if a dragon had just passed by. The few bleary-eyed witnesses assumed the strange ship was merely a part of the Carnival, one more amazing spectacle.

Behind them, the world leaders finally stepped outside, free of their death trap. Breathing the open air, they looked as bedraggled as the battered city buildings. But they were smiling.

As the morning brightened, the people of Venice—many of them nursing a variety of injuries, as well as hangovers—began to pick up the pieces.

Finally submerged and heading back out into the Adriatic Sea, the *Nautilus* powered into deep water. Its engines and propellers drove it forward at maximum speed.

But the stolen nautiloid had a substantial head start.

Nemo called the remaining members of the League into his stateroom. While they watched, he slid back a large panel to reveal a contour map of the ocean floor; he had drawn it personally, based on data he and Ishmael had collected over the years and their many thousands of leagues journeying under the sea. Two spidery mechanical pointers drifted across the contour lines, a large *N* signifying the *Nautilus*, and a lowercase *n*.

Nemo gestured to the smaller pointer, upon which the larger one was slowly gaining. "That's the nautiloid. We'll be upon it soon."

Tom Sawyer was eager for the hunt, but he noted Mina Harker's sadness. She seemed paler than usual, quiet and withdrawn. "Are you all right, Ma'am?"

"I'm a little shaken. Just . . . *Dorian*. I can't believe what he did."

"Not all fellows wear two faces, you know," Sawyer said, clearly meaning himself. "Some are perfectly honest and upstanding people."

Mina looked into the young man's blue eyes, then turned away. Private gloom hung around her like a pale burial shroud.

Then, while they were all intent on the undersea map, a high-pitched whistle resonated through the stateroom chamber. Nemo looked up, puzzled. The sound seemed to be coming from far-off, but somewhere *inside* the vessel.

"Nemo?" Quatermain said. "What is it?"

"It is nothing of mine. I know all the sounds on my ship."

A crewman named Patel raced down the outer corridors, urgency written on his face. Patel dodged other uniformed men, pushing past them to get to the captain's stateroom. The noise followed him, growing louder at first, then higher in pitch and harder to hear.

Nemo opened his cabin door just in time for the

crewman to rush up. He carried a flat leather case, which he held out in front of him, as if afraid it might explode at any moment. Thankfully, though, the high-pitched sound had grown so thin and weak it could no longer be heard.

Patel came to a breathless halt and spluttered his report. "Captain! The noise came from this." Nemo took the leather case from him, and the crewman seemed glad to be rid of it.

Inside the stateroom, he gingerly opened the case to reveal a wax disc. He picked it up and studied it in the light. "It is a recorded disc. Someone has left us a message."

"But, don't recordings come on cylinders?" Sawyer asked.

"It is a gramophone disc, of the type invented by Emile Berliner," Nemo said. "I adopted the technology in my vessel some time ago. The Fantom—M—knows that." He placed the disc on a player that rested on the small bureau in his cabin and started the machine.

As he listened, Sawyer tried to imagine the gloating man who had recorded the words specifically for them to hear. . . .

32

M's Private Headquarters

In a dark parlor, M sat in a padded leather chair, his long, thin fingers laced together. All around him, the furnishings were deep crimson and burgundy, from the thick curtains on the wall to the Persian rug on the floor. He had dispensed with all pretense of his Fantom mask or false scars. His heavy brows drew together, furrowing his high forehead.

He sat near a gramophone recorder, which was operated by a lady recordist. She seemed pale and listless, without heart or hope. M paid no attention at all to her until she had finished adjusting the smooth, blank wax disk and placing the needle in its position.

"Ready, Professor?" she said, lowering her voice to a whisper. "Recording."

M began to speak and, with a faint scratching sound, the recorder needle began scraping a thin spiral of wax from the gramophone disc.

"Gentlemen. If you're hearing this, then every step leading up to it has gone as planned, even if you do not realize it. Yet."

Smiling coolly, Dorian Gray stepped from the shadows in the den to amble around M's leather chair. "And I have been true to the goals set me, as well." He spoke in a dry voice, making sure the gramophone picked up his words, his irony. "Yes, it's me—Dorian. You know by now that I'm no loyal son of the empire."

He casually lifted an apple from a bowl of fruit on the mahogany table, set it back down with disinterest, then walked over to stand behind the high-backed leather chair where M sat.

"In fact, my loyalty to Mr. M comes in no small part from his possession of something I hold dear to my heart." From behind, Dorian looked down at the cadaverous leader. His eyes flashed, as if he could barely suppress an impulse to strangle the man. "Something I'll do anything to regain."

M leaned forward like a vulture, as if the audience listening to his recording could actually see him. "Everything so far has been misdirection." He smiled over at Sanderson Reed, who also stood in the room for the recording. "My 'bumbling bureaucrat assistant,' Sanderson Reed, who so easily recruited Mr. Quatermain. The assassins in Kenya. Your whole mission, and the excuse I gave you. Venice. Even the assembly of the League of Extraordinary Gentlemen."

He chuckled with a sound like witches' brooms rattling together. "*There is no League!* There never was. A few old paintings, an unused meeting room in the basement of the museum, and a dashing good story. It was just a ruse to get me closer to my real goals.

"You see, I want *you*. Each of you, even tired old Quatermain. I have no doubt he'll capture the bestial Mr. Hyde in Paris, where the others have so far failed.

That doddering Monsieur Dupin has been blundering about for months in Paris, ascribing the murders in the Rue Morgue to a wild monkey!"

Realizing he had strayed from the point, M sat straighter in his chair; the leather upholstery creaked. Gray picked up the apple from the bowl after all and bit into it with a loud crunch. Sanderson Reed looked at him, offended by the suave man's attitude.

M, seeing that the gramophone disc was nearly full, the needle approaching the center of its recording surface, continued. "So, my avid listeners, the important question is—why? Why all this cloak and dagger, masks and mystery? And why did I select the group of you, in particular, instead of, say, Sexton Blake, or Robur the conqueror, or Frankenstein's monster?"

He grinned, spreading parchment lips to reveal a row of tiny white teeth. "Because in the war that is to come, I have already acquired many grand and innovative weapons from the most brilliant scientists of all nations of the world. However, I intend to wield the greatest weapon of all—the power of the League itself. And to that end, I set my wolf among you sheep. He will lead you far from green pastures."

"Growl," Gray said, then took another bite of his apple.

33

The *Nautilus*

Listening to the recording in Nemo's stateroom, the members of the League looked at each other and recalled details of their interactions with Gray, as all the pieces clicked into place . . . like a bomb ready to detonate.

"Gray played like he was bored in his library, ready to turn us down, and then he claimed the battle with the Fantom's marksmen was just the spur he needed to change his mind." Quatermain put a hand to the aching shoulder wound. "He knew it was going to happen all along."

"So that was his plan if I hadn't shown up," Sawyer said, crossing his arms. "Shucks, I should have known better."

The gramophone recording continued to play. M's voice sounded superior and dismissive. "—And all the while I would collect *you*, thanks to Mr. Gray. The parts of you that I need. Nemo's science . . . Skinner's skin sample."

Mina looked shocked as the realization dawned. "Magnesium phosphorus. Photographers' flash."

Nemo's hands twitched as he remembered standing with Ishmael in the control room, sniffing samples of the powder they had found. "Yes, he must have photographed the details of my *Nautilus.*"

Quatermain nodded, also remembering. "And in the ice room, where we kept Hyde chained, Skinner said that Gray had scratched him. *Accidentally,* he said. Must've used a little scraper to collect cells from the invisible man."

Jekyll blinked his saucerlike eyes, then swallowed hard in his scrawny throat. "That's what happened to the missing vial of elixir in my medical bag. Gray took it." He rubbed his temples, as if a massive migraine were growing behind his eyes. "He's stolen us. And we let him."

Then, with greatest triumph, Gray's voice finished on the recording, "And, of course, dear Mina's blood."

She limited her reaction to a faint gasp as she recalled how he had handed her a glass of amontillado sherry, how the glass had so easily broken, slicing her palm, how Gray had been concerned and attentive, pressing his handkerchief to the oozing blood. . . .

The League members remained stunned in the captain's stateroom, all of them exhibiting signs of dismay. Nemo summed up their reactions by announcing with cold threat, "And now we all have our sufficient reasons for wanting to kill him."

Bothered by his oversensitive ears and the incessant, increasing pain in the back of his skull, the fidgety Doctor Jekyll looked out a dim porthole; he saw much more than just deep water and the faint shadows of fish outside. He caught a reflection of Hyde's twisted and demonic face. In the image, his brutish alter ego clapped both spasming hands to his temples, pressing against his hairy ears, grimacing in agony. Inside Jekyll's head, Hyde roared. *Turn it off, Henry. Turn it off!*

Lifting her head out of the feelings of betrayal and anger that Gray's words inspired, Mina noticed that Dr. Jekyll was standing away from the others, clamping his palms against his ears as if trying to keep his skull from flying apart. "Henry? Are you all right?"

Startled by her question, Jekyll turned away from the porthole, blinking. "My ears hurt. It goes through my whole skull." He tapped at his ears like a swimmer with water in them. "It's nothing," Jekyll said.

On the recording, the evil mastermind continued, "If you fail to save Venice, then I will get my war. And if you succeed—well, it's a small price to pay for giving Mr. Gray the luxury to go about his main task. War will come sooner or later, as inevitably as summer turns into autumn."

"M sure likes the sound of his own voice, doesn't he?" Sawyer said.

He continued, like a stern schoolteacher lecturing a group of disappointing students. "Now some of you—perhaps Quatermain, if he isn't dead, or maybe Skinner, who by all accounts is a sneaky, despicable chap—will pause to ask why I'm letting you know all this. What fool reveals his gambit before the game is over?"

M's voice paused, as if giving them a chance to answer the gramophone disc. "Because, you see, it *is* over. For you. The alarm tone that revealed this recording's existence to you has automatically sounded when certain sensors determined that the *Nautilus* is now deep under the ocean."

"Under a great deal of pressure." Gray's voice broke in. "Which is why I'll take the nautiloid, so that you'll follow and get yourselves into deep water. Perfectly predictable, perfectly boring."

Nemo and the others listened with dawning horror as M continued to relish his explanation.

"I'm sure you're aware, Nemo, how sound can affect certain crystals? Resonance frequencies? The pitch of this particular sound is higher than humans can hear. You won't even notice it. And all the while it continues to grow louder, out of range. More powerful . . . and more destructive."

Jekyll cringed from the reflection of an agonized Hyde in the porthole glass. *I can't bear it, Henry! Please!*

"Dogs and lower animals can hear it with their base instincts. But not men. Hence, while I've rambled on and you all have given me your rapt attention, a secondary layer of inaudible sound is pounding against a sequence of delicate crystal sensors dotted about your vessel."

Gray's voice came again, sounding thoroughly entertained now. "Sensors that are attached to bombs. *Bomb* voyage!" The crude pun seemed incongruous from the erudite man.

Sawyer hurled the gramophone to the floor and stomped on the wax disk. But it was too late.

In the complex maze of ducts, conduits, pipes, and cabinets aboard the *Nautilus,* Dorian Gray had secreted three compact explosives, rigged to shimmering crystalline detectors. Without a complete overhaul, not even Ishmael would have found the bombs deep in the submarine's workings.

Now, although Sawyer had destroyed the player and the recording, the crystal sensors trembled, clicked—and activated the destructive devices.

A huge thunderclap of force, noise, and fire erupted from the rear midhull. The fireball split through the armored side of the *Nautilus,* punching out into the ocean and then imploding under massive water pressure. Metal and ceramic shattered and spewed from a huge hole in the curved wall.

A column of water hammered inward like liquid cannon fire, instantly filling the corridor. The shock wave wrenched the underwater vessel back and forth like a piggy bank being shaken by a child. Glass shattered. Sparks flew.

Inside Nemo's stateroom, the members of the League were thrown off balance, careening into each other. The contour map that tracked the fleeing nautiloid was wrecked.

And then the second and third bombs exploded.

34

The Nautilus

Although the lower chamber was on fire, cold sea water rolled into the rear engine room like a wall. Smoke gushed from the site of the first explosion and poured through ruined turbines. Sparks flew, crackling in the pools and spray.

The metal-walled room filled rapidly with the pounding water. Engineers died screaming, some trying to flee, some giving their lives in attempts to save the undersea vessel.

Two crewmen dashed for the aft bulkhead door. They leaped through the door and tried to swing the heavy hatch shut, but the force of inrushing water swept the door open and smashed the men backward.

Responding together, the League members rushed onto the bridge, where crewmen struggled with the controls. More than ever, Nemo wished Ishmael were here.

"Midhull sealed, Captain. But the doors aren't holding!" a redheaded crewman shouted. "The water keeps rushing into the breach."

The *Nautilus* shuddered and began to sink. The deck tilted at a steep backward angle. Charts and tools clattered off of shelves and tables, pitched aside as the wounded, tail-heavy submarine vessel sank.

"Nemo, we have to surface!" Quatermain stumbled, fetched up against a bulkhead, and then grimaced at the renewed pain in his shoulder wound. "Get back up to the air."

"We've taken in too much water. The controls are no longer responding." Despite his own words, Nemo worked with the vessel's control panels, but the systems remained dark and inoperative.

The *Nautilus* sank through the water, like a shot pheasant tumbling out of the sky. Three jagged holes had been blown out though its stern. Oil trails and fire spilled out; fragments of ceramic armor flaked off like broken bits of eggshell.

Drenched and battered, Crewman Patel—the provisional replacement for the murdered Ishmael—rushed to the bridge, looking about for Nemo. "Primary engine room almost full, sir, and the aft bulkhead is still open! Pump valves are jammed."

"Seal it off," Nemo said. "That is the only way we can stabilize our descent."

"But there are crewmen inside there, Captain!" the acting first mate said. Patel's eyes were sunken, his face frantic. "We never let a man—"

"For the greater good, you must seal it! The pressure will crush us within minutes, if we don't all drown first."

Squaring his shoulders, Patel rushed out, past a shaken Jekyll who huddled in the corridor.

On the bridge, sparks sprayed, panels groaned, water spurted. Quatermain, Sawyer, and Mina hung on as the vessel pitched even further. The room was already thick with smoke, and the pressure outside squeezed the walls harder, like a giant crushing them in his fist.

"It'll be fine, Mina," Sawyer said, sidling closer, as if he could comfort her.

Mina Harker, though, was not interested in such reassurance. "I'm a scientist, young man—that makes me a realist." She turned to Nemo. "Can nothing save us?"

"Only a miracle," Nemo said.

The haggard Jekyll wrestled with his fears. He had already proved completely useless in Venice, and now he damned himself for not understanding the problem swiftly enough; Hyde's bestial senses had heard the deadly high-pitched tone, but his rational mind had not understood the treacherous sabotage in time. He could have prevented this disaster.

And now he meant to do something about it.

Inside him, the snarling presence of Hyde agreed. *We can do it, Henry! Just let me! Let me!*

In the corridor outside the control bridge, Jekyll whirled, saw Hyde's reflection in polished metal on the wall. "What are you on about?"

You know, Henry. We can do it. Together.

Shaking with inner turmoil, Jekyll raced from the bridge. Inside his mind, Edward Hyde roared with impatient glee.

When he finally reached the hatch of the primary engine room, Jekyll fought his way through spraying water and desperate crewmen. The corridor was almost vertical as he reached acting First Mate Patel, who was struggling to close the hatch.

"I'm going inside there." Jekyll's voice was a mere squeak amid the chaotic noise.

"But I've orders to close it!" said Patel. "You won't get back out!"

"Then do it! Don't worry about me." With surprising energy, the skinny doctor sprang into the waist-deep water filling the engine room. Three mangled crewmen were already dead inside, floating up against the walls. Sparks showered from the controls. Oily black smoke clung to the large pumping pistons.

"You'll never survive!"

"Maybe not." Jekyll still sloshed forward. "Or maybe we all will."

Patel realized that there was no time to evacuate any-one else. He cursed, then used all his strength to shoul-der the hatch closed after the doctor had entered. He knew that the *Nautilus* itself had only a few more min-utes before it imploded in the depths. He didn't suppose Jekyll would die much sooner than the rest of them. . . .

Inside the engine room, only a hellish air-pocket of steam and fire remained above the water. Drowning crewmen splashed and struggled for last gasps. Only one man still worked at trying to restart the unsalvageable machinery.

Jekyll dragged himself along the riveted wall. With his free hand, he reached into his shirt pocket to remove a glass vial and yanked out the stopper with his teeth. For a split second he hesitated, wondering if this was worse than a simple death of drowning. His hand trembled. If he dropped the vial into the water, everything would be over. . . .

Come on, Henry! Hyde was like a caged animal throw-ing himself against the bars. *They need me.* You *need me!*

Jekyll faltered a moment more, but the men kept

screaming, the water continued to pour inside, and the *Nautilus* sank ever deeper. More people would die if he didn't do his part. Many more. He gulped the bitter potion.

Without waiting for the elixir to work, he took a deep breath, swelling his narrow chest. He dove under the murky water and swam down through floating debris, grabbing handholds on machinery to drag himself against the rush of water. His muscles were weak. His arms started to shake.

Then his body began to change: Bones lengthened and thickened, muscles swelled and bulged. His hair coarsened and sprouted black from his hands, knuckles, and neck. His head grew larger, more apelike. He convulsed and spasmed, clamping his lips shut to hold in the air. Each time he suffered through this, the transformation brought him more and more agony.

Finally, Jekyll could not help himself. He screamed underwater, but let out only a mouthful of bubbles as his back arched and limbs thrashed. His eyes began to bleed.

When his form bulked up to twice its normal size, his prim clothes tore apart and floated in rags from his body. Yet all the while, his determination held. He kept going downward, handhold to handhold, until at last he reached the bottom of the flooded engine room. The submarine vessel tilted at an ever steeper angle, sinking fast.

He had to reorient himself, looking through the watery gloom to find his destination.

Deep under the swelling cold water, when he reached the wide-open aft bulkhead door, it was Edward Hyde who grabbed hold. With a silent, slow-motion stroke, he swiped aside two drowning crewmen who were still struggling to seal the bulkhead with their last breaths.

Driven by instinct now, Hyde would have preferred to rip things apart, bend pipes and girders, smash open windows. But he knew that he had to close the breach and seal off the flood.

The hatch was heavy, forced aside by the continuing rush of water from the explosion's gaping hole. The beast-man's gnarled and hairy hand gripped the edge of the metal door, and he strained to swing it shut, groaning and spitting bubbles from between his cracked and uneven teeth. Hyde strained to push the hatch, and finally slammed it shut like a man closing a door against a brisk wind. He twisted the wheel to seal the sturdy hatch in place. Safe.

But he could not go back to the surface yet. Dimly, he realized the *Nautilus* would continue sinking as long as its tail section was full of water.

Hyde found the jammed pump valves, tried to turn them so the pistons and gears could work again. The valves remained stuck, as if welded shut. That didn't stop him.

He roared, and the last trickles of air escaped from his mouth in a cloud of bubbles. His muscles bulged as he tried again. He hammered with his fist to loosen the valve, but the thick, cold sea water stole much of his strength. Hyde's vision grew dark, his anger increased, and he forced himself to think of the pump valve as an enemy to be defeated.

Then slowly, inch by inch, the valve wheel started to move, cranking clockwise. Snarling silently, dizzy from lack of oxygen, Hyde gave the lever another shove.

Suddenly the valve came free, spinning loose, as the undersea vessel's huge vents opened, hurling the massive man away. Screaming turbines began to evacuate water from the chamber. He hooked his hands around a sturdy pipe and clung to it with all his remaining strength to keep from being sucked out.

Hyde worked his way upward as the water level inside the sealed chamber dropped. High above, he could see the silhouettes of struggling crewmen splashing about on the surface. *He needed air.*

Higher and higher he climbed, until finally his shaggy, misshapen head burst out into the air above the water. He spat spray and heaved a huge breath to fill his starved lungs.

Heard only inside his head, Jekyll's thin voice yelled over the sound of the rushing water. "Bravo, Edward! Bravo!"

35

The wounded *Nautilus* rose under a dawn sky, breaking the surface of the choppy ocean with a clumsy gasp and a groan. Air hissed out, water sprayed, and the scarred and damaged submarine vessel sprawled on the sea as if exhausted. The slow chug of propellers moved the ship drunkenly forward, and the engines coughed.

Crewmen vented the vessel's foul interior to release smoke and stagnant atmosphere, pumping in fresh air. They flung open the upper hatch as the engines and pumps continued to labor. Haunted-looking men pressed their heads out into the open breezes, amazed that they had lived to see the surface again.

In dire need of repairs, the wallowing *Nautilus* creaked and moaned on the high seas. And Nemo and his men were the only people on Earth with the knowledge and skills to fix the exotic vessel.

Taking shifts inside, the surviving crewmen moved about in a daze, replacing broken fittings, resetting furnishings, and mopping up the last standing pools of sea water that had flooded the corridors.

Quatermain, Sawyer, Nemo, and Mina met in Nemo's

stateroom to discuss the larger implications of M's schemes, and to make plans of their own. With the exception of the ever-optimistic young American, all of them wore an air of defeat. Seeking an outlet for his anger and helplessness, Quatermain took the damaged gramophone disc from the player, and made a point of grinding it under his heel.

Looking shell-shocked, a restored Dr. Jekyll was the last to arrive. After his exertions, the elixir had worn off, leaving him in his frail and fidgety body. But he had served his purpose well. Quatermain nodded to the doctor in silent acknowledgment of his valor.

Jekyll shrank away, embarrassed. "Well . . . let's not make a saint out of a sinner. Next time, Hyde may not choose to be so helpful." Avoiding further discussion, he turned his attention to the damaged undersea map. The indicators of both the fleeing nautiloid and the larger vessel had fallen off, lost somewhere in the jumble of debris on the floor. "Can—can we still follow Gray?"

Mina made a disbelieving sound as she sat in Nemo's desk chair. "Even if the tracer could still get a signal from the nautiloid, we barely have enough engine power to keep us moving."

"We were faster," Quatermain said. "Now we're a tortoise to his hare."

"Not even a tortoise. We are practically dead in the water," Nemo said.

"So we're . . . just done?" Jekyll said. "We give up?"

Sawyer took the challenge. "No, we're alive. If M has ideas to the contrary, that gives us an edge. He shouldn't be making assumptions." He grinned, trying to rally them. "After all, we're the League of Extraordinary Gentlemen, aren't we? That stands for something."

Captain Nemo, though, was not impressed. "The sea is vast, young man. Even if the ship could move, Gray—and M—could be out there anywhere."

"Well, I'm an optimist. Maybe that's a crime to you twisted so-and-sos, but being the way I am keeps me from going crazy." Sawyer looked at Allan Quatermain, expecting to find support there . . . but he received none. "We'll figure out something."

"Your cheerfulness is out of place, Mr. Sawyer," Mina said.

"You're wrong. We *will* get our man—at least I will. Tom Sawyer of the American Secret Service." A shadow crossed his expression. "You all aren't the only ones with a grudge, you know. Remember when we first met, the other agent I told you about? The one who was first assigned to investigate the Fantom? Well, he was my childhood friend. He and I were agents together, until that masked madman shot him dead." He wrestled with his emotions, trying not to get choked up. His freckled face flushed red. "The rest of you may be done, but I'm not. I swear I'm going to avenge Huck Finn's death."

"But this isn't about any one of us, Tom. Certainly not anymore," Jekyll said. "It's bigger than that."

"Yes, it is, Mister. The fate of the world is in our hands. *The world!*" Sawyer looked at all the others, wanting to shake them out of their gloom. "Okay, so Dorian Gray was a traitor. And M tricked you into joining him, and you walked straight into his trap." Sawyer showed them a determined grin. "But the way I see it, that was his big mistake . . . he brought you—*us*—together."

The League members looked at each other, considering.

"He . . . he has a point," Jekyll said.

Quatermain cocked a brow at Sawyer, then finally responded with a wan grin of his own. "And the boy becomes a man. Perhaps a leader of men."

"And women." Mina stood again and smoothed her skirts down. "So now what do we do?"

First Mate Patel suddenly burst in. "Captain! We're getting a signal! I think it's from the nautiloid."

"M gloating, no doubt," Nemo said. "He'll want to know if we survived."

Patel shook his head. "I don't believe it's from the Fantom, sir—and not Mr. Gray either."

Spurred to action, the remaining members of the League rushed to the *Nautilus*'s radio room. A communications operator adjusted his headphones as he jotted down a message on processed kelp paper, one painstaking letter at a time. The radio apparatus emitted beeps and clicks.

Quatermain recognized the chatter he had heard at numerous African outpost telegraph stations. "Morse code."

"What's it say?" Mina asked.

The radio operator read all the words he had so far transcribed. "It says, 'Hello my freaky darlings.' "

Sawyer and Mina said in unison, "Skinner."

"So the invisible man has joined M's treachery after all," Nemo said.

That didn't make sense to Quatermain, though. He scratched his head. "Maybe . . . or maybe not."

The communications operator continued reading off

the Morse code message. "Hiding on board little fish with Gray and M. On way to base. East by North East. Follow my lead."

"He stowed aboard!" Sawyer said.

Quatermain clapped the young man on the shoulder. "Our ace in the hole. You were right not to give up hope, lad." The American agent beamed.

"You heard him, Mr. Patel," Nemo said. "Fix our heading at East by North East. All repair crews get to work on our engines, highest priority. I want this vessel moving with every ounce of speed the engines can manage, as soon as possible. Once we begin the chase again, we will make the other repairs while we're under way." The new first mate rushed off to follow his orders.

As the *Nautilus* floated on the surface of troubled seas, the reenergized crew worked to repair holes in the hull, reattach armor plates, and shore up structural braces from the inside decks. But the damaged engines were the highest priority and underwent an urgent overhaul: Wrecked components were replaced with spares, pistons and shafts were ground and refitted, oil reservoirs refilled, and fresh lubricants applied.

On the bridge, Nemo worked alongside the men to rewire circuits and connect pipes and conduits. Because the entire submarine vessel was of his own design, the detailed plans remained in his memory. First Mate Patel tested the patched controls while plotting coordinates.

Mina and Jekyll tended to the severely wounded crewmen, saving many of them, though several of Nemo's longtime comrades had died. The dead heroes were buried at sea in a solemn ceremony the following foggy morning at dawn. Nemo allowed the desperate work to pause for only a few moments before sending the crewmen back to their tasks.

Inside the sooty and stained engine room, Tom Sawyer lent exuberance, if no particular expertise, to tightening pipes and fixing gauges, wiping away excess lumps of fresh sealant, and polishing the equipment to bring it back to a semblance of the way things had been.

Still, with every instant the nautiloid drew farther and farther away.

When all the members of the League had gathered in the control room, along with First Mate Patel and other *Nautilus* crewmen, Quatermain addressed the group. "Good work. All of you. Captain?"

Standing on the bridge, Nemo activated the controls. The tense and exhausted engineers and mechanics looked at the captain and at Patel. Then, with a throb and a hiss, the engines engaged, pumping with an ever-increasing roar until they reached full power.

Finally, the vessel began to move, straining with the effort. The *Nautilus* crossed many leagues, picking up speed as each additional repair was completed. The open seas posed no hindrance to the Sword of the Ocean. Her jagged bow sliced through the waters like a shark in pursuit of prey.

The map of the ocean inside Nemo's stateroom was partially repaired. Relief plates of the sea floor and longitude lines shifted to the left as the *Nautilus* traveled further east.

36

Despite the submarine vessel's rushing speed across the ocean, those aboard could do little but wait. Some gathered their energies for the coming battle against the Fantom and his forces; others studied plans, assessing their options; many could not sleep because of either dread or impatience.

Quatermain retreated to his cabin where he once again pored over issues of *The Strand Magazine,* Scotland Yard crime reports, and even old records of the first appearance of the real Phantom that had plagued the Paris Opera House. Obviously, they were different men, but M had taken the other villain as his model.

Quatermain turned the magazine's pages with the hand of his uninjured arm. On Nemo's spare gramophone player, he listened intently as a cracked fragment of M's recording replayed over and over. The female recordist's drab voice said, "Ready, Professor . . . Ready, Professor . . . Ready, Professor."

When Nemo entered, Quatermain lifted the needle. He could see immediately that the captain did not have good news.

"Skinner's signal has stopped," Nemo said. "We no longer have any way to track them."

Outside, on the ship's observation deck under mockingly sunny skies, Sawyer stood staring at the horizon, as if hoping to see the distant and still-fleeing nautiloid.

Mina Harker came up to him in full green skirt and petticoats, with a bright red scarf wrapped primly around her pale throat. "Thank you," she said.

The young American turned to her, startled. "For what, Ma'am?"

"Your fearlessness." Mina stopped close beside him and looked out at the sea. "I've lived such a life of sorrow and regret—a long life—that I've always been rather afraid to step into tomorrow."

Sawyer's chest swelled. "Shucks, tomorrow's where I live and breathe, Ma'am."

"Yes. I see it's not so bad a placc at all." The *Nautilus* struck a set of heavy waves, and spray hissed from its bow, but none of the water droplets splashed them. Mina gripped the rail to steady herself against the choppy motion.

Sawyer touched her gloved hand with a fingertip. "Hey, if my earlier . . . attentions offended you in any way, I'm sorry."

"I am disappointed." Mina smiled up at him again. "I didn't think Americans gave up so easily."

Sawyer blinked his blue eyes again, liking what he heard.

Off to one side, Allan Quatermain lay in a deck chair beside which he had stacked his research books and files. Lying in the warm sunlight, the old adventurer appeared to have dozed off, but as he eavesdropped and watched them through half-opened eyes, he allowed himself a small grin.

Later, in the thrumming communications room, the radio operator settled his headphones in place again and continued to adjust the frequency, listening for the tell-tale clicks of a coded signal.

Behind him, Nemo waited patiently, silently, watching with his coal-dark eyes. Quatermain tried to match the captain's calm, but found it extremely difficult.

The radio operator suddenly sat up straight with his full attention. He gave the communication knobs a delicate twist, then gathered his paper and lead pencil. He spared only a fraction of his attention to glance back up at the captain. "It's Mr. Skinner, sir."

Then he began marking the dots and dashes of the Morse code signal, translating letter by letter. Finally, he read the message. "Sorry. Took a nap. Sea of Okhotsk. Tartar Strait. Amur River. Mongolia west of Hailar."

Nemo turned to hurry back to his bridge. "Come, Quatermain. We must set a course."

The engines continued to chug, nursed along by the un-easy engineers. The propellers drove the armored vessel forward through the waves. They were closing in.

Quatermain and Nemo surveyed gigantic map books that the dark captain had compiled over his years of exploration. Nemo's finger traced a line on the charts. "Our route will take us past the Kuril Islands into the Sea of Okhotsk. The communal waters of China, Japan, and Russia where many cultures merge and shift." He stroked his dark beard. "Then south through the Tartar Strait between Russia and the island of Sakhalin, entering the Amur River at Nikolayev."

Quatermain nodded, following the long and convoluted route. The names sounded strange and exotic, like the lands and tribes he himself had encountered in darkest Africa. Many of the places on the map remained mysteries, uncharted blanks. He almost expected to see the handwritten notation, *Here Be Monsters.*

Nemo now traced the dark line of a river leading deep into the wildest parts of East Asia. "The Amur will take us inland to remote Mongolia, which was once ruled by ruthless Cossacks. Their fortresses still stand as arrogant monuments to power and cruelty. No doubt, that is where M has built his lair."

"I can hardly wait," Quatermain said. "Let's go."

37

The Mongolian Wastes

As silent as a sea monster, the *Nautilus* cruised the water's surface along far-flung shorelines, past the snowy land masses of Eastern Russia, where smoky and firelit port towns were visible on the horizon. Small fishing boats braved leaden, wintry currents and the fog, never noticing the armored vessel that passed so close.

At first the ports were substantial towns, the last bastions of civilization on the fringes of the primitive wastes. Seen from the *Nautilus,* the prominent architecture included Russian spires along with touches of Japanese influence; a webwork of docks spread out, holding scores of boats.

But as the vessel passed farther northward, the ports took on the more primitive look of remote China, with rough-hewn wooden walls or stacked stones, woven roofs, and pointed arches. All of it was blanketed by snow.

Concerned about being seen as they drew closer to their quarry, Captain Nemo ordered the *Nautilus* to submerge and proceed along its course. It wouldn't be long now before they found where Dorian Gray and M had gone to ground.

*　　*　　*

At the Amur River at dawn, a curving silver-blue line of frozen water cut through a windswept landscape of snow and jutting gray rock. A few gnarled trees, bent low from the ever-blowing wind of the constant winter, dotted the monotonous steppe.

Today, even the ravens had taken shelter in the scrub brush, too miserable to search for carrion. Silence pervaded the frigid atmosphere.

Suddenly, with a cracking roar and the creak of broken slabs of ice, the *Nautilus*'s reinforced conning tower hammered through the frozen surface and rose into the air with a shower of snow and a spray of icy river water.

The vessel's upper hatch opened with a clang, and five people emerged, climbing up into the chill northern air. They all wore thick arctic clothing, heavy gloves, and hooded jackets. The wind whistling across the steppes carried with it a deeper chill, but even the biting cold could not bring a rosy flush to Mina Harker's pale cheeks. The others shaded their eyes from the glare of sun on endless ice and snow.

Skittish Jekyll slipped on the slick coating of fresh-frozen ice that covered the armored upper deck, but Quatermain caught him. "Careful, man. You wouldn't last a minute in water that cold." The slushy Amur knocked ice chunks against the side of the *Nautilus*, and Jekyll looked down wide-eyed at where he had almost fallen.

Nemo took his binocular device and scanned the landscape. "According to my charts, we should be very near to our destination."

Sawyer, Jekyll, and Mina shared a telescope that First

Mate Patel had brought up for them. Jekyll peered toward a distant rocky ridge. "Aren't the Fantom's manufactories over there?" He had a difficult time holding the eyepiece steady in his trembling hands. His teeth chattered.

Nemo nodded. "We may have to set off overland."

Quatermain took the binoculars to see for himself. He focused on snow-frosted piles of rock and stripped logs that had once been clustered homes, but had now fallen into complete disrepair. "Deserted peasant settlements."

Mina took the telescope from Jekyll. "Completely empty, no sign of life. They're close to a river, probably on a trade route. The houses themselves seem habitable."

"Well, with a bit of fixing up," Sawyer agreed, lowering the binoculars.

Mina continued to stare, using only her sharp green eyes. "Still, why would an entire village be deserted?"

Then oily smoke rose up in angry black whorls over the rim of the jagged rise, accompanied by a fiery glow, as if a doorway to Hell itself had been opened—just a crack.

"Fear, no doubt," Nemo said.

The icy plains of Mongolia were a far cry from the African veldt, but Quatermain still led the expedition.

Sawyer, Jekyll, and Mina trudged after him, picking a path over the treacherous ground: slick ice, uncertain rocks, deep snow. Nemo brought up the rear with a squad of *Nautilus* crewmen, all of them warmly dressed and well-armed. They ascended the steep hillside to the top of the rocky ridge beyond the abandoned peasant village. Behind them, the conning tower of the submarine vessel protruded from the Amur ice, like the ruins of a castle battlement.

One by one, the group struggled up through a windswept crack in the snow. Sawyer politely helped Mina, though her grip was stronger than his. Loose rocks tumbled from ledges, bouncing and picking up speed as they rolled down the slope.

After cresting the rise, they looked down to see a Cossack fortress, the lair of the counterfeit Fantom. *M.*

The giant structure seemed to be an amalgamation of a blocky gothic castle and the industrial revolution's dirtiest factory nightmare—a black stone folly of an exiled czar, built to rule over the landscape. Great bulbous minarets spired skyward, and huge blasts of fire coughed forth from tall chimneys atop foundries and processing lines. Its workshops, living quarters, and dungeons glowered out at friend and foe alike. The industrial fires of smithies, smelters, and incinerators made M's fortress look like a restless volcano, accompanied by a loud clamor and the syncopated puffs of small explosions.

Overhead, the wide sky was thick with gray clouds and the wind picked up as the storm gathered, carrying the metallic scent of impending snow.

"M's summer retreat. Can't say I care for the color." Sawyer made ready to move. "Let's nail this son of a bitch."

"Unprepared and unplanned? No, lad." Quatermain looked around the gnarled rocky outcroppings, the stark lichen-encrusted boulders. The first heavy flakes of snow began spitting down on them from the dark clouds. "This is where Skinner signaled he'd meet us. So we wait."

Later, the League members and Nemo's armed men gathered around a meager campfire inside a rock cave, surrounded by snowdrifts. Sawyer and several crewmen carrying axes had volunteered to go back to the empty peasant village to chop some of the frozen wood into chunks and splinters. As the storm grew worse, filling the air with pelting snow, the group had laboriously brought the pieces up to their makeshift shelter. Although the light from their fire seemed a mere spark in the vast emptiness of the steppes, for those huddled close to its warmth, the effort had paid off.

They melted snow and boiled the water, which Mina used to make tea. After taking a long swallow of straight whiskey from his hip flask, Quatermain offered it to fortify the brew, then went out into the continuing blizzard to stand guard.

The old adventurer sat on a rock at the cave entrance and kept watch, in spite of the freezing cold of the blustery night and blinding snow that whipped all around him. Though M surely believed them all dead and the *Nautilus* sunk, he refused to let down their guard so near to the enemy's fortress. He would take no chances.

Quatermain hunched over his rock, clenching his mittened hands together, his faithful elephant gun Matilda leaning against him. He was unused to such severe cold, and his wounded shoulder sent twinges of pain down his arm, reminding him that he was no longer the young, resilient man he had once been. He gritted his teeth and ignored the pain.

The heavy storm blocked the stars, rendering the skies a grayish black. Blowing snow smeared out details in the distance, too, muting the fiery fortress to a sore red-orange glow that could not penetrate the blizzard. None of M's men could possibly see the tiny, sheltered campfire in the cave.

Suddenly, Quatermain heard a noise. Swift and silent, the hunter yanked off his mittens, dropped them to the ground, and grabbed the elephant gun. He brought it to his shoulder and swept the barrel in a slow arc, looking for a target out in the blowing snow. In a low voice that the wind snatched away, he called out furtively, "Skinner?"

From out of the blizzard, an old white tiger appeared. Its camouflage had changed to winter coloring, pale as shadows on ice. It was powerful, dangerous, a hunter out in the emptiness, probably hungry enough to kill human prey. Quatermain sighted along Matilda, not needing his glasses now. The magnificent Siberian tiger was unnervingly close and utterly silent. It made no growl, no sound at all as it moved through the snow.

Keeping his breaths steady and even, Quatermain locked eyes with the tiger. It was motionless now, watching him. Its whiskers moved as it snuffled more of the man-scent. Snow eddied and swirled around the two hunters, sealing them in a curious, timeless moment, as if their tableau had been captured inside a child's snow globe. Quatermain closed one eye to take better aim, tentatively fingered the trigger.

But he couldn't do it.

The old adventurer had faced many deadly beasts before, yet he and the tiger shared a strange kinship. Perhaps they were meant to meet, in this far-off place. . . . With a sigh he lowered the elephant gun, looked once more into the tiger's eyes, and prepared to accept his fate. A few seconds passed.

Then the beast turned and stalked back into the blowing white wind, seeking other prey.

"We heard a noise," Mina said from the edge of the

cave, startling him. He turned to see her standing there beside Nemo. The captain, his scimitar ready, stared off into the darkness.

"It was . . . nothing." Quatermain's throat was dry, his heart pounding.

"Just an old tiger sensing his end," Nemo said with eerie insight. He indicated a track of paw prints heading away into the snow.

Quatermain rested the elephant gun's stock on the ground and retrieved his mittens, tugging them over his numb fingers. "Perhaps this isn't his time to die after all." Nemo nodded wryly.

Suddenly, Mina stifled a cry as she was goosed from behind. She leaped awkwardly forward in alarm, skittered around while regaining her balance, then crouched to defend herself.

"Aheh! I've been waiting all week to do that," Skinner's voice said. He stepped back out into the wind, and his man-shaped outline was visible in the blowing snow.

"Get a grip, man," Quatermain said, furious with him.

"I thought I just did," Skinner said. "Never thought I'd get away from that damned tiger. He's been tracking me for a mile. Smelled me but couldn't see me. Heh!"

"Report," Nemo said, sheathing his scimitar. "Tell us everything you—"

The invisible man interrupted him. "Hello to you, too, my dear captain." He came closer, leaving bare footprints in the drifted snow outside the cave. "Need I remind you that I'm naked in the snow in this bloody freezing wasteland. I can't feel any of my extremities. *Any* of them."

38

While thawing out by the fire after shouldering various crewmen aside so he could hold his invisible hands and other extremities closer to the warmth,
Skinner donned spare clothing and once again reap-
plied his white face makeup. He looked like a frozen
corpse, but at least he had stopped shivering, unlike
Henry Jekyll.

"Ah, the things I do for the Empire." He was deeply
disappointed to learn that his comrades had finished the
last drops of whiskey in Quatermain's hip flask.

When the other League members listened to the
scraping whisper of the blizzard outside, Nemo was the
first to demand answers. "So, if you weren't among the
traitors, how is it you knew to follow Gray?"

"Heh! He was the only one creeping around as much
as me." The invisible man turned his ghostly painted
face to Mina, and his lips curved in a broad smile. "He
has quite a way with him, eh, Mina?"

She didn't answer. She was dressed warmly, though
the cold of their surroundings did not seem to affect her
anyway.

Sawyer expressed indignation on her behalf. "So why didn't you just tell any of us?"

Skinner snorted at the suggestion. "With all the suspicion on the ship, I knew you'd never believe I wasn't the spy. You've been such dear friends, after all, aheh! So, I did what I'm good at. I thought it best to 'disappear' and wait for the real traitor to show himself."

Mina's face remained hard, and she stared at him with icy green eyes across the firelight. "Why not do something to the nautiloid? It sounds as if you had plenty of opportunities."

"I'm invisible, not heroic," Skinner said.

Quatermain shifted his position, mentally reassessing everything they thought they knew. "Skinner, we need your information. What are we dealing with? Tell us everything you saw and learned while you were out sight-seeing."

"Sight-seeing? Why don't *you* try creeping around naked in the snow for hours?" He scowled at Quatermain's empty silver flask, then grudgingly accepted a cup of fortified tea. "All right, I'll describe everything for you as best I can. That fortress is an awfully big place."

"Where did it come from?" Sawyer asked. "Did M design it himself?"

"I was built long ago by a czar who allied himself with Cossack bandits and warlords in an attempt to conquer Europe and Asia. But they caught him cheating at a gambling game and slit his throat in his sleep. Not very good at thinking ahead, those Cossacks. Without the czar, they were left to do their raping and pillaging across Mongolia on a more customary scale.

"The citadel was abandoned . . . and M simply

couldn't resist its allure. The place has all the amenities a discriminating mad genius bent on world domination could ask for." The invisible man slurped his lukewarm tea. "He's made a few modifications and improvements, of course."

Using words as an artist might use a fine brush, Skinner painted detailed verbal pictures of all he had seen inside. Foundry furnaces stoked by Mongol laborers produced fresh iron for making M's weapons of destruction. Sweating and straining in the simmering orange heat, they poured molten metal into large casts. After the molds were quenched and cooled with icy water pumped from the nearby Amur River, muscular laborers used hammers to break the components free. Parts for M's war machines.

Chains dangling from winches and pulleys raised the heavy iron pieces and shuttled them over to a maze of lathes, drills, and presses on the factory floor, where they were pieced together. Some workers constructed massive land ironclads, such as the one that had smashed through the Bank of England vault; others assembled monstrous long-barreled cannons, smaller guns, and rocket-launching tubes. Outside in the frigid daylight, teams test-fired the weapons, launching explosive artillery shells and shrieking rockets, using the empty peasant dwellings as makeshift targets.

"Worst of all," Skinner continued, "in the dry dock beneath the fortress, I saw M supervising laborers riveting hull plates in the diabolic heat and shadow. The vessels are still under construction, but soon M will have a fleet of armored submarine warships of his own."

"They've copied my *Nautilus,*" Nemo said, pained.

"*Nautili*, actually. Eight of them for now," Skinner said. "But, heh, I'm sure he'll build more."

Even in the firelight, Sawyer's face was flushed with anger. "Nemo, can you fire rockets from your own ship, like you did in Venice? Blow that whole place to Hell?"

"We are out of range, Mr. Sawyer. And all those people inside . . . surely some of them must be innocent slaves." Nemo turned to Skinner. "What of the kidnapped scientists?"

"M holds their families hostage inside the fortress. The men are forced to work, or the women and children die. Simple and straightforward."

Nemo's face darkened with fury, and he shook his head. "Monstrous. I see M has learned much from his barbaric predecessors."

The invisible man rubbed his unseen hands together. "Aheh! That isn't the half of it. M isn't just mechanically inclined when he designs his new weapons. He uses biology, as well. He's forcing the captive scientists to work night and day—to make new versions of *us*. As if one of me wasn't quite enough."

"What do you mean?" Quatermain said.

"You should see the chemicals and substances he is mass-producing. All distilled from our best—aheh!—traits. He will create invisible spies, an army of Hydes, vampiric assassins . . . and send them all off to wage war in a fleet of unstoppable submersibles." Skinner turned the tinted lenses of his glasses toward them. "Delightful, eh?"

Jekyll knotted his hands together, and his face sank in dismay. "I won't let my evil infect the world."

"Think any of us feel differently?" Mina looked at her

pale palm, where the cut from the broken glass had long since healed, leaving no scar whatsoever. She felt as if Dorian Gray had violated her again.

Sawyer was impatient. "I'm tired of just sitting here in the cold, when we know M is just over there all cozy inside his fortress. What are we going to do?"

"We put an end to him," Nemo said with quiet force.

The invisible man, at least, continued to think pleasant thoughts. "Chimney pipes lace the buildings, factories, and foundries—so a few well-placed bombs in the furnaces would make quite a bang. Heh!" As if in agreement, the wood in the small campfire suddenly crackled and snapped. Skinner held his transparent hands over the warmth. "I know the way down, and I'm least likely to be seen."

"Skinner, I didn't know you were such a barefaced liar." Quatermain surprised the invisible man, then gave him a sly smile. "All this time, declaring you weren't a hero."

"Shut up, or I'll come to my senses." The invisible thief actually seemed embarrassed. "Besides, any more like me, and I lose the franchise."

Tom Sawyer, holding his Winchester rifle, cocked it suddenly with a loud sound. Ready to go, he stood. "That man killed Huck Finn. I'm not gonna let that pass. He's mine."

But Quatermain reluctantly touched the young agent's rifle barrel, forced him to lower it. "This cannot be a hunt to the death, lad. More's the pity." Sawyer looked as if the old adventurer had betrayed him, but Quatermain remained firm. "We must take M alive, if his secrets are to be uncovered."

Mina's green eyes looked feral in the firelight. "Not Gray, though." She stood, like a vengeful spirit rising from the grave. "He's lived long enough."

"I'll handle him—" Sawyer said.

"No," said Mina. "Dorian is . . . my business."

Sawyer understood and nodded grimly.

The storm outside seemed to be lessening, but their work had just begun. Quatermain said, "M decided that he could use our particular abilities to help him wage war—it's time we demonstrate just how right he is. Only *we'll* be waging war on *him*."

"Right!" Sawyer shouldered his Winchester. "If we work together, getting into that fortress of his should be a piece of cake."

Quatermain strode to the cave opening and led the way out. "The game is on."

39

M's Fortress

With the first light of morning dazzling on the fresh snow, a Mongolian guard stood vigil at the foot of the black fortress. He had dark eyes, a long drooping mustache, and stiff leather armor that kept out arrows and knife blades, but not the cold. He carried a sleek new-design automatic weapon from the master's arsenal.

When he stamped his feet, the iron nails of his boot soles rang on the stone path. His toes were numb, his belly rumbled with queasy hunger, and his head pounded from the effects of too much drink the night before. Though no enemy had crossed the empty windswept wasteland in recent memory, he stood at his post and kept guard.

He would rather face an onrushing horde alone than incur the Fantom's anger. The masked man was a demon, the stuff of nightmares.

The guard was stationed at the opening to a roaring meltwater sluice. A canal diverted part of the river channel into the foundry forges and the factories, and dumped water into turbines and storage tanks. The air was bitterly cold, and spray from the surging water rimed the fortress's dark stones with thick frost and coated the walkway with treacherous ice.

One of his fellow guards took up a post deeper inside the sluice tunnel, where the surging flow made the cold air clammy, the stone walls slick and slimy. At least here, outside the fortress walls, the air was clear and fresh.

The guard scanned the open, rocky landscape all around, dazzled by the white glare. Then he saw two figures in the distance, black shapes: a woman and . . . something massive. He frowned, stroking one end of his ice-crusted mustache, then called out to his partner deeper inside the tunnel.

Oddly, he saw another set of footprints much closer in the fresh snow . . . coming all the way up to the sluice gate. Made by naked feet.

Though the guard saw no one, he heard a noise. "Who's there?" He extended his high-tech rifle, narrowing his eyes to scan for any target within range.

Suddenly, something yanked the long gun right out of his hand. The weapon floated in midair for a second, while he stared at it in astonishment. He snatched for the barrel, but the gun danced out of his reach, then turned itself about.

With a resounding smash of bone and a spray of blood, the haunted weapon clubbed him in the face. It struck again, battering the guard until he fell unconscious.

Responding to the call, a second guard came running out of the dark tunnel. When he saw his collapsed comrade, he skittered on the ice-slick walkway. Before he understood what he was seeing, he let out a yell, but it was lost in the roar of the meltwater sluice.

Then his warning cry shriveled to a squeak, and the guard stopped in his tracks as he became aware of something . . . *huge*. There was a bloodcurdling roar of challenge, a meaty arm covered with coarse black hair, a flash of jagged teeth designed to bite off flesh in dripping, painful chunks.

Terrified, the guard scrambled back into the sluice and ran toward the end of the tunnel until he reached a bolted gate. He dragged at a heavy iron pin, struggling to open the barrier.

A moment later Edward Hyde loomed behind him and let out a low grumble that sounded like boiling mud. He reached out to clench both the hapless guard and the metal grating in one massive fist and wrenched the sluice open. The guard broke before the latch did, and his screams abruptly ceased.

Hyde tore the gate free and tossed it aside along with the man's corpse. Then he bellowed for the others to hurry up.

At the top of the sluice tubes deeper inside the fortress factory, a third man, having heard the awful cries of his fellow guard, turned from his station. He felt even greater uneasiness as the noises were cut off. With wide eyes adjusted to the torchlit shadows of the deep tunnels, he peered down the sluice hole.

He caught a frantic rustling, high-pitched squeaking and buzzing just beyond the edge of his ability to hear. His breath caught in his throat as he realized something was coming up toward him—coming fast.

The guard scrambled backward as a black storm of flying creatures erupted up through the hole in a tornado of thin shrieks, sharp claws, and beating wings. Bats. Thousands of them.

And in the center of the swarm, he saw a whirling *thing* with piercing green eyes. He screamed, but he was trapped inside the crowded sluice tunnel. There was no place to run.

The bats enveloped the guard.

When they dispersed, the man's skin was a chalky, cadaverous white, pricked and punctured by scores of tiny teeth. And his throat had been torn out entirely. An expression of horror had frozen on his face.

Mina Harker crouched and wiped blood from her mouth. Then she adjusted her scarf and stood primly again, waiting for the others.

40

Even in the cold and uncivilized landscape of Mongolia, M had contrived to create a fine private parlor, full of rich wood and velvet. He reclined his gaunt body in a leather chair in front of a roaring fire. Here, the fortress's stone walls were thick enough that he did not hear the pounding clamor of the foundries and factories, though he could feel a reassuring industrial tremor through the floor. He smiled. Everything was proceeding very nicely.

He poured a glass of the finest sherry from a cut-crystal decanter on the table beside his chair, sniffed it, then enjoyed a long sip. "A woman's drink, indeed!" He would let Allan Quatermain have his bathtub gin, or whiskey, or whatever it was the old hunter preferred.

As he set the glass down, he winced, touching the tender pain of his dressed wound. Though his battle with Quatermain in the Venice cemetery had occurred several days earlier, he still nursed the injury. Luckily, his armored vest had mostly deflected the deadly blade, but unlike some of his recent acquaintances, he could not heal instantly.

The coffered wooden door opened quietly, and Dorian Gray, once again wearing fine clothing, entered the private parlor. His cool expression was a bit too tense to make a convincing show of his usual feigned boredom. In silence, he looked expectantly at the evil leader.

"All right, then." M sighed without looking around. "Your precious painting's in your room." It was pitiful how poorly Gray covered his relief.

"In return for the League. That was our deal, M, and I'm glad you honor it."

The mastermind took another relaxed sip of his sherry. "On the subject of honor—did it bother you at all? Betraying them."

"A little. I'd be lying if—" Gray cut himself off and paused to reconsider. "No, I'm lying now. It didn't bother me at all. Frankly, I found it amusing, all of them wrestling with past wrongs. . . ." He caught himself gloating. "I, on the other hand, am an unabashed villain. I need no justifications or rationalization."

"So what now for you?" M asked. "A man of your many years must have long-standing plans."

"London." Gray shrugged, as if the answer was obvious. "I've had my fill of violence. Now I'm in the mood for vice." He turned to leave.

"You could stay. Share my dream," M called to Gray's back. "You have many extra years to invest. Why not take a chance?"

M reached quietly for a pistol on his desk, laid his hand over it. He could snatch it up and fire in an instant. Though normal bullets had been harmless against Dorian Gray, this sophisticated projectile design—with higher velocity and marvelously explosive tips—might not prove quite so ineffective. Either way, he was curious to test his new toy.

Stopped at the door, Gray never turned, though he sensed the threat behind him. "It holds no interest for me." With a pale manicured hand, he gripped the end of his cane-sword and pulled the slim silver blade an inch from its sheath. His voice was dry. "I've lived long enough to see the future become history, Professor. Empires crumble. There are no exceptions."

M remained silent, pursing his lips, and finally he took his hand off the augmented pistol. Gray opened the door and took a step out into the hall without looking back. He seemed self-satisfied, superior.

"You think you're better than me," M said.

Gray paused to form a sarcastic retort, then thought better of it. "No, M. We're merely different men. Different goals, different personalities."

"Oh, you forget, Dorian Gray. I have seen your painting." M smiled coldly, raising his sherry glass again. "We're more alike than you know."

The observation stung. Gray hesitated for a long moment, then finally walked away with long, swift strides.

41

M's Fortress

Now that Skinner, Hyde, and Mina had breached the fortress's outer defenses and passed the guards, the rest of the League entered a vast hallway with silent granite walls. The place spoke of brute-force grandeur, majesty without finesse. Brooding statues of Cossack warriors stood along the corridor, petrified guardians carved full of intimidation.

Tom Sawyer stared around, open-mouthed. He almost whistled in admiration, but caught himself in time. He and his companions moved quietly ahead, backed up by armed crewmen from the *Nautilus*.

Quatermain once again fit his role of great white hunter, carrying Matilda over one shoulder, a Winchester over the other, and a Bowie knife in his belt. When they reached an intersection of large corridors, he stopped for a moment to listen down the halls. Without a word, he gestured to Skinner, asking for directions.

The invisible man indicated that Hyde, Nemo, and his crewmen should take the main artery, Mina a side corridor, and Quatermain and Sawyer a third hall. Quatermain nodded, and the three groups separated.

Before they could move away, though, the League members all paused and turned back briefly to look at each other, as if fearing it might be the last time they would ever be together. They suddenly seemed to be of one mind.

Breathing heavily, his nostrils flared, Hyde extended his massive hairy hand. Quatermain, without hesitation, placed his hand on top. Mina, Sawyer, Nemo, and finally Skinner, all did the same.

When they gazed at each other, determined smiles shone on their faces. Although the Fantom's gigantic fortress loomed all around them, it no longer seemed impregnable.

They had been a League before; now they were truly a team.

Reaching an echoing mezzanine on whisper-quiet footsteps, Quatermain and Sawyer crept past roughly shaped pillars. Beyond them, an expansive laboratory was filled with chemistry apparatus, crackling electrical devices, bubbling flasks and beakers. There, the miserable kidnapped scientists worked under armed guard.

The laboratory walls were covered with chalkboards which were, in turn, covered with furiously scribbled, and often erased, sketches and equations. Surly-looking guards holding the Fantom's sophisticated firearms kept watch over their charges, though the guards did not seem to have any interest in the science itself.

As they crept forward to get a better look, Sawyer pointed to the other side of the mezzanine, from which the loudest sounds and thickest smoke emanated. The factory floor below was filled with hundreds of Mongo-

lian workers, either slaves or sluggish laborers, who operated machines, presses, and pistons. Hissing steam
boiled out of jets, drenching the sulfur-smelling air with
its moisture. Sparks flew from grinders that shaped components to fit M's diabolical machines.

A swarthy foreman, high up in a caged control room,
barked orders in Mongolian over a tinny-sounding elec-
tronic loudspeaker. "Team Ten, move those parts to the
assembly area, now!"

"Do you understand what he's saying?" Sawyer asked.

The old adventurer shook his head. "At least he's not
raising the alarm. Come on, this way." He moved out.

"You lead, I'll follow." Sawyer crept after him in a
stealthy crouch. They moved on together, unnoticed.

The prison passage was silent and empty. The guards
were bored and sleepy; they did not realize the emergency until it was much too late.

Before they could call for help, Hyde had punched
them both and hurled the men against a far wall. They
could barely muster a whimpering groan while slumping
unconscious to the floor.

Hyde strode forward with a lurching, stalking gait,
forced to duck his massive head beneath a low ceiling. In
the beast-man's wake, Captain Nemo and several armed
crewmen entered the passage and approached the heavy
iron floor grates.

Nemo motioned the fearsome Hyde back as he
crouched on the grate and peered into the dungeons
below. He saw the hopeful faces of hostages turned up to
look at him. "These must be the scientists' wives and
children."

In a flash of memory, he thought of his own wife and son, both tragically killed. His fingers clenched, and he had to force the thoughts away. Nemo called upon his philosophy and his prayers, just to make his heart go numb again, his past go blank.

He put a finger to his lips, and the hostages inside fell quiet, stifling their confusion and joy. "We will rescue you. Do not be frightened." He signaled for Hyde to come forward, and as the brutish man's shadow fell over the grate, Nemo held out a hand to calm the captives. "Do not be frightened of *him*."

He and his crewmen gave Hyde room to work. Jekyll's monstrous alter ego bent over the grates and wrapped both of his hands around them. His back muscles strained, his biceps bulged, the cords in his neck stood out as taut as piano strings.

Then with a screeching groan, the metal grate tore free, ripping mortar and stones loose. Snarling at his own strength, Hyde lifted the heavy set of bars over his head and made as if to hurl them down the tunnel, but Nemo stepped in front of him, fearless, and gestured for silence. Disappointed, Hyde set the grate down with a thud on the tunnel floor.

Nemo extended a hand, and the first hostage reached out to take it. He helped her out of the cell, and the rest of the terrified captives began to stream out. "You are free now, but you are not yet safe."

He and Hyde kept watch as the *Nautilus* crewmen guided the escaping prisoners down the echoing tunnels. One by one, the captives climbed out of the cell chamber, blinking and frightened.

Karl Draper, disheveled and desperate, emerged from

the pit and clutched the sleeve of Nemo's uniform. "Please, sir—he has my daughter. That horrible Fantom . . . he took Eva!" His voice cracked with despair, as if he had already imagined endless nightmares of what M might be doing with her.

Beside him, Hyde growled.

"If she's here in the fortress, we shall bring her to you," Nemo said. He could see the anguish on the structural engineer's face. "Now go with the others. Get away from this place."

Though the group was large, they moved like phantoms down the narrow passage back toward the sluice gate—and their escape. Glancing over his shoulder for reassurance, bald and mousy Karl Draper scuttled after them. Hyde looked at the German scientist and sniffed, as if Draper reminded him of Henry Jekyll.

Neither the brutish man nor Nemo noted one of the two stunned guards recovering. Slumped against the passage wall where Hyde had hurled him, the guard stifled a groan. His head hurt, his jaw felt as if it had been knocked halfway around his head . . . not so different from a typical hangover.

But when he opened his eyes he was confused by all the people and the noise outside the prison pit. Next to him, his partner still lay crumpled, out cold. Then he saw Hyde, a misshapen anthropoid monster standing next to the torn metal grate while the last of the prisoners fled down the corridor.

Even before his focus and balance returned, the guard let out a yelping scream, stumbled to his feet, and turned to run.

Hyde grunted with surprise and turned his coal-black

eyes to see the man running away. Nemo, also startled, gave chase, but the frantic guard raced down the halls in absolute panic. He bleated for help like a terrified sheep. His wailing shouts echoed back through the passages, calling out a warning; Nemo didn't need to translate the Mongolian words to understand the message.

The captain came back, panting from the effort, adjusting the turban on his head. "We have trouble."

"Trouble?" Hyde said with a twisted grin. His eyes lit with anticipation. "I'd call it . . . sport." He cracked his hairy knuckles.

Inside the foundry, workers and guards labored under the intense heat and spraying sparks. Despite the flaring light of molten metal and furnace fires, there were still enough shadows to offer hiding places, if necessary.

Not that an invisible man needed the shadows.

A hot spark flicked through the air and settled on his bare skin. Skinner snuffed it out, restraining his reaction to no more than a hiss. It gave him all the more incentive to blow this whole place to Hell.

His invisible hands held three bombs that glided through the smoky air. He made his way behind the largest furnace and planted the first bomb at the base of the hot brick structure. Skinner hid the explosive and set the timer, already thinking of the best places to install the other two bombs.

One of the guards looked up, thinking he heard an amused chuckle and skipping footsteps that moved out of the foundry at a rapid pace. But he saw nothing, so he turned back to shout orders at his workers again.

42

M's Private Parlor

Moving with all the stealth they could manage, Quatermain and Sawyer left the dirty, industrial floors of the fortress and entered brighter, well-lit corridors with fine furnishings and clean white walls. It was in this area that the two men expected to find M.

They approached a set of opulent doors. The daring young American tested the scrolled golden handles and found the doors unlocked. With barely a click, they opened and quietly swung inward. Sawyer poked his head inside and stared in astonishment.

M's sumptuous boudoir contained a vast bed, paintings, vases, a red crushed-velvet divan, and fresh flowers and fruit that must have been worth more than gold here in this isolated winter landscape. In the boudoir's adjoining templelike bathing area, a warm-flowing fountain bath spilled a steaming cascade into a marble tub.

Quatermain waved his companion to utter silence as the two men entered, guns leading, alert for anything. The young man wrinkled his nose at the perfumes in the air. The hideous masked "Fantom" had not seemed like a man to enjoy a long scented bath. . . .

A human-shaped shadow flitted behind a painted silk screen in an adjacent side chamber. Quatermain froze, but the figure did not come closer. The two men hadn't been seen, and the sloshing of the waterfall bath muffled the sound of their approach. Together, they advanced toward the chamber door.

As the old adventurer reached for the door of the side chamber, the handle turned before he could touch it. He and Sawyer ducked into an alcove and flattened themselves against the wall.

The door opened, and a lovely young woman stepped out, her gaze fixed forward. She had long straw-blond hair that hung straight and limp, as if she no longer cared for it. Her loose gown was pale blue and should have been beautiful, but she wore it like a burial shroud. Like a wraith or a sleepwalker, she drifted wide-eyed and dazed past the two men in the alcove.

Quatermain recognized her from a sepia-toned photograph in the files M himself had provided, ostensibly to help them track down the heinous Fantom. How arrogant of the man! But Quatermain did not doubt the truth of the information. He knew who this young woman was: Eva Draper, the daughter of kidnapped architectural engineer, who had been abducted from the Valkyrie Zeppelin Works near Hamburg.

When she had gone, the two men slipped out of their hiding place and ducked into M's parlor to look around, ready for anything. Sawyer held his Winchester in a tight grip, eager to start shooting.

The Fantom's silver mask lay on a table, reflecting the candlelight.

Quatermain heard a noise, low conversation, movement from across the room in an antechamber. He hesitated, then crept forward so that he could see the angled reflection of an ornate dressing mirror. He got Sawyer's attention, and both of them watched.

The mirror's image showed the antechamber, where a fastidiously dressed valet was calmly shaving the cadaverous M, who lounged back in a chair. M seemed completely relaxed as the fastidious man stroked his cheek and neck with the gleaming silver razor, removing white cream. The man scraped away another swath, knowing it would mean his death if he so much as nicked the leader's skin. The valet had already helped M into his clothing, leaving only the black jacket and gloves on the vanity. It looked as if the evil mastermind were preparing to go to the opera.

The Fantom's lieutenant Dante strode into the parlor, carrying a bulky leather case similar to a doctor's satchel. Quatermain and Sawyer pressed themselves further into the shadows as the man walked past, but Dante was intent on M.

As the valet continued his work, Dante set the leather satchel on a table. "James, here's your box of tricks, as you asked. I think you'll find everything you need inside." He opened the case, tilting it to show M the contents.

M sat up, his close-set eyes vulturelike in the flickering candlelight. The lieutenant displayed each item, like a snake-oil salesman demonstrating his wares. "The brute's potion, the vampire's blood, the Indian's science, and mounted samples of invisible skin." He lifted liquid-filled vials, a scrap of bloodstained fabric, bits of ceramic, daguerreotypes, microscope slides, and rolled-up technical plans on thin paper. "No matter what else happens, you will have the most important components, sir."

With quick, confident strokes, the valet finished shaving M's upper lip. Though it was none of his business, the valet mused, "So much, and yet it seems like nothing. You're expecting trouble, sir?"

"Always." M regarded the kit with satisfaction. It amazed him that the future of the world could fit inside such a small bag. The valet wiped the last specks of cream from M's face and removed the moist towels. M ran a hand over his smooth chin and upper lip with pleasure, then sent the valet away with his shaving paraphernalia.

Before Dante could depart as well, a ragged-looking guard burst in. "Intruders! An Indian and a monster!" He reeled, holding his head as if he had just awakened from a bad dream, or groggy unconsciousness. "The prisoners are escaping!"

M groaned. "How many times must I kill these cretins?" He knew that if Nemo and Hyde were here causing trouble, the rest of the League would, in all likelihood, be inside the fortress, too. He turned to Dante, who could already see annoyance building to rage on the leader's face. The threat in M's cold voice seemed directed as much at Dante as at the intended victims. "Make this the last time. Be certain of it."

Leaving the leather satchel behind, Dante rushed out as the first shouts and sounds of battle echoed from the factory levels far below.

Alone now, the freshly shaved M moved to the table, pulled on his jacket, and reached for his silver Fantom's mask, ready for the show. He picked up the metal covering and glimpsed a distorted, moving reflection. He froze as a long gun barrel pressed against the back of his head.

"Don't move, M," Quatermain said from behind him.

Tom Sawyer stepped around the corner, also leveling his Winchester at the mastermind. He looked ready to use it. "You killed Huck Finn."

Caught in the line of fire, M froze, looking at both men as if they were large sewer rats that had found their way into a garden party. "Huck? Who?"

"Agent Huck Finn of the American Secret Service."

M shrugged. "I've killed so many people. I can't be expected to remember them all."

"Perhaps we can offer you a reminder, M." Quatermain stepped around, leaning closer and holding the cadaverous man in his hunter's gaze. "Or would you prefer that we call you . . . *Professor?* Professor James Moriarty."

Sawyer caught a breath, recognizing the name. "You mean . . . the man who killed Sherlock Holmes?"

M was shocked and inwardly furious that Quatermain had figured out his real identity. "Holmes, yes—I suppose you would have wanted him as part of your League, as well. As if even Holmes could have helped you!"

When he turned to look at them, the mastermind showed them a feral, calculating personality. Wanton. Spiteful. *Professor James Moriarty.*

Moriarty thought back to the rush of water like deadly white hammers, pounding over the sheer rocky walls. Reichenbach Falls, in Switzerland. A narrow path, slippery with spray, wound up the side of a cliff to the edge of the thundering cascade.

His archenemy Holmes had gotten there first—had been *lured* there—and stood just upslope wearing his dark green jacket, yellow vest, starched collar, and trademark deerstalker cap. He carried an alpenstock walking stick but no other weapon, though he must have known he would be in for the fight of his life. He seemed not at all surprised to see Moriarty there.

"Well, here we are then," Moriarty had said, facing his nemesis. His red-lined black cape flapped in the cold, wet breezes from the roaring waterfall.

Holmes had agreed. "Indeed. As closing acts go, I'll allow the scenery is more than adequate."

"Why, sir, it is Olympian! We tread the very borders of mythology!"

"I think you flatter both of us." Holmes had not been impressed. As usual, he had cut to the chase. "I'm tired with talk, Professor. So, then. To the death?"

"Oh, yes. Yes, absolutely."

They had struggled on the edge of the falls, Moriarty with a gold-hilted dagger, Holmes with his bare hands. But Holmes, damnable Holmes, had caught his wrist, knocked the dagger free, and thrown him over the ledge, where the professor had tumbled into the torrent of smothering spray . . . taking a long, wrenching plunge that had ended in sucking whirlpools, surging water, and hard bone-breaking rocks—

But he had emerged alive after all . . . irrevocably changed.

"You name me James Moriarty? The so-called Napoleon of Crime?" M took a step closer to Quatermain, who did not move. Sawyer loudly cocked his Winchester; M ignored him. "No, Mr. Quatermain—

that man died at the Reichenbach Falls. He died, and *I* was reborn. M. The Fantom. More than mere Moriarty ever was . . . more than you'll ever be." He gave a sneering sniff. "The League of Extraordinary Gentlemen! Ha!"

"He does like the sound of his own voice," Quatermain said to Sawyer.

At that moment, Eva Draper rushed into the room, blond hair in disarray, and charged at Moriarty. Her robe flapped around her, and she gripped a dagger in her hand. "Monster!" she cried in German.

Sawyer swung his Winchester aside, startled. Quatermain lifted a hand to stop the young woman's attack. "It's all right. We have him —"

But Eva threw herself on her captor. Grateful for the distraction, Moriarty knocked Eva aside and snatched up his box of tricks. Quatermain lunged after him, giving chase, but when Moriarty reached the door, he whirled and hurled a stiletto. The blade flashed through the air.

Sawyer tackled Quatermain to the floor, saving his life as the slim knife stuck into the wall. He grinned at the astonished expression on the hunter's face. "Eyes open, old boy. I can't protect you all the time."

43

M's Fortress

The Fantom's armed guards raced toward a corner of a low stone passage. Some carried high-tech automatic firearms; others wielded heavy Mongolian swords.

Instead of attacking the infiltrators, though, these guards were running *away* at full speed.

Gunfire cracked, and the men screamed and fled faster, fearing Nemo's crewmen behind them. They raced away—never realizing that they were running straight toward Mr. Hyde.

Fists clenched, the broad-shouldered, brutish monster stood blocking the passage. He grinned, showing crooked teeth, and roared with a powerful exhalation of hot breath. All around him on the floor lay the twisted and broken bodies of his earlier victims.

The guards scrambled to a halt. Some turned, running into the guards behind them. But they could not go back, either, meeting a blur of deadly blows from Captain Nemo's hands and feet. They were astonished by his power and speed.

Hyde came after them from the rear, swinging his fists

like big mallets. Heads knocked together, bones cracked, blood spurted . . . and Hyde chuckled.

"Where are the rest of the scientists?" Nemo demanded of his victims, kicking and pummeling the guards, then discarding them after he had beaten them senseless. Sooner or later, one of them was sure to talk before he collapsed into unconsciousness.

"You can tell him . . . or tell *me!*" Hyde's voice thundered in an avalanche of heavy words. He lumbered forward, shouting at the few remaining doomed guards. *"Where are they?"*

M's guards didn't resist much longer, and Nemo soon learned where to lead his men.

When they reached the mezzanine, Hyde punched open an iron door with repeated blows that resounded like heavy strikes on a gong. The metal barrier bent and twisted away as Hyde tore it from its hinges. As soon as the opening was wide enough, Nemo and his crewmen burst through, heading for the laboratory and the imprisoned weapons scientists.

Opposite them, Dante rushed down a steep stone staircase leading a cadre of hand-picked henchmen, who ran in lockstep. The Fantom's lieutenant saw the infiltrators and instantly barked a command. "There they are! Shoot! Full automatic fire!"

With the new-model repeating rifles, M's henchmen locked their weapons and opened fire, strafing the area around the *Nautilus* crewmen. Bullets ricocheted off the floor and walls and sang through the air, flashing sparks. Ducking for whatever shelter they could find, the crewmen drew their own weapons and returned the compliment.

Two of Nemo's men fell with mortal wounds, either from ricochets or intentional fire. A bullet cracked into the wall less than an inch from Nemo's turban. "We are too vulnerable here! There's no cover!"

Hyde growled as if a swarm of gnats was annoying him. He snatched up the fallen iron door and raised it to protect the crew. Muscles straining, he held the metal sheet up as a shield and listened to the hailstorm of bullets that vibrated against it.

Nemo touched the bodies of his two fallen comrades, searching for a pulse. When he found none, his expression darkened even further.

First Mate Patel and another of the *Nautilus* men moved closer to Hyde's hairy body so that they could fire around the edge of the door-shield. Across the open expanse, Lieutenant Dante dove for cover, and three of his men died in the crossfire. Their bodies tumbled from the staircase down to the factory floor far below. . . .

As the shooting continued, several bullets hit crucial gauges and spinning components in the industrial equipment. Shrapnel buzzed and bounced. Another of the Fantom's henchmen fell with a startled cry, headfirst, into a fabrication machine, shattering its front panels.

Steam built up from machine regulators that had been shot away in the gunfire. Whistling pressure grew unbearable, screaming through relief valves that were too hopelessly small—until finally two of the large tanks exploded in unison. Clouds of steam gushed out like fountaining blood from a severed artery.

As the chaos increased, several fuel barrels ignited. Flames followed waves of spilling flammable liquid. On the factory floor, teams of workers and armed guards alike lost their nerve and ran in every direction.

Defined briefly by a shower of sparks, Skinner shrieked, caught in the stampede as he planted another bomb under a fuel stack. "God, this hero lark is touch and go. Heh!"

The invisible man had to admit, though, that this was quite the little party.

44

M's Fortress
Dorian Gray's Chambers

In his sumptuous private room supplied by M, Dorian Gray packed his case with the barest of necessities for the long trip. He could always buy the essentials—both legal and illegal—en route. It was a long way back to London, and civilization, but he could make do.

Still, he abhorred being uncomfortable.

His bulky framed picture leaned against one wall, wrapped and bound up in burlap. It would be a devil to carry. Gray couldn't see the image on the portrait, though he could imagine his corrupted features, the weeping sores, the leprous face and age-withered skin. His immortality spell would be broken if he gazed on the painting, but he had no particular interest in seeing it. He would rather look in a mirror.

He smiled and did just that, fixing his hair, adjusting his collar. All ready to go. Gray snapped his travel case shut and moved to pick up his wrapped picture.

Far below in the fortress Gray heard the sound of gunfire, explosions, shouts of alarm, running feet. He shook his head. More of M's antics, convoluted plans, devious schemes . . . The leader made world domination into such a complicated and undesirable prospect. M was perfectly welcome to all the woes associated with his unhealthy ambition.

A dark wraith passed silently behind him, and he sensed it with a shiver. He glanced up in time to see his mirror glass ice up. Then, hearing the whisper of a noise, he whirled, catlike.

Mina Harker stood there, spectral and vampiric in the gloom. Her green eyes blazed, and she held a knife in her hand. "Hello, lover." Her voice was like the purr of a hungry lioness. She stroked the razor edge of the blade with her fingertip.

"You're alive," said Gray. He dropped his travel case and let the framed painting lean against the stone wall. Then he smoothly drew his cane-sword.

"I'm a vampire . . . part of me, at least. No matter what some traitor does to me, it's possible I can't die." She smiled, revealing her sharp fangs. "The same could be said of you, Dorian Gray." Mina stepped forward, never letting her gaze waver. "Let's put it to the test."

Snarling, she leaped at him, knife in one hand, claws extended on the other. Gray lifted his cane-sword just in time and parried, whipping the slim blade through the air. Her dagger clanged against it. Again and again, knife clashed against sword. They both panted from the effort. The flush on their faces came as much from their emotions as from the battle itself.

"It seems the League does not consider me much of a threat," Gray said, sounding disappointed. "They sent a woman to fight me?"

"I'm nothing if not emancipated."

Mina drove him backward, and he tripped on his

travel case. But Gray sprang back to his feet and jumped to the top of a table, kicking away the dirty plate and silverware from his afternoon snack. She ducked the flying utensils even as he continued their bitter conversation.

"Join me in London, Mina. Give in to your demons." Gray leaped backward to the floor, landing with perfect grace. "We will be a league of two. Just you and me."

"Dream on." Mina sprang over the table at him.

He slashed with his thin sword. "I don't dream. My body doesn't require sleep."

"You can sleep when you're dead," Mina said. "I'd be happy to help."

"You wicked tease. You talk as if you could do me harm," Gray said. Her dagger scored a red line along his left cheek. He flinched and countered her next strike with his cane-sword, but by then his cut had already healed.

"I'm a woman. I can do all sorts of things." She sprang into the air, skirts flowing, skittered upside down on the ceiling, and landed on her feet behind Gray. She drew back her arm before he could spin to face her, and plunged the long dagger into his back.

He gasped. "Minx!" He twisted around to drag the knife out of his back.

"Do you realize what you've done? What you've let out of me?" Mina snatched the knife blade out of his hand so fast that she broke several of his finger bones.

"A woman's wrath?" He straightened his fingers with a crackle and stood, letting the deep stab wound in his back heal. "Oh, I'm petrified."

Mina leaped at Gray again and slashed his exposed throat, splitting skin, throbbing blood vessels, muscles and sinews. Like a zipper closing, the wound healed.

Then, with a mighty thrust through the stomach, he impaled her on his long cane-sword. He shoved the blade all the way through, and she staggered away. But her wound healed as well.

"We'll be at this all day," Gray said with a sigh, then threw himself at her again.

45

M's Fortress

Through mazelike passages, Quatermain and Sawyer raced after Moriarty. The man moved like a ferret, streaking up the stairs, turning corners, dashing down hallways, always a few turns ahead of them. All the while, he never let go of his leather satchel that contained the items he needed to reproduce the exotic powers of the League of Extraordinary Gentlemen.

Though he was older, Quatermain pulled ahead of his young companion, concentrating only on catching the evil mastermind before he could find a way to escape, as he'd done so many times before. Quatermain shouldered his guns, saving his breath rather than shouting threats at the Fantom.

Sawyer lagged behind and held up his Winchester, hoping to fire it at M. The young American concentrated on his aim, still running headlong—and suddenly tripped on something unseen. His legs went out from under him, and he tumbled to the floor. His rifle clattered away. He heard a half-maniacal chuckle and saw the outline of an invisible man fall into a hanging tapestry on the wall.

"Skinner!" Sawyer cried in disgust. He sprawled on the floor, out of the chase now.

As Moriarty ducked around a corner, Quatermain looked back to make sure his young friend was all right. He couldn't wait, or the villain would escape. Sawyer waved to urge him on, and the old adventurer continued his pursuit.

The young American climbed to his feet and rounded on the unseen thief. "What the heck are you doing here, Skinner?" He brushed himself off, wanting to strangle the thief. "Now look what you did."

The invisible man continued to chuckle thinly, but the voice sounded very strange. "What makes you think I'm Skinner?" The transparent man untangled himself from the hanging fabric, and a floating knife came into view with him. "He's not here. My name is Sanderson Reed!"

The other invisible man attacked with the very visible weapon.

In the high keep of the fortress, an iron-hard door flew open, and Moriarty dashed into a stone-walled prison chamber. Quatermain bellowed after him.

This room had once been an impenetrable bastion of torture and horror, built by the Cossacks and their power-mad czar—but the place was now forgotten, cobwebbed and filled with opulent detritus. Snow blew through narrow spy slits and drifted over sealed wooden crates of books, tarpaulin-covered old furniture, and faded tapestries.

Plenty of places to hide.

Moriarty dove into the shadows, sinking down spider-silent as Quatermain entered, panting hard. He instantly quieted himself, trying to control his heavy breathing and the pounding of his heart.

Taking the time to study the room, letting his hunter instincts take over, he scanned for the dark-garbed man . . . and saw him crouching in the shadows. He raised the spare Winchester and drew a bead on his adversary. He couldn't possibly miss.

Quatermain had learned over the years that a hesitant shot usually let the quarry get away. He had tried to teach his son that lesson, too long ago, too late. And he had no intention of letting his quarry get away now.

"End of the line, Moriarty," he said quietly. M looked up, reacting with apparent surprise to see the heavy rifle pointed directly at him.

Quatermain pulled the trigger, and the Winchester let out a roar.

The evil genius shattered. Long pieces of reflective glass tumbled all around as the bullet demolished a mirror propped in view of the door.

Quatermain spun, taken aback as the real Moriarty charged out of the shadows with a wild yell, swinging a Mongolian mace. The deadly spiked chain-ball whistled through the air an inch from Quatermain's face.

The old hunter instinctively blocked the second blow with the Winchester in his hand. The heavy spiked ball smashed into the stock of the sturdy American rifle—demolishing both gun and mace handle.

Moriarty took a moment to recover, but he never fought with less than cold calculation. He tossed the mace handle aside and landed a heavy blow with his other hand, punching Quatermain square on the old shoulder wound, where the Fantom's stiletto had stabbed him in the Venice cemetery.

Quatermain roared in pain and swung the Winchester's broken stock at Moriarty. The evil mastermind sidestepped, moving with a feral grace. He stuck out a long bony leg to trip Quatermain, who fell, unable to get his elephant gun free in time.

As the old hunter went down, Matilda's straps snapped. The big elephant gun skittered into the cluttered shadows of the old torture chamber.

Moriarty stepped back and snatched up a wicked, bent rod of forged iron. It looked as if many times it had been heated red hot and used to sizzle the flesh off of pitiful victims. Though cold now, the iron bar was still capable of being an effective bludgeon.

"To the death." Moriarty advanced on Quatermain.

The hunter prepared himself for the fight. "*Your* death."

M gave a thin, cold smile. "You'll need Hyde here to make it *my* death, Quatermain."

46

M's Fortress

Under fire in the mezzanine, the *Nautilus* crewmen held their own, taking risky shots at M's henchmen whenever they could. But they could not last here forever. The tumult continued below them on the factory floor. Workers shouted and ran; steam tanks exploded.

Nemo himself saw a way down into the laboratory. "Hold them here, Hyde. I will take care of what we came for."

The brutish man grunted his assent, still holding the heavy metal door as a barricade against the furious hail of bullets. Hyde's muscles bulged, and veins stood out on his hairy skin, but he didn't seem at all flustered. "Go ahead."

Hyde coughed a mouthful of phlegm and spewed it around the side of the metal shield. Moriarty's men scrambled out of the way, as if the bestial man's fuming spit might be as deadly as bullets. They weren't necessarily wrong.

Dante called curt orders to his men. "This takes too much time. Summon the fighter, so that we may finish them off."

The shower of bullets ricocheting off the thick metal

shield in Hyde's grip diminished to an occasional patter. Nemo's crewmen tensed, wondering what other bizarre secret weapons the evil mastermind might have in store. Hyde growled and let the immense iron sheet rest on the flagstoned floor with a thud. He breathed stentoriously. Waiting.

Then a clanking noise boomed out even louder than the continuing explosions from the factory floor. Something huge and heavy plodded up behind the massed ranks of enemy soldiers. Dante whistled, summoning the massive mechanical threat forward.

Hyde peered around his shelter, and his bulging, bloodshot eyes widened. An ironclad "tank man" thudded forward, twelve feet tall—a man in a colossal, rivet-studded gladiator suit, powered by an electrical motor that crackled with blue sparks along its pistons and joints. Each footstep sounded like a falling boulder.

The tank man paused at the front of Dante's cadre, and the beleaguered henchmen backed away in awe. The Fantom's lieutenant grinned in anticipation at the fate of his cornered prey.

The ironclad tank man raised a titanic steel-plated arm, showing a circular cluster of long tubes—heavy-caliber gun barrels that rotated around a central axis. Captain Nemo would have recognized the design as an extension of the horrifically destructive Gatling gun introduced decades before in the American Civil War. Edward Hyde knew only that it was dangerous.

With a blast of steam and a crackle of power from thrumming electrical motors, the rotating Gatling launcher locked into position. Explosive artillery shells *thunk*ed into launching tubes.

Hyde had just enough time to pick up the thick iron shield again before the tank man opened fire.

Nemo fought his way to the guarded laboratory where captive scientists were being forced to develop ever-more sophisticated weapons for M's war against the entire world. Though he had reached his destination, the *Nautilus* captain's struggle was just beginning.

The Fantom's guards shouted, and Nemo crouched, keeping his limbs loose in his blue-sleeved uniform, his hands extended as weapons. The scientists watched the strange turbaned man, not daring to hope. Outside the laboratory prison, they could hear the clamor of continuing battles.

Nemo moved farther into the room. Seeing only one opponent, the guards drew their thick Mongolian swords and strode toward him. He gave them a welcoming smile.

In a flash, Nemo waded into the group of armed men, kicked a guard squarely in the chin with his left foot, and used his right fist to crush the larynx of a second. The bellowing guards swung their swords, but he moved too fast. Their curved blades swept like threatening whispers through empty air; some struck sparks from the stone wall.

Surging into the laboratory, the captain grabbed up a stool vacated by a scrambling scientist and punched a charging guard in the stomach with the long hard legs, then swung the seat around in a smooth lightning strike to his head. The guard crumpled to the floor, his skull split open.

Seven guards remained, but at the moment Nemo wasn't counting.

To a certain extent, he let his body act and react on a subconscious level, flying in an ecstatic release of blows and moves. He had seen the wild gyrations of the true Sufi dervishes in India, enlightened ascetics who threw themselves into a state of complete abandon. It was more than just dancing, it was a possession—like the berserkers on Viking battlefields. Nemo had incorporated elements of this approach into his fighting.

But he also prized his sharp and insightful mind. Even as the captain flung himself into a whirlwind of battle, he remained aware of himself and his goal. All the Fantom's henchmen together could not possibly withstand the onslaught of this lone man.

Nemo used tools and laboratory instruments to deadly effect, proving that a long metal T square from a blueprint table could be as dangerous as a sword. He smashed beakers, threw boiling acid into another man's eyes. A blackboard full of equations crashed down onto a guard's shoulders, and Nemo knocked him senseless with a sharp elbow blow to the temple.

Everything in his grasp became a weapon, and when he held nothing, his bare hands served him well enough. Before long, he had taken out every guard.

Catching his balance and his breath, Nemo turned to the stunned scientists who had watched him in awe. All around him the laboratory lay in ruins: tables splintered, chalk-scrawled blackboards shattered, notes and plans strewn on the floor.

The captive engineers and scientists stared, as speechless with fear of this stranger as they were of the masked Fantom—until he told them what they needed to hear.

"You are free."

*   *   *

Hyde struggled to hold the thick iron door steady against the coming attack. With a whistling cry in flight, the first of the large-caliber shells from the tank man's Gatling gun slammed into the heavy shield. Hyde staggered backward. The sound of the impact was deafening.

"Get back!" he snarled to the *Nautilus* crewmen, who still held their weapons ready, still hoping to take shots at Dante's cadre, though the remaining henchmen had taken shelter, leaving the battle to the armored colossus. "Go!"

Another artillery shell struck the iron shield like a meteor, making it shudder in Hyde's grasp. Two impact craters now bent the barrier inward, but the shield held. The high-caliber projectile ricocheted off to the side, striking high on a wall. A stone arch crumbled.

Hyde got the glimmer of an idea. It was enough.

The ironclad tank man took two heavy steps forward. The Gatling cylinder rotated, bringing the next shell into position. He fired a third heavy projectile, then another, and another.

The shells flew at him in rapid succession, and each time Hyde used the heavy iron shield to deflect them. One shell struck the ceiling, bringing part of it down. He tilted the door in a crude attempt at aiming the ricocheting shells.

The second caromed off toward Dante's huddled henchmen, detonated, and sent screaming bodies flying.

Hyde's third attempt flew true, blasting the ironclad titan in the armored torso and exploding with spectacular results.

Shrapnel showered everywhere. The remains of the

ironclad tank man toppled backward like a fallen Go-liath. Armor plates, weapons, and jointed metal lay collapsed in a pile of wreckage.

When the smoke and dust cleared sufficiently, Hyde surveyed the mess with pride and satisfaction.

The rest of Dante's cadre turned and fled.

47

M's Fortress

Sawyer scrambled backward as Sanderson Reed's dagger came down and slashed repeatedly on all sides. Reed's accompanying thin laughter sounded like breaking glass.

The young agent swayed, bent, and twisted like a willow tree, evading the deadly point. His Winchester lay across the hall, where it had fallen after the unseen killer sent him sprawling.

Seeing no other choice, intent on avenging his murdered friend Huck, the American lunged forward and grabbed the sharp dancing blade itself—the only part of his assailant he could see. Although his hand stung and bled, Sawyer never wavered. It was like teasing snapping turtles on the Mississippi.

Sawyer struggled with the invisible bureaucrat in a savage pantomime. Blood streamed from his slashed hand. He kicked out at thin air and sent Reed stumbling backward into the wall, stunning him for long enough that he could scramble over to snatch up his rifle.

Holding the Winchester out in front of him, he

backed away from the invisible Reed. He shot in the direction of the unseen killer, striking the wall, shredding the tapestries. The invisible bureaucrat's footsteps pattered down the hall toward a closed door. Sawyer ran after him, firing repeatedly. The murderous Reed already provided an uncertain enough target; judging by the sounds, Sawyer knew he had missed each time.

His rifle clicked empty.

The moment he stopped firing, he heard slapping footsteps and saw the floating dagger streak back toward him, gripped in Reed's invisible hand. Sawyer swung his Winchester around to block the main force of the knife as it slashed him once, twice, laying open his arm.

Hissing with the pain, the young agent swung wildly with all his strength, as if the long rifle were nothing more than a tree branch he had fashioned into a club. The Winchester made a loud and very gratifying sound as it connected with the invisible attacker. Sawyer drove him backward.

Reed's invisible body crashed through the door into a chamber filled with documents, parchments, and ancient writing supplies. Still reeling, Reed staggered backward, senseless, into a low shelf of ink powders.

Bottles and containers broke open and spilled around him, dumping lampblack and dried tints on Reed's transparent head and upper body. Groggy and injured, M's assistant struggled back to his feet. But now that he was smeared and dusted back to partial visibility, his advantage was gone.

Sawyer stood at the parchment room door with a look of determination. No scrawny little bureaucrat was a match for him. Even without bullets for his Winchester, he could take Sanderson Reed.

Suddenly a fireball erupted, splashing heat and flames like a wave of lava crashing against the wall next to the parchment room. With a yelp, Sawyer hurled himself to the side, barely avoiding another gush of fire. A few loose documents in the room ignited, and Reed himself scuttled out of the way like a half-dissolved shadow.

Sawyer glanced up, spluttering. "Now what?"

With heavy clanking footsteps, a second one of Moriarty's ironclad tank men advanced toward him down the corridor like an angry dragon. Instead of a Gatling launcher, though, this one had been rigged with a flamethrower.

Sawyer dove out of the way as another fiery river exploded toward him.

Circling and slashing, round and round, Dorian Gray and Mina Harker fought on wearily, like an old married couple—but with knives and swords. Each blow, each slash had only a temporary effect, but still they kept cutting.

Eyes flashing, fangs exposed as she grimaced with the effort, Mina managed to back Gray into the bedroom, much to his apparent delight. "The bedroom, Mina—does it give you memories?" He smiled as he swung his cane-sword again. "Or ideas?"

She leaped at him, whirled, and pushed off the wall with spiderlike agility. In a flowing movement, she ducked Gray's slash with his rapier and plunged her knife directly into his groin.

Screaming, he hunched over, backing away from her with his free hand pressed against his crotch. His fingers came away covered with already-vanishing blood. His pale face trembled with an unsettled expression. "If that had been permanent, my dear, I'd have been very upset."

A substantial explosion from the lower factory levels shook the whole room. The floor bucked and heaved, and dust showered down from the ceiling. Shouts and screams reverberated through the fortress.

Mina's momentary distraction gave Gray the perfect opportunity to skewer her in the chest. His long cane-sword thrust through her bodice, under the perfect milky breasts he had so thoroughly enjoyed, and straight through her vampire heart.

Mina gasped for air, her green eyes bulging with disbelief. She clutched ineffectually at the sword that had sprouted from her chest and out her back. Choking on words, she gave Gray one final glare of anger, then fell dead upon the bed.

Gray frowned down at her lying there. His expression was almost a pout. "I hoped I'd get to nail you one more time, dear Mina. Didn't think it'd be literally."

Inside the cluttered high keep, Quatermain and Moriarty continued their battle to the death. M clumsily swung his rusty makeshift sword, making up for any lack of finesse with unbridled violence. He slashed and parried against the old hunter's Bowie knife.

Moriarty poked viciously at his opponent's gut, but Quatermain blocked and twisted the flat iron bar aside. His move, however, gave M the opening to kidney-punch Quatermain repeatedly. With his bony knuckles, Moriarty hammered his opponent in any vulnerable place.

Fortunately, Quatermain was tougher than that. Grinding his teeth together with a wordless roar, he backhanded the gaunt mastermind with his Bowie knife, slashing at M's face. "I'll give you a real scar or two. Make you want to wear that mask again."

But Moriarty's crude metal bar blocked the knife with a resounding clang, and the impact sent both weapons clattering off into the darkness among the ancient torture paraphernalia.

M lunged after him like a madman, and Quatermain found himself on the defensive. Tripping through the clutter as he retreated, he used anything he could get his hands on, grabbing at books, lamps, iron tongs. But Moriarty was unrelenting and drove him back.

Finally Quatermain saw an opening. He managed to grab Moriarty's wrist and wrapped his other arm around his thin, sinewy throat. Pressing closer, he squeezed, trying to choke the life out of his enemy.

"I hope I have your fire when I'm your age," Moriarty said, wheezing the words through a constricted windpipe.

"You won't live beyond today. That's a promise." Quatermain pressed his angry face so close he could have bitten off M's ear.

Then from outside the chamber came a challenging roar—a voice that sounded like Hyde's. The impacts of a furious battle shook the whole room, giving Moriarty the chance to twist free again and suck in a huge gulp of air.

He head-butted Quatermain, who shook it off and head-butted Moriarty back. Moriarty staggered briefly, stunned and reeling.

Then they were both at it again.

48

After the armored colossus was defeated, Dante shouted for the rest of his fleeing cadre to turn around and redouble their attack against Mr. Hyde. "Use your bare hands if you have to! Would you rather face the Fantom?"

Many of the men clearly would, but they hesitated and came back. Then, gathering courage, they swept together, yelling as they charged forward in a concentrated offensive against the brutish man.

Now straining with the effort, Hyde protected the surviving *Nautilus* crewmen as best he could, using the battered iron shield to deflect a few frantic potshots. "Go find Nemo," he roared, and the crewmen ran to aid their captain in freeing the hostage scientists.

M's henchmen careened forward, stupidly attempting hand-to-hand combat with their monstrous opponent, but Hyde was brutal. He had no patience for the squirming annoyances that raced toward him.

Now that he no longer needed to protect the crewmen, he met their foolish charge by stomping forward and swinging the iron door like a ton-weight cricket bat.

He swatted away the first wave of henchmen, sending them flying like rag dolls over the mezzanine's edge and down into the ruined lab area.

Nemo had gathered the terrified hostage scientists and pushed them out the barred laboratory door, where they were met by his surviving crewmen. Behind him, Hyde's victims crashed spectacularly into the shattered glassware, destroying the last few scientific implements that had survived Nemo's battle with the guards.

Hyde hurled the metal door in front of him, crushing two of M's henchmen, then stalked toward the remaining few. His heavy feet trod on the fallen iron plate, under which the dying henchmen stopped squirming and started oozing. When he reached the last scrambling henchmen, his punches and blows sent battered victims flying in every direction.

Finally he faced Dante: the final man standing.

Seeing his doom approach, the Fantom's lieutenant scrambled backward, trying to find shelter as Hyde stormed in for the killing blow. Dante fumbled in his pockets, frantically searching. . . . He found it: an unbroken vial of Jekyll's potion, which he had kept for himself from the leather satchel he'd delivered to M. It was a desperate chance.

With Hyde's swollen form looming over him, Dante pried off the stopper and gulped down all the liquid.

"God, no!" Hyde howled, realizing what the man had done. "Not the whole thing!" Not even Jekyll in his weakest moments had ever consumed so much of the elixir at once.

Too late. Dante glared hatefully at him and wiped the last drops from his lips. Suddenly he writhed and screamed as the transfigurative chemical took hold.

A jet of curling flame rolled down the hall toward him, and Tom Sawyer dove headlong into the parchment room. He sprawled on the floor among rolled parchments and documents that Sanderson Reed had knocked from the shelves. But hundreds of ancient—and flammable—documents remained stored in the chamber.

The towering flamethrower man clanked to the doorway and raised a reinforced metal arm. With a whoosh, he unleashed another flood of incinerating fire, blasting the whole room while Sawyer scrambled for cover. A wall of parchments caught instantaneously.

Like a cornered river rat, Sawyer cast around for an escape route, but fireballs cut him off in every direction. The ironclad colossus closed in on him, raising the flame-throwing arm again.

From inside the armored walker suit, the voice of the Fantom's man sounded surprisingly thin and small. "You left your luck on the doorstep, boy."

Sawyer found himself trapped in a corner with nowhere left to go. The flamethrower man loomed through the burgeoning smoke and took aim with his jet arm. Just as he shot a spurt of flames, something knocked the reinforced arm aside, and the fiery blast went wide.

The walking ironclad roared in confusion, and his fire jet petered out after incinerating a wall of empty shelves. Sawyer opened his eyes and saw the armored titan struggling with an invisible assailant. A long knife protruded from between the walker's iron plates, shoved deep to reach the man's vulnerable organs. Rising smoke delineated the outline of the newcomer.

"Skinner!" Sawyer cried. "The real one this time, I hope."

"I thought you Yanks were supposed to be the cavalry," Skinner said. A grin was barely visible on his smoke-stained face.

The wounded flamethrower man spun his armored body and knocked Skinner aside with an ironclad arm. He turned his fiery nozzle in the direction of his unexpected opponent and blasted at the invisible man, who skittered away.

Skinner didn't move quickly enough, and the leading edge of fire scorched him. Large areas of his transparent skin were burned visible: a patch of his back and part of one buttock, now bubbling and blistered. He yowled and cursed in a drawn-out, incomprehensible wail.

Tom Sawyer acted without thinking. He grabbed a piece of shattered shelving and charged the armored flamethrower man from behind, rammed into him, and knocked him spinning. He whacked against the tank on the ironclad's back until he pierced the fuel reservoir. Sparks flying from the inferno in the room caught the flammable liquid and ignited the tank, causing it to spew fire like a Catherine wheel.

Sawyer rushed to where Skinner lay on the floor, burned and suffering. "Are you hurt bad?"

"Oh, no, it's really quite pleasant," the invisible man said sarcastically. "I can't wait to do it again."

Then Sawyer froze as another knife blade was suddenly pressed against his throat, drawing him up. He lifted his chin and swallowed hard.

It was Reed, still semivisible from the smeared ink powder. "You know what they say, Yank. Ask a stupid question, get a stupid answer."

49

M's Fortress

While in his excessively muscled bestial form,
Edward Hyde had never before felt intimidated. Now,
however, he staggered back from the huge and monstrous thing that Dante had become. The lieutenant's
metamorphosis left him in a horrific form that would
have made even a prehistoric carnivore tremble.

His face still rippling and writhing from the agonies
of the change, the Dante-beast loomed up, and *up*—
then he struck. The blow he landed knocked his opponent backward across the mezzanine. Hyde slammed
into a wall, smashing whole stone blocks into gravel, and
fell to the floor, stunned and drooling.

The Dante-beast lumbered forward to pummel him
again.

After Captain Nemo had sent the freed scientists fleeing
with their hostage family members, he rushed back to
the pillared mezzanine to help his fellow League member.

In his *Nautilus,* Nemo had seen awesome sights that few
men alive had witnessed: sunken cities, undersea moun-

tains and volcanoes, a horrific giant squid. But when he saw what Dante had become, he froze in disbelief.

The Fantom's lieutenant was now twelve feet tall, tremendously deformed, engorged with muscle and sinew. His spine had twisted, as if unable to support so much power and fury. His face, no longer even remotely human, was swollen with popped blood vessels and spiny facial hair that grew like a forest of bristles.

Hyde struggled to his feet just in time to meet Dante's next charge. The larger beast-man stormed at him. The force of his roundhouse punch sent the League member careening into a thick support pillar. The stone column cracked, teetered, and fell, bringing down a precarious arch. Hyde fell amid a shower of stones and rubble that blocked the exit passage.

A thick arm knocked the heavy blocks away, and Hyde hauled himself out of the rock pile. The Dante-beast immediately waded toward him and began his merciless assault once again.

Though he was being battered to a pulp, Hyde broke the attack and swung a powerful uppercut. "Come on, then, if you fancy a ruckus." The blow slammed the Dante-beast back into a structural column, toppling it and collapsing another section of the ceiling.

As Hyde continued to advance, Nemo joined him, a wicked scimitar held in his right hand, his left raised and ready to assist with the fight. Despite his martial arts skills and the curved blade, the captain looked absurdly small in the company of the two behemoths.

Hyde stopped him with an outstretched hand as large as Nemo's head. "No, no. Leave this to me." He cracked his knuckles. "This will be my pleasure."

Reeling to his feet again, the Dante-beast charged at Hyde. Hyde ran back at him. They looked like two stampeding rhinos.

On one voyage when he had visited mysterious Japan, Nemo had seen a match of enormously fat Sumo wrestlers. Although this colossal struggle brought back the memory, that contest had been a mere child's game in comparison.

Hyde and Dante collided like two locomotives, giving Nemo a ringside seat at their gargantuan battle.

Standing over his bed, Dorian Gray turned from Mina's body. She lay sprawled, impaled on the thin sword. Gray sighed wistfully. "You were so lovely."

"Why thank you." Mina stood and pulled the sword from her chest.

Gray whirled in disbelief.

"You stole my heart once a long time ago, Dorian. This time you missed."

She somersaulted from the bed and skewered Gray with his own rapier. The energy of the impact drove him backward, and they hit the wall together. Mina added extra force, shoving the point of the sword with all her vampiric strength.

Then she backed away and dusted her hands, as if trying to wipe away the contamination of his touch. Gray tried to move, squirming left and right, but found that he was firmly affixed to the wall, helpless.

Mina ran to the other side of the room and snatched up his wrapped painting, which still leaned against the wall. She turned it toward him.

"Mina," Gray said warily, then grew more frantic. He

tugged at his cane-sword to free himself, but to no avail. He was stuck like an insect pinned to a mounting board.

With razor-sharp nails, Mina tore at the burlap covering. "You spoke once before of wanting to atone, Dorian. You wanted to face your inner demon."

Gray's terror grew with each shred of cloth that she peeled away from his painting.

"Well, here he is!" Mina exposed the entire picture of Dorian Gray.

In the painting, Gray's face—barely recognizable as a corrupted version of his youthful, handsome features—was wizened with age, leprous, oozing, swollen, and rotted from the accumulation of decades of evil debauchery. It was a symphony of horrors wrapped in an approximation of human form, carrying the weight of far more age and poison and decrepitude than any one person could endure.

Gray was transfixed by the true appearance of his soul—the last thing he would see. As he hung pinned to the wall by his cane-sword, his perfect, youthful face began to crease and peel. He gasped, writhed, *screamed,* while his body aged and rotted, until he took on the precise appearance of the painting—its degeneration, the cracked and peeling texture.

Mina looked away, her face resolute, yet her eyes brimmed with regretful tears. Dorian Gray withered and shriveled and finally died as nothing more than a twisted mummy.

At the same time, the image on his portrait became younger, restored to the likeness Mina remembered . . . and loved.

50

Nemo threw himself into the titanic battle between Hyde and the Dante-beast, but the two mammoth combatants paid little attention to him. Dante knocked the captain aside with an offhanded smack, then began to pummel Hyde again. The two monsters had reduced the mezzanine to rubble. Rocks continued to fall from the unsupported ceiling.

Though battered and bloody, Nemo remained determined. He drew a deep breath, quelled the pain through direct mental effort, sprang to his feet, and dashed back into the fray. He had studied philosophy and mental discipline, as well as sophisticated fighting skills; he knew he was not as insignificant as the Dante-beast seemed to consider him.

With a mighty blow, the Fantom's horrific lieutenant slammed Hyde through another stone pillar. Nemo attacked Dante from behind, his scimitar flashing. Each slash with the curved blade drew a thin line of blood—little more than a shaving nick—but Nemo struck again and again. He scored the Dante-beast's tough hide.

Although each individual stroke caused only the

slightest of injuries and pain, the captain knew it to be a subtle technique, most often used for torture. The brutal ancient khans had called it the "death of a thousand cuts." Now it might be his only chance.

But before Nemo could wear down the enemy, Dante backhanded him. The beast's massive hand was like a battering ram, and the captain sailed through the air like no more than a leaf blown by a strong wind, his blue turban askew. Still grasping his scimitar, he tucked his head and arms, rolling as he struck the wall, and landed only partially stunned beside Hyde. They had both fallen into a cold, disused ash pit.

Hyde picked himself up and flexed his bulging arms, searching for something to hit. Grabbing a stone block that had fallen into the rubble around them, he hurled it at the near wall.

Nemo threw off his pain and groggy confusion, then made a rapid assessment of their situation. "We're trapped. He's too strong."

Dante continued to roar in his rampage. They could hear him crashing closer.

"Too much elixir. He's burning through the formula at an accelerated pace." Hyde shook blood and rock dust from his shaggy hair. "He'll soon change back."

"If we have that much time left," Nemo said.

Suddenly, the Dante-beast's huge claw burst through the debris and snatched Hyde's head and tried to crush his skull. Hyde roared and battered his opponent's arm, scraping and scratching.

Nemo thrust with his scimitar and stabbed Dante's swollen, hairy hand, plunging the point deep. The blade snapped in half.

Even so, the beast's unexpected pain gave Hyde the moment he needed. As Dante reacted by hurling himself forward at his enemy, Hyde grabbed him. He plunged ragged nails of both hands into Dante's flesh and used main strength to haul the whole beast over his head. Dante snarled and thrashed, until Hyde body-slammed him into the far edge of the pit with a sound like a cargo wagon crashing.

Knowing they could not fight Dante much longer, Nemo stumbled toward a low opening at the far end of the ash pit. He peered upward and saw bright daylight far overhead, illuminating thick layers of ice, frost, and long stalactites of icicles encrusted on the walls of an old, empty chimney.

Their only way out.

"Hyde, come on!"

His weakened, brutish ally staggered—and Nemo realized that the unsteady reaction was caused by more than his battle injuries.

Hyde winced, his face rippling, brow ridge convulsing, lips peeled back from crooked, squarish teeth. "I'm done. I've burned through . . . the . . . formula . . . too." He let out a yowl of pain and disappointment. His chest squirmed and spasmed in the sudden throes of transformation. "Damn!"

Behind him, the Dante-beast struggled to get to his feet. He shook his massive head and swatted shattered rock aside.

Nemo ran back and grabbed Hyde by the shoulders, helping him stumble to the chimney. "Come, we can hide. Maybe escape." They staggered along, while Hyde seemed to shrink in on himself, his body mass diminishing with each step. "Hurry!"

All too soon, he had reverted entirely to the small, shaking form of Henry Jekyll. He stood looking weak and forlorn, like a rain-soaked alley cat.

The Dante-beast charged at them.

Nemo pulled Jekyll with him through the fire hole into the ice-encrusted chimney, just as Dante hurtled into the wall. The beast slammed into the small fire doorway like a rampaging elephant, but only his monstrous head and straining neck passed through. His enormous arms and shoulders could not fit, though the force of the impact shook the chimney.

High above, a long, thick spear of ice snapped loose and fell, gaining speed, glinting in the reflected light from the sky.

"Look out!" Jekyll cried in a thin squeak. He shoved Nemo aside just before the icicle spike splintered into chips on the chimney floor.

"I thank you. I would have been killed."

Jekyll blinked, then smiled. "I'm glad that . . . *I* can be useful, too."

But the Dante-beast had also seen the thick ice spears on the chimney. He ground his shoulders into the opening and thrust himself through, breaking part of the doorway free. Inside, he reached up with one thickly muscled arm to grasp a gigantic ice spike from overhead and pull it down. The Fantom's lieutenant loomed, filling most of the room, and shoved his long frozen lance forward, intending to impale both trapped men in the confines of the chimney.

Nemo and Jekyll had no place to go.

Just then, on the factory level, the timers of all of Skinner's bombs finally reached zero.

51

Inside the high keep filled with crates and torture implements, Quatermain drove the mastermind back. Moriarty retreated, and the old adventurer snatched up the Mongolian mace and pressed his attack, swinging the spiked ball.

M scrambled backward, desperate but not yet defeated. "You think you can come in here and destroy it all?" He laughed. "I'll just start again, rebuild from scratch."

"Is that supposed to convince me?" Quatermain raised the mace to smash Moriarty. He had had enough of talking.

"There'll be another like me, Quatermain! You can't kill the future."

But Skinner's bombs could.

Thunderous detonations ripped through the foundry, the dry dock, and the factory area. As floor upon floor shook and support walls collapsed, the whole high keep fractured. Crates and rusty equipment fell in a jumble.

Quatermain and Moriarty were both hurled to the floor even as it split wide open. The explosions continued.

*   *   *

A wave of fire and debris consumed everything across the factory floor. M's black fortress exploded. Huge granite blocks coughed out. Flames reached huge tanks of fuel, turning them into firebombs. Compressed steam tanks burst open. Stored weapons caught fire and erupted with whistling shock waves.

Unprotected, the Dante-beast turned just in time to be impaled by red-hot shrapnel. He slammed against the chimney and dropped his lethal ice spear, which shattered on the floor.

The impact of the detonation snapped a further brace of ice spikes from high above in the curving chimney. Stone blocks and heavy spears of ice cascaded from high above onto the screaming Dante-beast.

Jekyll dragged Nemo to the center as deadly shards came crashing down along the wall. They listened to the falling rocks, the wet sounds of slicing flesh and muscle, the brittle crack of shattering bone. When the ice shower stopped at last, the two huddled men opened their eyes.

"I . . . I can't believe we're unhurt." Jekyll checked his body for hidden injuries. All that remained of his clothes were blood-smeared tatters.

Nemo gestured toward a part of the chimney wall that had crumbled open behind them, exposing a small but convenient escape hole. "Yes, we are very fortunate."

On the opposite wall, though, in the opening through which they had entered, the less-fortunate Dante-beast lay trapped and mewling, impaled repeatedly by slowly melting ice lances and heavy shrapnel. The wall above the doorway had slumped down in a precarious collapse, dumping a thousand tons of stone onto the beast's back.

The monster stared imploringly at them, its remaining bloody eye desperate.

Just then the formula finally wore off, and Dante reverted to his human form. The feral eye changed to the smaller, frightened eye of a dying man. His body shrank into itself, and the fallen blocks shifted again, crushing him entirely.

Nemo shoved Jekyll to safety through the escape hole as a mighty collapse of the whole chimney generated a huge cloud of dust behind them.

Continuing explosions literally shook apart the tower room. One half of the high keep broke away, then settled with a lurch several meters below the rest of the chamber. Daylight and sparkling snow streamed through great cracks in the stone walls, where all had been shadow.

Quatermain fell between a creaking torture rack and a set of long, sharp-tipped iron rods. Moriarty got to his feet first, saw his opponent's Bowie knife lying on the floor, and lunged for it. Knife in hand, he stumbled through dust and debris and snatched up his fallen silver mask and his leather satchel of the genetic and scientific information that had given the members of the League their special abilities.

Several thick wooden ceiling beams had already broken from the walls and fallen into the chamber. With scrambling, slipping footsteps, Moriarty started climbing to the high floor above, the top of the tower.

"Not so fast, M." Quatermain gripped a shaft of rusty pointed metal, which he aimed like a spear. "You've lost."

Moriarty turned to see the threat, Bowie knife at the

ready, and smirked dismissively. "I've lost?" He jumped back down from the stairs. "Not yet. Not nearly."

"I have you." Quatermain stepped over a fallen beam, pushing the rusty spear closer to his nemesis.

M rolled his eyes in their sunken sockets. "Do you ever tire of being wrong, old man? The League. Me. Skinner. *Wrong.*" He sighed. "And wrong about the young American, too."

"Sawyer?" A cold dread trickled like glacier water down his spine. "What about him?"

"He's a bumbling fool, just like his friend Huckleberry Finn. What a ridiculous name." Moriarty held up the retrieved Fantom mask where it gleamed in sunlight that filtered through the crack in the tower. "Do you think him ready and able? Ha! You didn't train him any better than you trained your son."

Quatermain saw Tom Sawyer reflected in the mask's mirrored finish—being held in the doorway with a knife at this throat by the powder-coated head and shoulders of Sanderson Reed. Sawyer struggled, but the knife pressed against his jugular.

Quatermain paused, knowing he had no choice but to surrender.

Moriarty laughed in his face. The old hunter locked eyes with his nemesis. M seemed utterly victorious, in spite of the explosions and the fortress crumbling around him. Quatermain wanted to kill him right then.

Instead, he spun and hurled his makeshift spear dead into Reed's chest. He missed Sawyer by a very comfortable inch. The invisible Reed writhed and wailed in pain, and his half-seen form slumped into death even before the spear stopped vibrating. The bureaucrat's knife fell to the floor, and Sawyer broke free, kicking his dying form for good measure.

But as Quatermain straightened, knowing he had made the right choice, Moriarty sprang at the old adventurer and plunged Quatermain's own Bowie knife deep into his back. He twisted the hilt, grinding the blade farther into the hunter's lungs, questing for his heart.

With a disbelieving gasp, Quatermain dropped to his knees. Sawyer ran to him, distraught to see his mentor fall, torn between attacking the Fantom and staying beside Quatermain.

"I thank you for the game." Wiping his bloodied hands on his trousers, Moriarty dashed over to where a wide crack in the tower wall offered escape. Carefree, he jumped out into the open sky, soaring high above the ground.

With an angry shout, Sawyer rushed to the crack, seized the edge of the broken stone, and pushed his head out into the cold daylight. He expected to see the evil mastermind falling to his death at the base of the fortress.

Instead, Moriarty sailed gracefully toward a safe landing far below, his black cape extended into a wind-resistant barrier, billowing out like the skin of a flying fox.

"Not . . . over . . . yet," said Quatermain.

Sawyer turned to see the deeply wounded hunter staggering toward him. The Bowie knife still protruded from the middle of his back; his shirt was soaked in blood. But he'd had the strength of mind to retrieve his elephant gun. He cradled Matilda in his hands.

He lurched forward. Sawyer grasped his arm and steadied him. "We need to get you help. Got to find Mina, or Dr. Jekyll."

Quatermain shrugged him off. "No. No time for that." He reached the gap in the tower wall and peered out through the crack. He reeled, struggled to focus his eyes. He saw the black Fantom sailing to the ground. "There's the bastard!"

Moriarty skidded to a landing and took off running across the snow-swept field toward the half-frozen Amur River, where the curve of the stolen nautiloid still poked up through the ice.

Quatermain held his rifle with trembling arms and tried to aim, but he couldn't see. Slumping, barely able to stay on his feet, he fumbled in his pocket with blood-stained fingers. When he drew out his spectacles, both lenses were broken, the frames twisted.

With a sigh, he pulled Sawyer close so that they could stand together. "It's on you now, boy." He guided the young man to help him take aim. "Look there, find him. Show the bullet where to go."

Sawyer was uncertain, wracked with grief for his mortally wounded friend, but Quatermain clenched him tightly until he submitted to the hunter's intensity. The American agent leaned in and sighted down Matilda's long barrel.

"So, take your time. Last . . . chance."

Sawyer squinted, aimed, and adjusted the elephant gun. He concentrated, but finally hesitated, unsure. "It's too far."

"No, you're ready," Quatermain said, urging Sawyer to aim again. "Got to be ready."

Moriarty kept running, his black cape flapping like a bat's wings behind him. Every step carried him farther away, closer to the small submersible.

"Take. Your. Time." Quatermain squeezed his eyes shut, fighting back the pain and the tide of weakness as his life continued to bleed away.

By now, Moriarty was so far away that he seemed barely a black dot. Exactly centered on the sight line. Sawyer accounted for breezes, the movement of the target—and took the shot.

With a loud crack the bullet whistled away from the rifle. An eternity passed.

Then . . . far off, Moriarty fell face first into the snow at the river's ice-crusted edge. The leather satchel filled with vital, stolen secrets skittered along, teetered on the thinnest ice, then broke through and sank forever into the frigid water of the gurgling Amur.

The Fantom's mask spun away, it's polished silver surface spattered with blood. It came to a rest, the empty eye-holes staring up at the clear sky. . . .

Up in the tower, Quatermain smiled with satisfaction. Then he collapsed with a dying gasp. Sawyer knelt by his side. The young man's eyes filled with tears, but there was nothing he could say, no way to help.

Quatermain clutched the front of Sawyer's shirt. "May this new century be yours, son—as the old one was mine."

"Allan," Sawyer said. "No, wait—"

And with that, Quatermain died.

52

In front of the smoking, crumbling fortress, a British soldier raised his head over the snowy slope. Beside him, another head appeared, peering at the destruction. Then another, and another.

Finally, two hundred soldiers in winter uniforms marched together through the snow: a combined British and American force that trudged across the wind-swept steppes.

Several heavy icebreaker ships were moored in the far distance at a wide point of the frozen Amur River. Slabs of white ice had ground up against their armored hulls as they had battered their way up the half-frozen channel, until they encountered the *Nautilus*. Soldiers and officers continued to disembark, though all that remained were the mopping-up chores.

A few surviving henchmen and Mongolian guards fled into the distance across the empty hills, searching for peasant settlements to pillage or take refuge in. Black, greasy fumes curled into the sky from a collapsed chimney. With a low rumble, another minor explosion blew out a side wall.

On their way back to the submarine vessel, the *Nautilus*'s crew had corralled hundreds of Moriarty's escaping workers and guards; other crewmen now tended to the rescued scientists who were reunited with their hostage family members.

An elegant portly gentleman disembarked from the largest icebreaker and brought up the rear of the marching soldiers. He had a neat mustache and goatee, a handsome face that had gained a fair amount of weight due to lavish living. His clothes were elegant, a fine dinner jacket, plaid waistcoat, a pocket watch on a chain. Reaching the top of the rise, he placed one ringed hand on his hip and studied the spectacle of the Fantom's fortress.

Bandaged and battered, the remaining members of the League of Extraordinary Gentlemen, no longer part of the military action, waited for the soldiers to meet them. They eyed the arriving troops coldly.

Quatermain's body lay nearby, wrapped in cloth. Tom Sawyer and Skinner had carried it out of the tower and into the open.

"Coming to rescue us, are you?" Mina said with undisguised irony. "It's about time."

The elegant gentleman smiled a warm greeting at her. "Sorry. Took us longer to get here than we expected. Russia was none too keen on the sight of our gunboats." He extended a hand to Mina and introduced himself. "Bond. Campion Bond. British Secret Service."

"Dollar shy, day late, I'd say," Sawyer said, his voice raw.

"Ah, you must be the American," Bond said. "How . . . quaint. Though I must say you've done quite a respectable job."

"Yeah. That's right." Sawyer was surprised that the elegant man knew him. He imitated the other's introduction. "I'm Sawyer. Tom Sawyer."

Bond glanced at his pocket watch to make sure the whole mop-up operation continued on schedule. "Yes, I know who you are. We've had a spy among you for the whole time." He snapped the pocket watch shut. The League members looked in unison at Skinner.

"Rodney Skinner. On her Majesty's Secret Service." Skinner's proud smile was only visible because of the smears of grime that covered his transparent face.

"Now I don't know what to believe." Mina's usually neat hair was disheveled from her battles; her dress was in tatters.

"Or who to trust," Jekyll added, looking cold and miserable.

Uniformed scouts and army engineers scoured the remains of the fortress. Even though the battle was already over, they were still needed for their muscle. Groups of men carted equipment, engines, and war machinery out of the smoking fortress and delivered them to the icebreakers. Campion Bond watched the work with glee, as if he could barely wait to inspect all the new toys in his possession.

Another contingent of soldiers took over tending to the former prisoners. Nemo nodded his permission to his crewmen, and the soldiers led the hapless scientists away, including Karl Draper, who refused to be separated from his daughter Eva. They looked haggard, but comforted to know that their ordeal was over at last. They had all seen the Fantom's body lying motionless on the riverbank.

Sawyer watched the scientists go. "Taking them into care? They'll need hospitalization."

"Oh, they'll be taken care of, all right." Bond beamed, looking immensely satisfied. "Just so long as they keep up the good work—for us, of course."

Racing across the snow and panting white steam in the cold air, an aide ran up from the nearest icebreaker. He clutched a flapping telegram in his hand. "Mr. Bond, sir! We just received this in the radio room."

Bond scanned the message, his smile broadening. "Gentlemen, Mrs. Harker. The Queen herself would like to congratulate you for your extraordinary actions, and she proposes to induct you as a real league. What an honor!"

Sawyer wasn't entirely overwhelmed. He looked down at the wrapped shape of the old adventurer's cold body. "I'd like to suggest a greater honor. Allan Quatermain should be buried in Africa, next to his son." His voice was now hard and determined. He raised his chin. "I aim to see that happen."

"And I would be honored to take you there," Nemo said. "My *Nautilus* is at your disposal."

Sawyer felt relieved, a small portion of the weight lifted from his shoulders. He turned to his fellow League members. "Who else is coming?"

Mina smiled at the young man. She took his hand as they moved toward the armored submarine vessel waiting at the edge of the Amur. After hesitating a second, Jekyll joined them.

Skinner stayed with Campion Bond, though. Sawyer looked back, frowning in disappointment. The other man shrugged his barely visible shoulders. "I am nothing if not a servant of my Queen."

"Skinner," Sawyer said sternly.

The invisible man quickly changed his mind. "Coming!"

Bond's brow furrowed with sudden concern as he read the second half of the lengthy telegram from London. He gasped. "Wait! You all may be needed anew!" He raised the sheet of paper. "Scientists have discovered hot flares on Mars, green flashes as if from launches of massive cylinders. The astronomer Ogilvy has theorized it could be the sign of a Martian invasion."

Jekyll's watery eyes widened, then he chuckled. "That's ridiculous."

Sawyer scoffed. "Martian invasions like world wars are the stuff of fantasy." Together, he and Skinner respectfully lifted the shrouded body of Allan Quatermain and carried it toward Nemo's waiting vessel.

As the snow blew harder and harder, the League turned their backs on Bond and began their trek back to the *Nautilus*.

About the Author

K. J. ANDERSON has written many original novels, novelizations, and media tie-in books. He is also the author of two other "fantastic historicals" in the vein of *The League of Extraordinary Gentlemen:* the critically acclaimed *Captain Nemo* and the forthcoming *Mr. Wells & the Martians* (due from Pocket in March 2004). Writing under the name Kevin J. Anderson, he is the coauthor of five bestselling prequels to *Dune,* with Brian Herbert, and the original novels *Hopscotch* and *Hidden Empire.* With his wife, Rebecca Moesta, he created and wrote all fourteen volumes in the award-winning series *Young Jedi Knights.* An avid comics fan, Anderson has also written for DC, Wildstorm, Dark Horse, Topps, and IDW. His website is www.wordfire.com.

Visit
❖ Pocket Books ❖
online at

....

www.SimonSays.com

....

Keep up on the latest new
releases from your favorite
authors, as well as author
appearances, news, chats,
special offers and more.

SIMON & SCHUSTER
A VIACOM COMPANY
www.SimonSays.com

Pocket
Books

2381-01